A TRAIL TOO FAR

Robert Peecher

For information the author may be contacted at

PO Box 967; Watkinsville GA; 30677

or at robertpeecher.com

This is a work of fiction. Any similarities to actual events in whole or in part are purely accidental. None of the characters or events depicted in this novel are intended to represent actual people.

For Jean,
Who reads first.

CONTENTS

The long prairie grass shimmered blue and then green as it moved with the breeze, rippling as if the hills and wide open stretches were alive, a shiver moving along the back of a stretching animal.

The lone rider followed the wagon tracks through the tall grass, keeping to a safe distance where he would not be seen. They called him Pawnee Bill, not because he had any Injun in him, but because he lived down on the banks of the Pawnee River in southwest Kansas. But that wasn't strictly true, either. He never really lived anywhere. Pawnee Bill drifted, mostly, and what he drifted toward always was trouble. If trouble wasn't where he was going, he manufactured it when he got there.

Presently, the trouble Pawnee Bill intended to manufacture had to do with the daughter of a sod buster.

For a week, Pawnee Bill and two hillbilly horse thieves from Arkansas, Chess Bowman and Dick Derugy, had been camping out at Six Mile Stage Station. They were on the dodge, riding stolen horses, and were trying to decide which way was best to go next when the daughter of a nearby farmer arrived on the afternoon stage. She was returning from a year spent with an aunt and uncle in Kansas City attending a women's school, and she was now coming home, accompanied by a young man she'd met in Kansas City. The pair were seeking her father's blessing on a marriage.

But at the stage station, she caught Pawnee Bill's eye. Pretty girls in real dresses were a rare sight on the Kansas prairie. More common, the women looked little better than over fed men, their skin battered by the winds and cooked by the sun, their hands rough from hard work. But Susan Raleigh had soft, pink skin, and pretty blue eyes, and curly blonde hair, and Pawnee Bill decided when he saw her that he would have her.

Tommy Raleigh, Susan's older brother, drove the buckboard to the station to collect her and young Matthew Rose, who intended to marry her. When the three left out from the station in the buckboard, Pawnee Bill mounted up on his horse and followed them.

Pawnee Bill was a stout man, strong but not particularly tall. He carried a mean look on his face the way a snake does, nature intervening to offer protection to those who would be prey. As such, for most of his adult life, folks gave Pawnee Bill a wide berth even in those places where he did not have a reputation. And those places were running low. After the sacking of Lawrence, Pawnee Bill had been steadily building a reputation for hard violence. If Kansas was bleeding, as Horace Greeley claimed, Pawnee Bill was one of them making the wounds.

He sat his horse on a grassy hill overlooking the farm where the buckboard wagon stopped. An acres of waist-high corn, some wheat, other vegetables. A few heads of cattle, and enclosure of horses. It was not a bad little farm, but the family lived in a sod house. Pawnee Bill had contempt for sod houses. People living in dirt was something he could not understand.

When they came to the prairie just a few years before, the Raleigh family brought with them enough timber to frame out windows and a door and a good support beam for the roof. The roof itself was made of timber, and there were shingles. But the rest of it was all cuts of sod. The barn, though, was all made of timber. This was one more reason why Pawnee Bill hated sod busters. Putting up hay for cows and horses and stowing the wagon in a better building than the one where the people lived was just plain foolishness.

Marking the spot where the sod house stood, Pawnee Bill mounted his horse and made the trek back to Six Mile Station.

"They'll have money," Pawnee Bill told Chess Bowman and Dick Derugy. "Money and valuables. I guarantee they brought valuables with them from back east."

"You don't even know how many menfolk they might be," Dick Derugy said. "Might be the two you saw, surely she's got a pa, and on a farm like that there could be six or seven brothers."

Pawnee Bill shook his head in disgust. They were camped about sixty yards from the station, outside of the enclosure that housed the station house, the stables, the paddock, and the eating house and rooms for rent for stage passengers. There were not passengers letting rooms presently, and the three drifters could have had a room except that they had little money for anything beyond meals. Now, sitting around their campfire within sight of the stage station, Pawnee Bill was working out his plan.

"It don't matter how many menfolk they might have," Bill said. "We have two six shooters and a rifle a piece. By my count, that's a total of more than eighty rounds of ammunition we can fire between us before we ever have to reload a gun. They ain't going to have eighty menfolk in that tiny old sod house. The pa, three brothers, and that man what rode in on the coach with her. That's all it'll be. Hell, I could kill all of them by myself."

Pawnee Bill took a drink from his jug. "Besides, you're thinking about it all wrong, Bill. The question ain't never how many men folk are there. The question always is how many womenfolk are there."

Bill guffawed at his own joke, and Dick had to give him a grudging smile.

"Well, you're right about that," Dick Derugy said. "Maybe the ma'll be as pretty as the daughter."

Chess Bowman sat quietly and listened to the other two talk. He didn't mind stealing horses. He'd been at Lawrence and Osawatomie, so he didn't mind murder and wasn't scared of a fight. But violating women didn't sit right with him.

"I might sit this one out," Chess said. "You boys go on without me, and I'll just wait for you here."

"We ain't coming back here when this is over," Pawnee Bill said. "My plan is to ride out west. Let the station manager and the hands see us go that away. Then we'll cut north to the farm. We can make it look like Cheyenne Injuns did it, burn 'em out, scalp 'em, loot the house, drive off their stock."

"You're talking about killing everyone there," Chess said.

Pawnee Bill looked surprised. "Well, yeah. If you're going to try to cover something up by making it look like Injuns did it, you can't very well leave witnesses alive to say different."

In the firelight, Chess looked at Dick to read his old friend's thoughts. He'd known Dick since way back. They'd come up from Arkansas together to join the Border Men in Missouri and help with the free-staters in Kansas. They met Pawnee Bill on the Lawrence Raid, and they'd ridden with him for most of the time since, sometimes joining the pro-slavery militia and sometimes doing their own thing.

Pawnee Bill's own thing seemed to be getting more reckless and more brutal.

Dick Derugy's face showed no indication of surprise or disgust.

"You're okay with violatin' women?" Chess Bowman asked.

Dick's head lolled back and forth from one shoulder to the other in an indecisive fashion. "It's been a long time since we've been up to anything," Dick said. "I'm feeling restless. You ain't got to do anything you don't want to do."

***

The next morning Pawnee Bill, Dick Derugy, and Chess Bowman took their breakfast and coffee in the station house.

"We're headed west," Pawnee Bill told the station

manager and his wife, who did the cooking. "Going to ride west to see what we can get up to in Denver City. I ain't never been there, but I've heard tell that there ain't better saloons until you get to San Francisco."

The station manager said he'd been to Denver City.

"Easy for a man to get into trouble there. You boys be careful."

An hour later, the three men rode west, making a production of waving goodbye to the station manager as they did.

They rode two miles west and then cut off the stage road and headed north. Pawnee Bill had done enough wandering in the prairies that he was pretty good at finding his way in a land where men could get easily turned around. To Dick and Chess, accustomed as they were to mountains and hills and trees to serve as landmarks, one rolling hill covered in long grass on the prairie was no different than any other, and the few trees that dotted one bottom were indistinguishable from the trees dotting another bottom.

After a couple more hours, Pawnee Bill led them directly to a buffalo trace. "This is what I was looking for," he said. "We can follow this and come up on them." But they topped a hill not far from the farmhouse and there encountered just a few yards away Matthew Rose and Thomas Raleigh, Susan's father, in conversation.

Thomas Started when he saw the riders appear on top of the hill.

"Hello there," he called to them. "Are you lost?"

Pawnee Bill, who knew his own appearance and how people took him, put on as big a smile as he could and rode directly to the two men. Dick and Chess held back at the top of the hill, neither knowing how to deal with the unexpected appearance of the two men.

"No, we ain't lost," Pawnee Bill said as he reined in his horse in front of the two men. "We know exactly where we are. But we did not expect to see you here."

"I have a farm here," Thomas Raleigh said. "My home is not far from here. Are you looking for something or someone? Is there something I can help you with?"

Pawnee Bill threw a leg over the side of his horse and slid down out of the saddle. He opened up a saddle bag and reached a hand inside. He had there a knife he acquired some years ago when he traded with Cheyenne Dog Soldier. He'd given the Cheyenne a half-drunk bottle of foul whiskey. He liked the knife but had already made up his mind it would be the evidence he would leave to convince others that whatever he did here to these sod-busters would be blamed on raiding Injuns.

"I do have something you could help me with," Bill said, his hand still in his saddlebag.

The younger man wore the appearance of a city dweller, not the sort of man who would handle himself in a prairie fight. Sod busters, generally, weren't much for fighting, but they were typically tough men. So Pawnee Bill decided his first victim needed to be the older man.

Thomas Raleigh stepped forward to see what Bill had in his saddlebag, and in a quick turn, one fluid motion, Bill Pawnee spun in the spot, drawing the knife from the saddlebag, and sliced a deep gash right across Thomas Raleigh's midriff. The older man clutched at his stomach as it opened up and spilled blood. Now Bill lunged for Matthew Rose. Just moments ago, Matthew Rose had confessed to Mr. Raleigh that he was seeking the older man's blessing to marry Susan. And now, inexplicably, Thomas Raleigh was doubled over and bleeding to death.

Matthew Rose was too slow to process the sudden violence. He never even moved. Pawnee Bill clutched him by the front of the shirt, and with one hand he dragged Matthew Rose toward him, and with the other hand he plunged the knife into the young man's throat.

Both men were dying, but neither man was dead, when Pawnee Bill began to slice skin and hair from the tops of their heads. His throat full of blood, Matthew Rose squirmed and spluttered but made no real sound. Thomas Raleigh screamed and cursed, but Pawnee Bill was strong and there was no way the man could put up a fight.

In just a couple of minutes, the gruesome work was finished, and Pawnee Bill let out a hoot of victory.

"Come along, boys!" he shouted up to Dick and Chess. "This ain't even the fun part!"

Pawnee Bill climbed back into the saddle and started for the farmhouse. Dick Derugy bounded along to catch up to him, and Chess Bowman reluctantly followed behind.

Two more rolling hills brought them to within sight of the farmhouse. Tommy Raleigh and his younger brother Doug were both going through the vegetable patch, baskets in hand, and picking what was ready. Doug was just fourteen years old, but Tommy was twenty. The middle brother, Joe, was digging potatoes in the potato patch.

Outside the sod house, Susan Raleigh and her

mother were snapping beans.

"When we ride down there, I'll get the two in the vegetable garden," Pawnee Bill said. "Chess, you go after the one digging potatoes. And Dick, you get those women and don't let them get away. Try not to bust up their faces if you have to be rough with them. Especially the younger one from the stage station."

Chester Bowman had a sick feeling. He knew what Pawnee Bill was planning, and what Dick would do, too. He didn't even mind killing them – folks got killed all the time. But for Chess, there was some invisible line, and violating women was on the other side of that line.

They rode down the slope at an easy pace, drawing the attention of all the remaining Raleigh family members. But they did not look particularly threatening, just drifters riding across the prairie. Visitors were uncommon, but not unheard of.

"I guess that was your pa we was just talking to out across the hills over there," Pawnee Bill called to Tommy Raleigh, the oldest male at the homestead. "He invited us to stop by here and maybe get a bite to eat. We've been riding for a while."

Tommy eyed the strangers with suspicion, but Pawnee Bill's ruse – that Tommy's father had sent them – too him off his guard.

But Mrs. Raleigh, with a pit in her stomach, knew immediately that something was wrong. Her husband would never have invited three strange men to their home when he was not there. He might have walked with them, but he would not have sent them on ahead.

"Susan, go into the house and get the scatter gun over the mantle," Mrs. Raleigh said. "Be sure there are shells in it, and bring it to me, directly."

Pawnee Bill rode to the edge of the vegetable patch. He was close enough that both of the brothers there would be easy targets. His hand was already on the grip of his .44 caliber Colt Army. Bill waited just a moment while Chess and Dick got close. He noticed the girl had gone inside the sod house, but it didn't worry him any.

In a moment Chess would be up to the boy with the spade.

Tommy Raleigh started to say something, but Pawnee Bill didn't hear it. Chess's horse stopped at the edge of the potato patch, and Pawnee Bill jerked his Colt from its holster. He shot Tommy in the chest at such close range that it snapped the young man backwards and he fell to the ground.

Chess was watching Pawnee Bill, waiting for the moment. When Pawnee Bill shot the boy, Chess drew his revolver. But the boy in the potato patch started to run, and Chess had to ride after him. The horse easily caught up to him, and Chess simply leaned over and fired a shot right into Joe's back. The boy fell forward, and Chess reined in his horse. He leapt from his saddle and holstered his revolver. Chess used his Bowie knife to cut Joe's throat.

Doug, the youngest of the Raleigh boys, also started to run, but Pawnee Bill turned in his saddle and fired a shot. The first shot struck Doug in the back of thigh. Doug limped and stumbled until Pawnee Bill fired a second shot that exploded into the back of the boy's skull.

Dick Derugy came out of his saddle like lightning, and before the mother even had time to react to the slaughter of her children, Dick knocked her in the side of the head with the barrel of his Colt Army, leaving her senseless and sprawled over a basket of beans.

Susan Raleigh stepped out of the sod house with the shotgun leveled at Dick, and he shot her in the stomach. Susan fell back against the door frame, and Dick Derugy took the shotgun by the barrels and jerked it from her hands.

"What did you shoot her for?" Pawnee Bill demanded. "I told you not to touch them."

"She had this shotgun," Dick said.

"You can't take a shotgun away from a girl?" Pawnee Bill demanded, storming toward Dick and the injured girl.

Pawnee Bill shoved Dick out of his way and snatched Susan Raleigh by the wrist. He dragged her into the sod house. Shot though she was, she still fought, and Pawnee Bill used his knife to cut her throat.

Then he came out and took the girl's mother into sod house.

When it was over, and both Pawnee Bill and Dick Derugy had done to the mother what they came to do to the girl, Bill went around and took the scalps of all of the Raleigh family.

Chess Bowman refused to go into the sod house, but he collected straw from the barn while Bill and Dick looted the house.

Other than a couple of pocket watches and a good Enfield rifle, there were no valuables in the house. Each man took a spare horse from the herd, and the other animals they stampeded away from the farm to wander out across the prairie until someone found them or they became some predator's dinner.

When they were finished with all they cared to do, Dick and Pawnee Bill set the straw inside the house alight, to burn everything in the sod house that would burn. Bill left his knife beside the body of one of the boys. Then the three men rode east.

-2-

The old man couldn't be found in his upstairs office above the mercantile, but some people on the street directed Amos Cummings to the saloon down the street. The saloon offered a free lunch buffet, and Albert Huntsdale took a meal there just about every day. It was his excuse to get an early start on his drinking.

The street was crowded with people, all seeming to be in a hurry to get somewhere, but Amos Cummings did not think any of them could relate to the rush that he was in. He was bordering on desperation. His spring and early summer were marred by delays and disappointments.

The first delay was a late snowfall that kept his family from getting started on their journey for three days.

The second delay was a washed out bridge that cost him an extra day of travel.

When his daughter fell ill with a fever, he lost a week.

There had been some debate about whether or not

to take the train to St. Louis and then travel up river by steamboat to Independence. But Amos Cummings, always thrifty, believed the family could make the initial journey west by wagon and save money on supplies. The supplies they would need, not just for the journey but once they arrived in California, would cost much more in Independence – maybe twice as much – than they would at home. So Amos decided to make the overland journey by wagon, starting from his own front door.

And then came the delays, so that when Amos Cummings and his family at last arrived in Independence, Missouri, Amos was in a panic.

He paid in advance to join a wagon train headed down the Oregon Trail. Having thoroughly planned his journey, Amos Cummings expected to arrive in Independence with more than a week to spare before the wagon train left out. Now, he was almost a week late.

His family camped east of Independence, about fifteen miles, and Amos rode on ahead to try to find Albert Huntsdale to see what could be done.

He knew that sometimes trains were delayed and didn't get off in time. He suspected that happened most of the time. He hoped this one had been delayed a week. And if not a week, at least a few days so that he might catch up to them.

Short of that, Amos Cummings had paid in advance. The contract protected Huntsdale from refunding the money, but Amos was hopeful that if the train had already left then Huntsdale would see his way fit to let the Cummings party join up with the next train.

The saloon was a reeking place, swamped by the stench of old liquor and bodily fluids. It was dark and crowded and noisy. The only thing more foul inside the saloon than the smell was the language, and every conversation seemed to be conducted from across the room at a shout. The saloon itself was long and narrow, and the bar running along one wall from front to back made the rest of the place even more cramped.

"I'm looking or Albert Huntsdale," Amos said several times as he moved through the crowd. "Albert Huntsdale. Can anyone point me in the direction of Albert Huntsdale?"

At last, near the back of the saloon, an old man with a dingy and crumpled hat, long white hair and a thick white beard raised up a hand and called out, "You've found him, mister. I'm Al Huntsdale."

Amos breathed a sigh of relief. He pushed his way past a couple of men and slid into a chair at the table where Huntsdale was drinking a whiskey and beer.

"I am Amos Cummings, Mr. Huntsdale."

The old man gave Cummings a long appraisal. Huntsdale wore a fine suit, and though it was wrinkled and had a fine layer of trail dust, a man couldn't help but see that Cummings was a professional of some sort, a man accustomed to cleanliness and tidy about his appearance. Huntsdale could not place the face, which was strange because he was usually better about face than names.

"I know that name, Amos Cummings. But you'll have to remind me how. Where have we met before?"

"We've not met before, but we have corresponded. Amos Cummings – surely you remember. I reserved a spot on the wagon train bound for California on the Oregon Trail."

The old man nodded, remembering now. "You're

the one who didn't show up."

"That's right," Amos Cummings said, his thoughts a mixture of relief and renewed concern. "We were delayed in getting here. But we are here now, and ready to depart as soon as possible."

The old man had more teeth missing than present, but he had plugged the holes with sodden chewing tobacco, and Amos Cummings found the man's appearance too distasteful for conversation. Amos forced himself to look at the old man's forehead to spare himself a view of the mouth. Nevertheless, his eyes kept wandering down to the thick, white beard stained yellow and brown from tobacco juice that had drizzled from the man's mouth.

"Train's done left," Albert Huntsdale said. "Been gone almost a week now. Almost a hundred wagons headed down the trail." Albert Huntsdale closed one eye and leaned forward, giving Amos a suspicious look. "Ain't no returns on the money. That's in the contract."

Amos shook his head in confusion. "But you are still here in Independence. How did the train leave without its wagon master?"

The old man laughed, giving Amos a second glance at his mouth full of missing teeth and the black wad of chew. Amos was disgusted when he watched the old man take his whiskey and beer over and through the tobacco.

"I ain't a wagon master," Albert Huntsdale said, still laughing as if the notion were preposterous. "I ain't never been no further west than Atchison. I just arrange things, see?"

Amos was crestfallen. "Very well, then. The next train. Surely we can go with the next train."

16

Albert Huntsdale again greeted Amos with derisive laughter. "You can do that, and I won't charge you no extry for the inconvenience to me. But you'll be staying for a while. Next train going along the trail don't leave until next spring."

Amos shook his head in disbelief. "But that is impossible. I must be to California before the start of the new year. I have accepted a position, you understand? I have been engaged with the University of the Pacific as an instructor."

"Are you a teacher?"

"I am. A professor. Yes. I serve as both chaplain at the university chapel and a professor of moral philosophy."

Albert Huntsdale shook his head. "While I congratulate you on your teaching engagement, your first lesson will have to be on tardiness, schoolmaster. You won't be going with one of my wagon masters this late in the year. It's too late to start now. You run into any trouble, any delays, and you'll be stuck in a blizzard in the mountains."

Amos sat back in his chair and felt the back give way. He pulled himself forward in time to avoid toppling over backwards. He shook his head in disgust. "I have to leave now," he said. "I have accepted a position. This is very important to me. It's my entire life, my entire career. Surely there is a way. Is there some guide I can hire to take just me and my party?"

"You're too late getting started," the old man said. "You'd never make it over the Sierra Nevada before the snows."

Amos Cummings nodded his head in frustration. "Yes, you've said that. But what I'm asking you is whether or not there is a guide who can take us now, even though we are starting too late."

"Ain't no guide going to take you now. It's too late in the season. If you went all the way through, no problems and no delays, you'd pass the mountains before the snows. But you have to give yourself a week or two to be ready to deal with troubles. Any kind of troubles can come up – a broken wheel, a team of mules get scared by the buffalo and skedaddle, Indians pester you for days trying to trade or steal. All of that could hold you up. And then you get caught in a blizzard and you're dead before the thaw."

"I will pay very well," Amos said. "I don't mind paying beyond the normal rates, beyond what I have already paid. It is very important to me, and I would pay you – and any wagon master you could find – very well."

"Hush, you," the old man hissed, and he looked around viciously to see if Amos had been overheard. "You want to get yourself scalped before you're ten miles past the Kansas River? They's men in here would scalp you if they thought you carried that kind of money."

"I am just trying to impress upon you the urgency of my desire," Amos Cummings said. "While I realize that we are getting a late start, I certainly do not think my request is impossible."

The old man rubbed his face vigorously with his rough, calloused hand. The request, supported by the promise of money, had clearly put him in considerable consternation.

"They's Injuns, and troubles in Kansas, and weather. You get to the Sierra Nevada and you're liable to be snowed in. You've heard stories of what happens to those what get snowed in, ain't you?"

Amos Cummings knew the man was referring to the infamous Reed Party. "I've heard stories," he said. "That was a very long time ago. Surely things have improved."

"Things have improved, but blizzards is blizzards and they don't get better. Kit Carson couldn't get you to California safe this time of year. You can get to the Truckee Pass just fine. But you wouldn't get there before the second week in October. So you never would get on into Californy."

Amos nodded his head again, his frustration had peaked.

"It is simply not an acceptable proposition to me that I cannot make it to California before the first of the year," Amos said, and he spoke slowly and with purpose. "I have paid you a considerable sum of money already. And I am now telling you that I understand your objections, but I am asking that the money I have already paid to you would be sufficient to purchase solutions, rather than objections."

Albert Huntsdale looked at the ceiling and stuck a finger under his hat to scratch at his hair.

"I don't know if I can find him, and I don't know if he could be persuaded, but I might have a solution for you."

"What is that solution?" Amos asked.

"It ain't a what," Albert Huntsdale said. "It's a who that's your solution. A man I know. His daddy was a missionary among the Injuns. He's walked ever mile from Mexico City to Oregon, San Francisco to St. Louis. He's Kit Carson and Dan'l Boone all rolled into one. I heard tell the other day he was planning to take the Santa Fe Trail to New Mexico Territory and that he was planning to make that trip by hisself. If it were anybody else, that would be a foolish undertaking. But this boy could do it. If you could compel him, he could get you from Independence to Santa Fe. From there, you could follow the Southern Route into Californy. That's the same trail the Butterfield Overland uses to deliver the mail. You would need to find a guide, or maybe convince this man to do it, but you could make the Southern Route and get to Californy before the end of the year. Ain't no snows that away. You might die of thirst, and there will be Apache, but you won't freeze to death in no blizzard."

"Can you find this man?" Amos Cummings asked.

"If he ain't left, I can track him down. Where will I find you?"

"I've told my party to camp on the road east of town. We have with us six wagons, a dozen cattle, oxen and horses. We should be easy enough to find," Amos said.

"You'll be the only wagon train around, that's for sure!" Albert Huntsdale laughed. "E'ry other train is already bound for Californy."

*　*　*

The six wagons were arranged along the side of the road in a flat, dry space. There were trees enough nearby, and room for foraging for the animals.

Already the boys had managed the livestock.

Amos Cummings had bought oxen and mules to haul the wagons. He had spare animals that could relieve the others in case of illness or injury, and during their trip from their Ohio home, they had alternated the animals. He also had three good saddle horses which had come useful whenever the mules wandered. There were a few head of cattle, milk cows that could become meat if necessary. He had been told not to bring more than the one cow, but he reasoned that a dozen would not be difficult to keep up with and would be useful.

But it was difficult to keep them all corralled. The boys had found the easiest way was to rig up a temporary rope fence, and that is what they'd done here. They had a few posts they used and ran a rope at the top of the posts and another midway down. The cows had, a few times, slipped through the ropes or knocked down the posts, but for the most part the rope fence kept them in one place. And when it did not, they never got too far.

The horses were harder to keep corralled. They liked to wander, and when they went to running, the rope fence did nothing for them. So they slept with the horses tethered.

Beyond his own family – his wife, three sons, and daughter – Amos Cummings' small party consisted also of his assistant, a young man and former student Graham Devalt. Graham chose to make the journey so that he could continue studying under Amos and hoped to get a teaching job at the University of the Pacific as well. Stuart Bancroft, Amos' brother-in-law, was also coming west with his family, two sons, a daughter, and his wife.

Stuart, who was also an academic, intended to take up farming in the fertile California valley. He had studied and taught agricultural methods his entire adult life, but he had never put them into practice. When Amos received the engagement with the California university, Stuart viewed it as an opportunity to join his brother-in-law in California and make a try at farming.

Between them, they occupied six wagons loaded

with supplies for the westward journey.

Martha Cummings saw her husband on the road and walked out to meet him on the edge of the camp. The look on his face told her what she needed to know.

"We've missed the wagon train," he said.

"Oh, Amos. I am sorry," Martha offered. It was not much. The days that their daughter, Rachel, was sick with a fever had been hard days. They knew as each day passed that their chance of making the wagon train diminished. But she was so weak with the fever. The couple had lost a daughter three years before. Their youngest child. And so when the doctor said she needed rest and could not endure the journey, they stayed put. That was in a town in Illinois. Even after the fever broke, the doctor insisted Rachel was too weak to move.

And so they waited. More days. More delay.

"What are we going to do?" Martha asked.

Amos climbed down from the saddle. "There is a small chance. Huntsdale said he knows of a guide who is planning to go down the Santa Fe Trail. He might be enticed into taking us."

"I will pray that the Lord's will be done in this, and I will hope that His will matches with our will," Martha said, and she gave her husband a small smile.

"That is all that can be done," he said.

"When will we know?"

"Huntsdale said he would try to find this guide if he has not already left, and he said he would come and find us here."

"There is still some hope, then," Martha said.

Amos nodded agreement, whether he believed it or not. Martha Cummings could see that her husband felt dejected, and she wanted to find some way to cheer him up. If they were still at home, she might have suggested a lecture or a concert or maybe a stroll through a park. Here, though, on the edge of the frontier, it seemed that the only diversions were drink and bawdy dance halls.

Their youngest son, Paul, now fifteen years old, was toting buckets of water up from a creek and pouring the water into a trough for the animals to drink.

The middle son, seventeen year old Matthew, was rounding up firewood.

Twenty year old Jeremiah, Amos Cummings' oldest son, was just finishing tying off the rope corral.

These three boys were the real reason the family was coming west. The professorship at the University of the Pacific was the destination, but the boys were the reason.

Amos had followed the news of events in Kansas very closely. He kept up with the debates in Washington D.C.

Amos Cummings had foreseen trouble on the horizon for several months now. Most men could at least guess that it was coming. But Amos' intuition told him that the trouble would escalate to full scale war and that it would not be a simple, short-lived thing as some predicted. Instead, he believed that the war would rip the nation from the Mississippi to the Atlantic, and carry away its youth. He envisioned invading armies of free-staters going South and invading armies of pro-slavery Southerners coming North. And Amos believed their home across the Ohio River would be swept away with the ebb and flow of the armies.

Further, he believed his sons would follow their friends and join the army to fight. His family, for generations now, was an abolitionist family. Amos himself had helped people who helped runaway slaves. His family was also a peaceable family. Amos Cummings had raised his sons to abhor violence, but he knew that the pressure from peers and society to join the army would be tremendous. If they did not, peaceful principles would be shamed and they would be called cowards. But Amos Cummings was unwilling to sacrifice his sons on the altar of freedom, even freedom for the Negro — a cause that he held dear but believed it should be made real without violence. And so he sought safety for his sons in the farthest away place he could take them. In California, he believed, his sons would be untouched by a war.

So while he was desperate to get to his new professorship in California because it would provide the wages that would sustain his family, Amos' true urgency was in putting as many miles as possible between him and the conflict that he believed was coming to the east. The forthcoming election, he knew, could be the spark that ignited the powder keg.

Martha's younger brother, Stuart Bancroft, also believed war was coming. His children were younger and not in imminent danger of being recruited or conscripted into the army, but Stuart also lived across the Ohio River from Kentucky, and all indications convinced both men that Kentucky would side with the south. They knew what had happened in Lawrence when pro-slavery border ruffians from Missouri had come into Kansas, and they feared a similar fate would befall them.

So when Amos announced to his young brother-in-law that he was heading west, it did not take much to convince Stuart that his family should come along as well.

And likewise Graham Devalt, who had to fear conscription himself. As his assistant, Graham was privy to Amos Cummings' thoughts about the eventual conflict, and Graham had been easily convinced to come west.

But now Amos Cummings had to wonder what he had brought these people to. Would they be stuck for the winter in Independence, Missouri, on the border with Kansas, in the very place where the fighting had already begun? Amos had to wonder if there could be a worse place in the entire country to have to be when the election came.

"Stuart, Graham," Amos called to the other men. "Let's have a word."

They walked away from the camp, out of earshot of the women and children, and Amos told them what he had learned when he rode ahead into Independence.

"So our only hope of going farther rests with this guide who may have already left?" Stuart summarized.

"It seems so," Amos said. "Unless we decide that we will travel on our own, without a guide."

"How dangerous is that?" Graham asked.

"Certainly it is a risk," Amos conceded. "But we have come this far without a guide, and we have done well. And I believe the danger here, on the Missouri and Kansas border, could prove to be greater than anything we might face on the open prairie."

"There are not hostile Indians here," Graham noted.

"No, but there are hostile pro-slavery factions that

25

have already sacked a town. How would it go for us if we are camped here for months and people here discover that we are abolitionists from Ohio?"

Stuart nodded his agreement. "Our best hope is to keep moving. With or without a guide, we do not want to winter here."

Graham was a respectable and intelligent young man. Good looking and industrious, he had a bright future ahead of him in the academic world. Amos Cummings was pleased that during the journey so far he and Rachel had grown closer. Amos liked the idea of a blossoming romance between Graham and his only surviving daughter. His wife, Martha, also approved of the match and often compared Graham favorably to Amos himself. He was not much of a hand on a wagon train, it had to be admitted. Graham drove his wagon only with oxen attached because he could not manage the stubborn mules. But once the journey was made, a man's ability to manage mules was not nearly as important as his ability to provide for himself and his future wife. With Amos lending a guiding hand, surely Graham's abilities as a provider would be sufficient.

-3-

The man at the livery saw an easy mark in the youthfulness of the man looking at his horses, but he misjudged his customer.

"That gelding there is ideal for making the trip," the livery man swore. "He ain't but ten years old, and you can see how tame he is."

The young man shook his head, a grin on his face. "That gelding there is twenty-five years old if he's a day, and he's so tame because he's tired out from doing nothing all day. I get fifty or a hundred miles on to Santa Fe, and he'll be exhausted and ruined. That's assuming he makes it so far, which I doubt he will."

"Maybe fifteen years old, but he's spry enough."

"He's not spry enough to get out of his stall," the young man said. He reached into his pocket and withdrew a pipe and tobacco pouch. He pushed the pipe bowl and his thumb into the tobacco pouch and packed the bowl. He lit it with a match and puffed on the pipe a few times to get it going.

The young man was not particularly tall nor particularly broad, but he had a way of carrying himself that made him seem bigger than he was. He had long hair that spilled out from under his hat and fell straight down past his shoulders. His eyes were brown and thoughtful, and his face seemed fixed with a permanent grin, as if he was in on some joke that others were just about to find out about.

"No, sir," the young man said. "Ain't interested in an old hawss that can't make the journey. I need two hawsses, geldings or mares, something around ten years old, that will tote a pannier or a man or will be driven easily. They've got to have the endurance to make this trip with some speed, too."

The livery man shook his head. He was already getting frustrated that his customer was not going to be as easy as he thought. "You want one that can also make your coffee?"

"That one out yonder can make the coffee," the young man said, not missing a beat. "I ain't got time to break 'em in. I need good hawsses now. If you ain't got them, I'll go on to find someone who does."

"How about the bay there?"

"That bay sitting yonder in that stall is a fine looking animal," the young man said. "He's not been cared for particularly well, which is a shame because he might be a good animal otherwise."

"What do you mean?" the livery man demanded.

"I done looked him over. He's got cracked hooves. Only a blind fool would buy such a hawss to go on a thousand mile journey."

The young man said it all in an even tone. There

was not even any hint of accusation in what he said. "You should have a farrier come see to him. If you don't have any stock that's fit, I'll go and look elsewhere."

The livery man hemmed and hawed and tried to stall the young man, but the fact was he did not have a decent horse for sale. When the last of the wagon trains of the season supplied itself, they took his better horses. Those that were left were too aged for long travel or, as the young man said, in need of a farrier's attention. The only decent horses were the ones not for sale, these were the ones the livery man kept for his personal use or let out for local travel. Good horses were too hard to come by to go selling the best.

The man from the livery followed the young man out of the stalls to the street, and he saw the young man take a beautiful blue roan from a hitching post. It was as pretty a horse as the livery man had ever seen, a deep shade of blue like you wouldn't believe was natural. Its face was full black. When he saw the horse, he knew immediately who the young man was.

"Hey, boy, are you Rabbie Sinclair?"

The boy stopped, his horse's lead in one hand, his pipe still smoking in the other.

"That's right," Sinclair said.

"Why didn't you say so? Tie up that horse there and come with me out back. I've got a couple of horses in the paddock, my private stock. I don't normally sell those, but I could sell you two. Give you a good rate for 'em, too."

Rab Sinclair hitched up the blue roan and patted Cromwell on the neck. The blue was still a colt. Rab had him since he was a foal, and he'd started training him when he was just a yearling. Rab Sinclair was no wrangler, but he had a way with most animals, and a mutual trust existed between Rab and the roan. "I'll be back presently, maybe with a couple of riding partners for us."

Rab followed the man back through the livery to the paddock behind.

"I don't sell from the private stock, but I'll make an exception for you."

"I'm obliged," Rab said. "What made you decide that?"

"I knew your father, the preacher."

Rab Sinclair chuckled. "He weren't really a preacher," Rab said.

"Well, whether he was a preacher or not is neither here nor there. My wife's brother was among that stranded party up in the San Juan Mountains six years ago. I reckon there ain't much I wouldn't do for Preacher Sinclair's son."

It seemed wherever he went, Rab encountered someone who was either with the party in the San Juans or was related to someone who was. His father would have said it was God's hand guiding him, but Rab suspected it had more to do with the size of the wagon train. More than a hundred wagons following a bad trail with no decent guide, and they got stranded in a blizzard. Preacher Sinclair was with the Utes that winter. Rab was there, too. A Scotsman who fancied himself a Presbyterian missionary, Preacher Sinclair convinced the Utes to take in the stranded folks and shelter and feed them through the winter. More than three hundred white emigrants survived that winter because of the decency of the Ute people, and Preacher Sinclair got all the credit.

"Did you recognize me by my hawss?" Rab asked, puffing on his pipe.

"Surely did," the liveryman said. "When you're in the horse business, as I am, you hear about special horses. A couple months back they was in here talking about that pretty blue roan that Preacher Sinclair's son was riding. I saw that one out front, and I knew right away what horse it was. So you're going on the Santa Fe Train, are you?"

"I reckon so," Rab Sinclair said. "I heard there was a gold strike at Pinos Altos in New Mexico Territory, and I thought I might wander down that way and see if I can't put some gold in my pockets."

"Whatever became of your pa, Preacher Sinclair?"

"Pa died about four years ago. We was living among the Kiowa and he took a fever."

"I am sorry to hear that," the liveryman said. "He was a hero to those people he helped out of the mountains that time. You been on your own since then?"

"I have," Rab said. "The Kiowa turned me out after my pa died. They liked his Bible sermons, but I didn't do no preaching so I wasn't any use to them."

"What about that one there? The buckskin? That's a good gelding and would make a good trail horse. You can put your pannier on him, or saddle him up. And that sorrel, that's a mare. Both of those would be good trail horses. You can lead 'em, pack 'em, or ride 'em. I'd sell both of them to you for an even hundred dollars. I could sell them to anybody else for sixty dollars apiece, so that's a good price."

Rab looked over both horses, ran his hands along their legs and over their sides. They had good, strong hind legs. The hooves were clean and clipped.

"You take good care of these hawsses," Rab said. "You should take as good a care to the ones in the livery. I'll spend a hundred dollars on the sorrel and the buckskin."

"You think you'll find gold in New Mexico?" the liveryman asked.

"It's hard to say what will happen when it ain't happened yet," Rab said. "I know I have a better chance of finding gold in New Mexico Territory than I have of finding it here. Anyway, it's something to do."

The liveryman took his money, and Rab led the horses out to the roan. He climbed into Cromwell's saddle and led the buckskin and sorrel, and he started to ride out of town. Both horses were in good shape, old enough that he didn't expect they'd give him any trouble by running off, but young enough that they could endure the long distance. They were well built, strong horses. The sorrel was a pretty red with a light red mane and tail, and the buckskin was a light, even tan with a black mane and tail and four black socks.

He'd gone no more than a few blocks when he saw Albert Huntsdale over on the boardwalk in front of some offices waving to him and calling his name.

Two years ago, Rab had worked as a guide for one of Huntsdale's big wagon trains when one of his usual guides took ill. With his father, Rab had made the Oregon Trail journey twice from start to finish, and he'd lived in the area of the trail almost all his life. His youth had been a problem for some of the people in the wagon train, but by the end of the journey, Rab had won them over by passing the ultimate test, he safely deposited them in California.

He returned from California the next year by the Southern Route and the Santa Fe Trail, and had been in Independence ever since. Albert tried to entice him to serve as a guide on a wagon train again, but Sinclair declined. When they'd last encountered each other, Rab Sinclair had told the old man that he intended to go back to New Mexico.

Like most folks who met him, Huntsdale took an immediate liking to Rab Sinclair.

"I was worried you'd already left Independence," Albert said.

"Leaving out in the morning," Rab said.

"Still planning to take the Santa Fe Trail?"

"I'll go another way if you know a shorter route to New Mexico Territory," Rab said.

Huntsdale laughed. "I don't know a shorter route, but I might know how you can make it more profitable to yourself."

"How is that?" Rab asked.

"I've got a small group that missed the last wagon train to California," Huntsdale said. "They showed up in Independence yesterday. They're desperate to go now, even though they missed the last train."

"If they go by the Oregon Trail they'll never make Truckee Pass before the snows."

"That's what I told them," Huntsdale said. "But they're insistent. I remembered you saying you were planning to go the Santa Fe Trail. I'd pay you fifty dollars to guide them to Santa Fe. Once you're there, if you would help them find a guide on to Californy, I'd be obliged."

Rab looked behind him at the two fifty dollar horses he'd just bought. Supplies to get to Santa Fe and two fifty dollar horses had tapped out almost all the money he had. He knew once he was in New Mexico he would need money for prospecting tools – a pan and digging implements.

"They would slow me down something fierce," Rab Sinclair said.

Albert Huntsdale nodded his head. "They would do that, I reckon."

"I ain't going to be responsible for their care, nor will I round up the animals they let stray off," Rab said.

"They should plan to be responsible for their own stock. I agree," Huntsdale said.

"If they fail to ration water and food, I'll not suffer by giving them mine."

"You ain't carrying that much anyways, not if you're packing on the trail," Huntsdale agreed.

"I reckon they might take some of the loneliness out of the trip, though. Eight weeks is quite a while to be alone with yourself."

"Eight weeks is long enough for a man to forget the language if it ain't spoke at him," Huntsdale said.

"I'll not ride behind 'em and eat their dust the whole way. They can follow along behind me."

"Be hard to guide 'em from behind, anyway," Huntsdale said.

"If they're inclined to follow me, I suppose I can't stop them."

Huntsdale spat tobacco juice into the dirt road.

"Beggars can't be choosers, Rab. If that don't meet with their approval, then they can camp in Independence through the winter and go with the first train out next spring."

-4-

The buckboard was loaded with flour, salt, lamp oil and other supplies. Ted Gibson was in no hurry. He'd make it home in plenty of time to beat the dark. The ride to town was two days there and two back. He rose early on his second day and was making good time. He didn't like being away from the farm for any length of time and hated these four-day treks to get supplies. Indian raids were rare but not unheard of, and it always worried Ted to leave his wife and children. She was a strong woman and would do what she had to. She'd stared down Indians with a scattergun before, and she could do it again. Still, Ted preferred to be at home.

But he did enjoy the solitude of the ride across the tall grass prairie. Off in the distance, ominous clouds colored the sky dark gray and black, but Ted had been watching the storm through the morning and believed it would blow north of him.

Riding out across the prairie, the terrain looked flat as it could be, going on forever to the horizon as one long, flat green place. A stand of trees, that usually indicated the presence of a creek, was an occasional break on the horizon. But Ted Gibson understood that across that flat looking plain there were plenty of low hills and hollows, all subtle and nearly invisible until a man was on top of them. Those hollows could hide creeks, trees, a herd of buffalo, and even a hundred Indians.

The buckboard wagon, loaded with supplies that would see his family through the winter, creaked and rocked as the mules pulled it through the tall grass. If there'd been more rain this summer, the mules might have had more trouble cutting through the grass, even with the wide wheels of the wagon. But he rolled along pretty well, making good time.

When he topped a hill overlooking a deep meadow with a small creek running through it, Ted did not at first see the three men and the six horses. They were standing under a stand of cottonwoods, watering their horses at the creek. He saw the three men when one of the horses wandered away from the creek to graze.

Ted put the break on the wagon and pulled back on the reins to stop the mules. He sat for a moment, looking down at the trees, and then he spotted the men.

Right away, Ted had an uneasy feeling about the three men. Strangers were an uncommon sight.

He was thinking about turning the mules and fording the creek a little farther to the south, hoping to avoid any contact with the strangers. But he was too late in reaching his decision.

"Howdy!" one of the men called up to him.

The man started walking up the slope toward Ted. He wore a broad smile, but even so his face gave an appearance of hostility.

"How are you?" Ted called back to him.

The other two men were now out from under the trees, watching. They made no greeting.

The man coming toward him wore a Colt Army revolver on his hip.

"Just watering our horses," the man said, still walking toward the wagon.

"I didn't expect to see anyone out here today," Ted said. "I make this journey to town a few times a year, and I can't recall ever running across anyone other than a few Indians looking to beg or barter."

"We ain't Injuns," the man said. "My name is Bill, and down there are Dick and Chester."

"Pleased to meet you," Ted said. "I'd love to stay and chat, but I'm trying to beat that storm." Ted nodded his head at the clouds off to the west.

Bill turned and looked at the clouds. "Those'll blow north of us," he said. "You should be fine. How far is your place?"

"It's a ways, still," Ted said.

"How many people you got at home?" Bill asked.

It seemed a strange question, and Ted was uncomfortable offering an honest answer. "Just me and my two sons."

In fact, waiting for him at home were his wife and daughter, his wife's mother and sister, and four sons. But only one of Ted's sons was big enough to heft the Enfield rifle and put it to any good use. Ted still did all of the hunting.

"Your sons ain't got a mother?" Bill asked.

"She took ill and died a year ago," Ted said.

Maybe it was the meanness in Bill's face, but Ted's intuition told him it would be unwise to let this man know that there were women at his homestead.

With Dick Derugy and Chess Bowman watching from down at the creek, Pawnee Bill walked around to the back of the buckboard wagon. He took out his Bowie knife and cut one of the ropes tying down the oilcloth.

"What are you doing?" Ted Gibson asked, and he leaped down off of the buckboard and went toward Pawnee Bill.

"I'm just looking to see if you've got anything I might could trade off of you," Bill said. He was working to keep the smile on his face, but it was slipping.

Pawnee Bill flipped back the corner of the oilcloth and looked into the wagon.

"I'm not interested in trading," Ted said, but he did not take a step more toward Pawnee Bill, nor did he make a move to stop him.

"Well, you don't know what I might have to trade," Pawnee Bill said. "You don't know that I might have just the thing you're looking for, and if you've got just the thing I'm looking for then maybe a trade might do for both of us."

"I just have supplies," Ted said, but there was a tone to his voice that caught in Pawnee Bill's ear. It was a tone of pleading. It was a tone of weakness that Pawnee Bill like to hear.

"You don't think I'm the kind of man who likes to be supplied, too?" Pawnee Bill asked. His tone carried a note of harshness, a note of challenge. The smile was gone.

"I don't mean to insult," Ted Gibson said, and he held up his hands in a gesture of surrender.

Pawnee Bill reached across and grabbed the farmer by the wrist and in a swift motion lifted Ted Gibson's arm up over his head. With his other hand, the one holding the knife, Pawnee Bill swung and plunged the knife into Ted's exposed armpit.

Ted Gibson screamed and tried to wrench his wrist from Pawnee Bill's hand, but the wound under his arm had stolen all the strength. Bill twisted the knife as he jerked it free, and then he swung it a second time, driving it into Ted Gibson's side, under his ribcage.

When Pawnee Bill jerked the knife clear again, Ted Gibson collapsed to his knees in pain.

Now Pawnee Bill's face broke into a genuine smile, and he laughed heartily at the struggling farmer.

"Now let's see what you've got in here that's worth trading for."

He cut more ropes from the oilcloth and pushed it farther away, exposing more of the contents of the wagon.

The farmer struggled to get his breath and hugged his wounded arm and side.

"There's nothing in there," Ted Gibson said.

Pawnee Bill ignored him, picking through the sacks and boxes. "Why, there's a tent, and flour, and lamp oil. I ain't got a lamp, but I might find one. There's lots of things in here a man might use."

Pawnee Bill lifted the flap on his holster and slid

out his Colt Army.

"I'll tell you what I'll do. I'll trade you everything inside this wagon – and the wagon and mules, too – for one of the lead balls in this gun."

He drew back the hammer, pointed the gun at Ted Gibson's back, and pulled the trigger.

The explosion made the mules dance, but they didn't try to run.

"Bring up them wagons," Bill called. "We're going to take this wagon. There's supplies enough in here to last us for months. There's even powder and balls. I've got an idea."

Dick and Chess collected the horses and walked them up the hill of the hollow. Dick stuck the toe of his boot against the farmer and kicked him over onto his back. "I think you've killed him," Dick Derugy said.

"Well, I hope so," Pawnee Bill answered. "I stabbed him twice and shot him. He'd better be dead."

Chess was almost afraid to ask. He'd grown wary of Pawnee Bill's ideas. "What's your idea, Bill?"

Pawnee Bill smiled at them, but it just made him look meaner. "Why don't we ride down the Santa Fe Trail to New Mexico Territory? I've had enough of Kansas."

-5-

Amos Cummings led Albert Huntsdale away from the camp to speak to him privately. They left the young guide standing beside one of Cummings' wagons.

"Mr. Huntsdale, I appreciate that you've found a guide so quickly who can take us along the Santa Fe Trail, but I have to question whether or not this man is fit to serve. He is no older than my own son, and that is not an age that I would trust to see to the safety of my entire family."

"It's like this, Mr. Cummings," Huntsdale said. "I ain't got guides or wagon masters that work for me who will take you down the Santa Fe Trail. They's others leave out of Independence, and maybe you can find one who will take you, but you'll have to pay them without getting a return on your payment from me. If that's what you choose to do, then farewell and good luck to you. But because you've paid me up front, and even though you were late and it weren't no fault o' mine, I did what I could for you. I've told Rabbie Sinclair that I'll pay him to guide you to Santa Fe, and he's agreed to help you see about a guide to get you on to Californy.

"He's young," Albert Huntsdale continued. "I'll grant ye that. But if I was going to make a journey west, by any trail with any destination in mind, Rabbie Sinclair is the first guide I would look to if I wanted to get there in safety. But it's your choice."

"It very much seems to me that your business practices would come under suspicion of the law if we were back east," Amos Cummings said. "Though I certainly acknowledge that I signed a contract, I cannot help but feel that I have been the victim of a swindle. And now you offer me a boy as a poor substitute for the wagon train I should have been on."

Albert Huntsdale deliberately spit between Amos Cummings' feet, leaving a black spot of tobacco juice in the dirt road.

"Do as you please," Huntsdale said. "Rabbie Sinclair is riding off to Santa Fe in the morning. You can go with him or not. He'll lead the way so long as you keep up with him. Two days ago you come and find me at the saloon, all fired ready to head out for Californy. I told you I'd find you a guide, and that I've done. Today, you don't like the guide and you accuse me of cheating you when no man on this earth forced you to sign that contract. Do as you please. If you decide to winter here and go in the spring, you've paid your passage and I'll put you on with the first wagon train going west in the spring. Otherwise, I have no business more with you."

With that, Albert Huntsdale waved to Rab Sinclair.

"I hope to see you again one day, Rabbie. Good luck to you."

Rab returned the wave.

Amos Cummings watched Albert Huntsdale climb into the seat of a buggy and drive off back toward town.

Rab Sinclair dug his pipe into his tobacco pouch. He struck a match and held it over the bowl to set the tobacco alight.

"Mr. Cummings, I can see you're not pleased with me as a guide," Rab said. "I don't blame you none for that. I'll allow I'm a bit young. I ain't here to convince you. Mr. Huntsdale has paid me, whether you follow me or not. I'll camp over there across the way. That'll leave you and your people in peace tonight to speak free and decide what you want to do. I'll leave out at sunup. If you're coming with me, you should be ready to leave as soon as we see the sun. All these animals and wagons you've got, we won't get ten miles into Kansas tomorrow because you'll be all morning ferrying across the river. And ten miles into Kansas is a poor place to be these days."

"Why is that?" Amos Cummings asked.

"All along the border, here, you've got some bad sorts. A team of six wagons looks like easy prey to men like that. I don't know them to attack emigrants, so much, but I also don't know them to have any rules against attacking emigrants."

The young man pulled his slouch hat with the dome crown down over his eyes and led the three horses away to a clear spot on the opposite side of the road. Amos Cummings watched him as he cleared out a spot for a fire, unpacked his gear, and began heating a pot for coffee. Then he turned to his family and traveling companions to seek their counsel.

"I'll tell you straight away, I think he's too young

and I don't like it," Graham Devalt said.

Amos appreciated his young assistant and he valued him, but he did not know how much weight he gave the young man's opinion in this issue.

"Tell me why you don't like it," Amos said.

"He must be at least three or four years younger than I am. I'm a university graduate, and I wouldn't have any idea how to guide a wagon train to New Mexico Territory. I'm not sure I could even find it on a map."

Stuart Bancroft, Amos's wife's brother, took a different view.

"If we're going to make this journey successful, we need to be to Santa Clara before spring," Stuart said. "If my intention is to see to planting a farm, that's spring work. If we wait until spring to make the journey with another wagon train, that will put me off an entire year. And your position at the university could be in jeopardy."

"I agree with you about that, Stuart," Amos said. "We have been besieged by delays from the very beginning, and further delay could be ruinous. But I am hesitant to put the lives of my family in the hands of a boy."

Stuart nodded thoughtfully. "I understand, Amos. But their lives are still in our hands. He's just giving us directions. If you drove your wagon into a strange town and needed to find a hotel, but the only person who offered directions was the same age as your son, would you not follow those directions because he is too young?"

"Finding a hotel in a town is not nearly the same thing as getting across the prairie and the mountains to find a territorial capital."

Martha Cummings, Stuart's sister and Amos's wife, was listening to the conversation. She had been present when Albert Huntsdale introduced the guide, and she had listened to Huntsdale praise the boy's knowledge of the wilderness.

"He has made the journey on the Santa Fe Trail already," Martha interrupted. "Is that not the case?"

"That is the case," Amos Cummings said. "Insofar as we know, he has. Mr. Huntsdale said that he has, and the boy himself said he has."

"He's not really a boy," Martha said. "He is young, certainly, but he is a man."

"True. It is hard not to think of him as a boy, though."

"I also think it suggests something about his abilities that was intending to make the journey by himself. He obviously has confidence in himself," Martha said.

"That confidence might be misplaced," Amos said.

"It might be," Martha conceded. "But if he is as experienced as he has given us cause to believe, he would know if he was suited to make such a trip alone."

"He does not inspire confidence in me," Graham Devalt interjected. "His is slovenly, his clothes are soiled, and that constant grin upon his face is cavalier to the point of being boorish. Is he even the sort of influence you want around Rachel and your sons?"

Martha noted Graham Devalt's consideration for her daughter. She knew that Amos envisioned a time when Graham would be a son-in-law, but Martha's intuition made her suspicious if it was only Amos who viewed Graham as a suitable match for their daughter. She'd not yet seen evidence that Rachel felt the same way about it.

"I will grant you that he is rude," Martha agreed. "The way he smokes that pipe and leans so casually against the wagon, his shoulders slumped forward in such a manner. But if he were the very picture of New England virtues and mannerisms, we might not wish to have him lead us across the prairie."

"I must agree with my sister," Stuart said. "If his clothes are soiled, we might suspect that our own clothes will need washing before we have reached Santa Clara."

Amos Cummings knew that it was on him to make the final decision. As the head of the household, the oldest, and the man who fronted nearly all the money for the journey, the decision was his alone to make.

The sun was setting in the west now. It had already dropped below the trees so that everything was cast in shadow. But for the small fire burning across the road and the silhouettes of the three horses, he would not know the young guide was across the way.

"It does us no good to stay here. We cannot afford to try to buy our way in to another wagon train bound for Southern Route, nor can we wait for spring. Everyone should be prepared to be up and ready to leave at sunup."

Later that night, on bedrolls next to each other and near their wagon, Martha spoke to her husband in a soft whisper.

"I have a good feeling about the guide," she said. "Something about him struck a good chord with me. I believe he is more competent than his youth would suggest."

"I hope you are correct," Amos said. "I am not as assured as you are, but our options seem woefully limited."

***

Rachel Cummings sat on the driver's bench of the wagon beside her mother. It was still morning on the fifth day out from Independence. That first morning had been a horror attempting to ferry across the Missouri River, but the road was good from Independence to Lawrence, and they made excellent time. They were beyond Lawrence and cutting along a well-worn trail, if not exactly a road.

Rachel and her mother Martha drove the first of the wagons. Stuart's wife, Rebekah Bancroft, and daughter Faith, drove the second wagon. Amos and Stuart were currently on the horses pushing the cattle along.

Ahead of them, pushing his pack horse and his spare mount, and riding the beautiful blue roan, Rab Sinclair sat dozing in his saddle.

"Mr. Sinclair!" Rachel called ahead.

Rab jerked his head up with a start and turned in his saddle. He checked the two horses ahead of them, and both were maintaining the trail, so he wheeled Cromwell and rode back toward the wagon.

"Yes, ma'am?" he said.

"I have heard that the prairie and plains do not support trees, and yet I see stands of trees off in every direction."

Rab looked around, though he knew there were

plenty of rows and stands of trees within sight.

"Miss Rachel, we're not properly out on the prairie yet, exactly," Rab said. "When we get another two hundred miles or so west of here, you'll wonder where all the trees went. It's not exactly correct to say that there are none, but they are so few as to be worth very little beyond a shady spot to escape the afternoon sun. When we get farther to the west, we'll be in among the long grass, and that will be the prairie, proper. This here is just the prelude, you might say."

"Do you prefer living on the plains, Mr. Sinclair?" Martha asked.

Rab had grown accustomed to the questions from the women. Mrs. Cummings, the older woman, was gentle and kind. The girl seemed to always have a motive to tease when she went to asking questions, and Rab was all but certain Martha now asked about where he preferred living to divert the girl's questions.

"It's a hard life on the plains," Rab admitted. "My preference is in a mountain valley, if you want to know the truth. I like the scenery better in the mountains, and I like having forests around. It's easier to hunt and survive in places where water and trees are more plentiful. But I enjoyed my time among the plains people. The Arapaho, in particular, are a colorful people and very skilled at riding hawsses. I learned a great deal about riding from them."

"Did you always live among the savages?" Rachel asked.

"Most of the time," Rab said. "My father fancied himself a bit of a missionary. I lived with the Ute around the mountains for the longest time. They are a good people, also."

"Was it not difficult for you to be reared away from your own people?" Martha Cummings asked.

"I never really saw it that away," Rab Sinclair said. "We went to towns often enough, but when we lived among the Indians, they were my people. I fished and hunted with the Indian boys and didn't think of them as anything other than my friends. I never considered them to be savages, as you say."

"Are they dangerous?" Martha asked. "Should we be afraid of encountering them?"

Rab scratched at his chin as he rode along.

"Ma'am, that's hard to say," Rab said. "Are white men dangerous? Should you be afraid of encountering them?"

"Some of them," Martha said. "Some of them live outside the law. I would hope, though, that when I encounter a white man, I could have an expectation that he would treat me as a friend."

"Well, I'd give the same answer back to you, then. The Indians, some of them, are dangerous. But you can always hope when you encounter them that they'll treat you as a friend."

Martha Cummings smiled at his answer, but her daughter was frustrated with it.

"You just talk in circles sometimes, Mr. Sinclair," Rachel said.

"I don't mean to, ma'am," Rab said.

"Are there some tribes that are more dangerous than others?" Martha asked.

Again Rab scratched at his chin. "I reckon I would not want to turn my back on an Apache or a Comanche," he said. "I did not live long among either of those tribes. Some tribes welcomed my father and his teachings, but other tribes made it clear that we were unwelcome. In particular, the Comanche and the Apache had little use for us. What I would say beyond that is that when we stopped being a curiosity to them, some of the people in the tribes – and it didn't matter which tribe – began to have less use for us."

"What do you mean a curiosity?" Martha asked.

"With him being a preacher, the tribes mostly respected my father's medicine. They'd allow him in and let them talk at them some. My father was a Scotchman, and so he never took up the languages of the people much. He couldn't get his mouth to pronounce anything that didn't sound like Scottish. But they'd listen to him and respect him and treat him decent just because he had big medicine. But when more white folks started showing up, digging up the land looking for gold or digging up the land to plant crops or killing everything that had fur and taking only its pelt, the people stopped being curious about us quite as much. They never had to go too far to find more white people. And so about a decade ago, when I was about ten years old, that's when we never stayed with one tribe for more than a few weeks."

"It sounds like a very lonely way to grow up, Mr. Sinclair," Martha said.

"It wasn't so bad," Rab said. "Maybe if I'd known some other way I might think different about it, but it was the way I knew."

"What about your mother?" Rachel asked. "Did she object to moving about among the Indian tribes?"

"I didn't have a mother, exactly," Rab said. "My father took up with a number of different squaws, and I suppose some of them was mothers to me. But they never objected to living among their own people that I recall."

It was a scandalous statement, and even Martha Cummings, who seemed to have a kindness toward Rab Sinclair, was appalled at what he said.

"Mr. Sinclair, I do not think that's an appropriate thing to say, either to me or to my daughter."

Rab smiled at her in his easy way.

"I didn't mean to give offense, ma'am," he said.

He squeezed Cromwell's sides and urged the horse to run on ahead. The sorrel, carrying the pack, had stopped to munch some grass. Rab got up to the sorrel and gave it a tap on the rear.

"Come on, you!" he called to the horse. "It ain't supper time yet."

The sorrel started on its way, but Cromwell dropped his head into the grass and began to eat. Rab took the moment of still air to dig the bowl of his pipe into his tobacco pouch and light the pipe. Then he pushed Cromwell on ahead while he smoked the pipe. Like most men who spent hours of solitude in the saddle, Rab had a habit of talking to his horse.

"How do you think about that, hawss?" Rab said to Cromwell. "Not appropriate to say the truth. That's white women for you. They ask you a question, and when you give it to them straight with a true answer, they chastise you over it. Remind me not to accept too many more questions in the future," he said.

-6-

The small collection of buildings could not rightly be called a town or even a settlement.

A store and a tavern, a cluster of sod houses all tucked down in a hollow under some cottonwoods near a creek is all it was. The place had no name that anyone used. It sprang up as a stop along the way to Colorado Territory for those off to seek gold. Abner Spears set up the place near a well-used trail to sell tools and supplies to gold seekers trying to get into the mountains. For a while he did good business, and he found travelers paid best for other services – repairing wagon wheels and offering fresh mounts made good profit, but nothing beat the business he did in always having something warm to offer for supper.

But when Denver City began to thrive, the traffic into the gold fields of the mountains shifted north and the collection of buildings that wasn't exactly a town or a settlement began to suffer. Abner and his family and the few folks who still lived in the place managed to eke out a life trading with the Arapaho and the few white folks who sometimes passed through, but the heyday was over.

And with the diminished prospects, a meanness had settled in to life around Abner Spears' little collection of buildings. The half dozen men who called the place home usually spent their days sitting and drinking.

Pawnee Bill, Dick Derugy, and Chess Bowman fell in easily with the other men here.

For a couple of days now, Bill and his two companions had put aside their thoughts of traveling to New Mexico Territory. They'd taken to drinking with Abner Spears and the others, and it was easier to sit and drink than to hitch the wagon and keep going.

Mickey Hogg was among those men living in the hollow with Abner Spears, and Pawnee Bill had taken an immediate liking to Mickey. Crass and vulgar, Mickey Hogg was unapologetic. He drank and chewed, and he spoke his mind on issues ranging from women to Negroes to Injuns, and he had no love for interfering Yankee foreigners coming to Kansas to sway votes. He did not have the same animosity for interfering pro-slavers coming to Kansas from Missouri and Arkansas.

"I've been living in this territory most of my life and come from Missouri," Hogg proclaimed in one of his many drunken speeches. "If I see a man from Pennsylvania or Ohio, why he's as foreign to me and as foreign to these parts as the King of Russia would be. And he deserves neither respect nor hospitality, and he'll get none of both. Some Yankee bastard wants to tell me how I can live and how I can't or what I can own and what I can't, that ain't none of his business."

The saloon was nothing more than a sod hut, and the grease paper windows left the place dark. Only three lanterns burned – one at each end and one behind the bar. The bar was two old water casks set side by side with a couple of plank boards laid down over them. Everything about the saloon was cheap. But the nine men inside were a raucous and ornery bunch, made hard by the winds that whipped the lonely prairie and made irritable by the lack of womenfolk. Abner Spears' wife and a half-breed whore who worked in a lean-to out behind the saloon were the only two women who lived down in the hollow.

Besides Pawnee Bill, Dick Derugy and Chess Bowman, a half-dozen others were drinking in the saloon. Abner and his son Waymond took turns as bartender, but both were also drinking heavily. Mickey Hogg was holding court. Abner's cousins Wesley and Earl Spears were in the saloon, and a rough man named Wallace was also drinking.

Wallace had come to the hollow the previous summer and had built himself up a little hut up creek some. The rumor was that he had a squaw that he kept at his hut. He came to the hollow to drink and sometimes buy supplies. Abner and the other men figured he was running from the law. He always toted with him a Kentucky long rifle and two Colt Paterson five-shooters that he'd had in the war with Mexico. Wallace was a grizzled man, in his late thirties though he could have passed for fifty, and he'd hinted several times of having been with the Texas Rangers in the Mexican war back in '46 and '47.

"What would you do about it?" Wallace spoke up, startling everyone.

"What's that, old man?" Mickey Hogg asked.

"If a Yankee, or the King of Russia, was to walk into this sod saloon right now and tell you that you couldn't own Negroes no more, what would you do about it?"

Mickey Hogg laughed derisively. "Don't you ask questions unless you want to know the answer."

"I'm askin'," Wallace said. "Every time I come in here for a drink, you're mouthin' off about what you'd do about this and what you'd do about that, but all I ever see you do is toss back drinks. So I'm askin' what you'd do about it. Let's say I'm the King of Russia. What are you going to say to me?"

Pawnee Bill licked his lips. The tension in the small saloon grew palpable in the space of a breath. Everything suggested to Pawnee Bill this was bound to be some excitement, the first he'd seen since they took that wagon off the sod buster.

Abner Spears felt it, too. Drunk though he was, he raised up a hand to intercede.

"Boys, now, there ain't no call for disagreement."

Abner couldn't even remember what was said, now. He'd only been half listening but he was full drunk. All he knew for sure was that both of these men were carrying guns.

Mickey Hogg toted a double barrel scattergun with the barrels sawed short. Wallace toted those two Patersons.

Dick Derugy and Waymond Spears were sitting either side of Wallace, and as one they both stood from their chairs and backed away from the line of fire.

"Don't press me old man," Mickey Hogg said.

Wallace intended to jump to his feet, but it was more of a scramble than a leap. He threw one of those five-shot Patersons as he stood, but the barrel was so long, and it got hung up on the table.

A sober man would have been able to say that Wallace was faster on the draw, but he couldn't beat the table.

Mickey Hogg, who seemed genuinely shocked that Wallace was moving, grabbed at the shotgun. He'd rigged up a hook on his belt that allowed him to swivel the gun but not easily remove it. Younger and maybe a little less drunk, Mickey Hogg got to his feet more easily than Wallace had, and he mule-kicked his chair to send it flying behind him. That gave him clearance to swivel up the double barrel scattergun.

Mickey Hogg thrust his hip toward Wallace, cocking back both hammers, and he pulled both triggers.

The shot from the two blasts spread out wide, but plenty shot from both barrels found Wallace. The older man's torso was shredded by the pellets. The force of it knocked him backwards and he stumbled over his chair and fell to the ground.

"The king is dead!" Mickey Hogg yelled, dancing a jig. "Long live the King of Russia!"

Pawnee Bill hooted in glee, and Dick Derugy and Chess Bowman both clapped their hands in time and joined Mickey Hogg in his dance.

"Dammit and tarnation!" Abner Spears shouted. "Mickey Hogg, you take your good for nothing ass out of this saloon before I flog you. Waymond, check Wallace and see if he's dead."

Mickey Hogg worked the shotgun out of its rig and ejected the two spent shells. He reached into his pocket and replaced them. The whole time he craned his neck to look past the table at the body on the floor.

Abner Spears' son bent down on his knee and looked at the older man.

"He's shot all to hell, pa," Waymond declared. "He's still breathing, but he ain't awake."

Mickey Hogg's face cracked into a smile, and he turned around and walked out of the saloon. Pawnee Bill followed him, and Dick and Chess followed Pawnee Bill.

"Drag him outside," Abner Spears said. "Drag him down to the creek a ways and leave him somewhere that we won't smell him."

There was no doctor in the hollow and Abner Spears wasn't about to go digging in someone's body to try to remove lead pellets. A gunshot wound like this was probably fatal in New York City where an entire army of doctors might tend to the man, but down in Abner Spears' hollow, it was unquestionably fatal.

Mickey Hogg was pleased with himself. This was the first real test of the rig he'd concocted for his scattergun. It was not innovative. The fact was, it was clumsy and inconvenient at all times except a gunfight, but in a gunfight it had served. It was nothing more than a clip attached to his belt that swiveled at the end so that the barrel could always hang toward the ground. He'd put a metal loop into the stock near the trigger so that it could hang on the clip.

"Did you see the look on his face?" Mickey Hogg asked. His teeth shone a dingy yellow behind his thick beard and mustache. "That old man couldn't believe it when his pistola hit the table. He knew he was done for then. Should have never tried to draw on me. Bam! Bam! I got him just like that."

"That scattergun makes it hard to miss," Pawnee Bill said.

"Bam! Bam!" Mickey Hogg said. "The King of Russia, dead down in a hollow on the Kansas prairie."

A moment later Waymond Spears backed out of the saloon doorway. He had hold of Wallace's wrists and was dragging the dying man out of the saloon. Abner Spears followed them out.

"Mickey Hogg, you ain't welcome back in this saloon. You ain't welcome in my store. And you ain't welcome in my town. Come sunup, you need to move out."

Mickey laughed in his face.

"This ain't no town," he said. "And it ain't no place for me to stay. I was leaving anyway."

Abner turned back into the saloon.

"What you goin' to do?" Pawnee Bill asked.

"I don't know," Mickey Hogg said. "Maybe go into Denver City. Maybe go into the mountains. They say there's still prospecting that's payin' off."

Pawnee Bill took a drink from the beer he'd toted out of the saloon with him.

"You could ride with us," Bill said. "We'd be happy for the company."

"Where are you bound for?" Mickey Hogg asked.

"New Mexico Territory."

"Leaving at sunup?" Mickey asked.

"We can," Pawnee Bill said.

"I guess there ain't no difference between Colorado

and New Mexico," Mickey Hogg said. "They's both territories, anyway. I'll ride with you."

"Do not grease them animals," Rab Sinclair said to Matthew Cummings, the middle son of Amos and Martha. "Wash the animals, grease the wheels."

"My father told me to grease them," Matthew said.

Rab Sinclair was idly smoking his pipe, sitting on the back of the sorrel. The small wagon train had stopped for the afternoon, having made only ten miles that day.

They were now seven days out from Independence, and the wagons were slowing Rab Sinclair's pace.

"I ain't one to tell a boy not to do what his pa told him to," Rab said. "But you ought not to grease them animals. When we stop for camp, you wash them with water, maybe a little soap every other day. Brush 'em down some. Take care of them live stock better, and they'll move us along faster. Leave off the grease, and don't mention it one way or t'other to your pa. And if he says anything to you about the grease, you have him come and talk to me."

Matthew stood for a moment, indecisive. Rab Sinclair was a guide and nothing more. He did not work around camp, he barely lifted a finger to help with anything along the trail. For seven days he had camped alone, away from the wagons. He took his meals by himself on his own fire. On the trail, Rab Sinclair talked to his horses more than he spoke to his traveling companions.

"Here, if I do it for you, then you won't have to explain to your father why you didn't grease the stock."

Rab Sinclair swung his leg over and slid down from his saddle. He took up a bucket of water and a brush and began washing an ox with water. He then brushed the ox. He went on doing it, moving from one ox to the next, until Matthew Cummings decided at last to give up with the grease and help him.

"Keep them clean with water and soap, brush them, and it will help them to avoid sore necks. If they ain't sore, you'll get more work out of them. They'll move faster and take the harness easier. The grease don't help keep down the sores. It's mistreatment, is what it is. Grease holds dirt, and dirt rubs the skin raw when the harness is on. Oxen are big, dumb animals, and they're slow enough on their best day. When they're sore and raw, they go slower. You move too slow on the prairie, and you die."

After some time, Amos Cummings came by.

"I thought I told you to apply grease to the animals," he said to Matthew.

"I told him to stop," Rab Sinclair intervened, though he did not look away from the mule he was washing. "Wash these animals, do not grease 'em."

Amos started to argue, but then thought better of it. Instead, he said to Matthew, "When you're done here, put them into the corral. Your brothers have finished roping it off."

"I wouldn't do that neither, Mr. Cummings," Rab said. "You need to turn out the oxen and the mules. Let them roam this night. We're coming through too late in the season and the good forage is all gone. You put these animals in that corral and they won't feed enough. The oxen and mules ain't getting enough to eat because you only turn them out at noon and then round 'em up after an hour or so. You need to leave them out all night."

"I'm not so sure that's a wise idea," Graham Devalt said, overhearing the conversation. "If the oxen and mules wander at night, we could be all morning trying to round them up."

Rab stopped washing the mule. He dropped his brush down into the bucket of water. He dried his hands on the front of his trousers, and then he produced from his pocket a pouch of tobacco and his pipe. Rab leaned easily against a nearby wagon and filled and lit his pipe. Rab had an easy, natural way about him, a manner that was learned from so many years living among the various tribes. He was unhurried and could not be baited into a disagreement. But beyond that, Rab Sinclair knew the subject he spoke on, and he knew that he was right.

"You don't have to do what I suggest," Rab said. "But your animals are giving out. We're still on a decent trail here. This is a good road we're traveling. In a day or two, this road will run out and we will find ourselves traveling through tall prairie grass, flatlands that are wet in some low places and difficult for oxen and mules to pull wagons through. But already, your animals are slowing down. Our second day out, after spending much of the first day on crossing the river, we made twenty miles or better. We did that again the next day. But we've gone less each day since. Today we didn't do more than ten miles. It's too early in the journey and the road is too good for the animals to be slowing down."

"If you're worried about slowing down, how fast do you think we'll go if some of the livestock wanders away?" Graham Devalt demanded. "We could be two hours rounding them up in the morning. We would lose two hours of traveling time."

Rab nodded thoughtfully, puffing on his pipe.

"You make a point," Rab said evenly. "It's not just the slowing down. You work those beasts too hard without giving them room to graze, and they'll stop going at all. If you're worried about them wandering too far, they'll not do that. You've had them walking ten or fifteen or twenty miles during the day, pulling the wagons. They ain't interested in wandering. But they will want to graze."

Amos Cummings listened to both sides of the argument and decided to split the difference.

"How about this, why don't we corral the mules and horses, but we'll let the oxen roam. If they do well, we can do it every night when we stop. That leaves more grazing in the corral for the horses and mules, and it gives the bigger stock more room to graze." Amos thought this was an equitable conclusion to reach.

"You're also overloaded," Rab Sinclair said. "You've got the wagons too heavy. You're doing right by making sure someone is always walking, but you've still got too much weight in the wagons. You're not feeding the animals enough and you're making them pull too heavy a load. You need to see what can be left here."

Amos smiled, but he shook his head. "I assure you, Mr. Sinclair, we were very careful to pack only the things that we needed. The wagons are not overloaded."

Graham Devalt couldn't explain it, but he was perturbed at being told what to do.

"Look, Sinclair – I know you think you're smarter than all the rest of us because you've lived with Indians, but these animals did just fine all the way from Ohio to Kansas. We corralled them, and they carried the same weight they carry now. We came a long way without your help."

"That's true enough," Rab agreed. "But you came all that way on good roads where there were supply stores and hay barns, and any needs you had could be seen to. And it could be that I misunderstood what Mr. Huntsdale told me, but I believe he explained to me that you were late in your arrival to Independence."

"Your only role out here is to show us the direction. We don't need you to look through our luggage or care for our animals. We're perfectly capable."

Rab shrugged his shoulders as he puffed his pipe.

"That's true enough, Mr. Devalt," Rab said. "But I have a problem. I'm packing, which means that everything I have to survive from Independence to Santa Fe is in the panniers on my hawss. That ain't much in the way of supplies," Rab said. "I have to make this trip as fast as I can before I'm stranded out here without food enough to eat. A wagon train is going to take eight weeks or more to get to Santa Fe. But a man packing, he can do it in 10 days or two weeks less than that. But if you slow me down, it makes it harder on me to survive the journey. I'd rather not leave you to find your own way, but if the choice becomes my life or guiding you, I'll ride on."

"You were paid to guide us!" Graham Devalt said, his voice full of outrage.

"If I have to leave you, I'll send Mr. Huntsdale his money back, and you can take it up with him."

Graham Devalt spun on his heel and walked away, back to where the women were getting out supplies to begin cooking on the fire that Stuart Bancroft was building. He had good flames already started and was now adding branches from the possum belly under one of the wagons.

"Tomorrow you should have your sons pick up any prairie coal that we pass," Rab said.

"What is prairie coal?" Amos asked.

"Dried buffalo droppings. They may have to spread out some away from the trail to find them. The trail has been well traveled already this season," Rab said to Amos Cummings. "Prairie coal burns as well as branches. Toss 'em in the possum belly up under your wagon. We'll run out of wood to burn soon enough."

"Thank you for the advice," Amos said.

"You should give some thought to the other things I've said to you," Rab said. "I know what I'm talking about out here."

"I'll give thought to it, Mr. Sinclair," Amos said. "Would you care to join us for supper?"

"Thank you, but I'll make my own," Rab said.

***

"I don't like him telling us what to do like he's the boss of this wagon train," Graham Devalt complained as the travelers sat around the fire. They did not continue to feed branches to the fire, saving what they had for cooking purposes.

"He is very rude," Rebekah Bancroft agreed. "He told me yesterday that if I was smart I would put on a pair of trousers."

Rachel Cummings laughed so hard she began to cough and had to cover her mouth with her hands. "Forgive me," she said. "He told me the same thing. How preposterous! I was riding one of the saddle horses for a spell, and he told me I should give up riding side saddle, put on a pair of britches, and ride the horse like a man. But he insists on calling it a 'hawss.'"

Faith Bancroft, the ten year old daughter of Stuart and Rebekah, giggled heartily at the notion of a woman wearing britches.

"It's too forward by half," Graham Devalt complained. "He should not address the women familiar, anyway. And he should certainly not be advising them as to their clothing. It's unseemly."

Stuart Bancroft cleared his throat, hoping that at least his own wife would catch on that he was uncomfortable ridiculing the young guide. "He does seem to know his way about, though. It might be that he has very good reasons for advising the women to wear trousers."

"Oh, Stuart, please," Rebekah said. "He's half savage. It's a wonder he hasn't encouraged us to strip naked."

"Enough of that kind of talk," Stuart said harshly. "Not in front of the children. Mr. Sinclair may not be as refined as we are, but he seems to have a thorough understanding of this wilderness."

Amos Cummings glanced out to the prairie where he knew Rab Sinclair had made his camp. There were no burning embers to mark the spot, and the moon gave off too little light for silvery shadows. But Amos realized he could see a glimmer of something, some darker shape. Then he realized it was one of the horses, probably the blue. It was a young horse, maybe even still a colt, but it stood by Rab Sinclair as he slept. Amos assumed he must have picketed the horse. He could not see any sign of the other two horses, no dark shadows standing nearby.

"We should turn in," Amos said. "Morning comes early. Mr. Sinclair makes a valid point about the delays. We're not moving as fast as we should. We've packed the bare minimum to get us to Santa Fe. If we delay him and he runs out of supplies, we will be obliged to share what we have. And that could cause us to run low. We must make the most of every daylight hour."

Amos stood up and walked away from the fire, but he touched his oldest son's shoulder when he did. He walked away from the wagons and the others, and Jeremiah, the oldest of the Cummings boys who was about the same age as Rab Sinclair, followed his father. When they had gone some distance and were out of hearing of the others, Amos said, "I want you to light a lantern or two and get Matthew and Paul to help you let the mules out from the corral. Keep the horses in it in case we have to round up the other animals in the morning. And tell your brothers that if Mr. Sinclair tells you to do something, none of you should offer him any argument but just do as he says."

As they turned in a short while later, Martha Cummings spoke in a soft whisper to her husband. "Are you worried that we will run out of supplies? I noted what you said about sharing our supplies with Mr. Sinclair. I also saw that you had the boys turnout the livestock."

Amos sighed heavily. "I don't want to say that I am worried about running out," he said. "Not yet. But I know there is some truth to what Mr. Sinclair says. He may be young, but he has made this crossing before. He does know more about it than we do. I am afraid we looked on this journey as a pleasure trip, but it is not that. Many men and women have perished on this journey. We might have approaching it too lightly. That's not to say that we have made a mistake. I still believe this is the best thing for us, and for our sons. Moving them to California may very well keep them out of a bloody conflict. But we should realize that the peril on this journey is just as real if we are not careful."

"Should I wear trousers?" Martha asked, and Amos could tell by the tone of her voice that his wife was smiling.

He chuckled quietly at the thought of it.

"Perhaps you should," he said.

"Mr. Sinclair also told me that I should be wearing trousers. And he said that I should wear a wide brimmed hat. He said all of the women were risking sunburns and exposure if we did not start wearing men's clothing."

"I have noticed these last two days that your face and shoulders are very pink," Amos said. "Are you burning?"

"A little. Not enough to complain about it. But so

is Rachel, and Rebekah, as well."

"Go through the boys' clothes tomorrow," Amos said. "The boys all have spare hats. See if you cannot find for the women trousers and shirts."

Martha was silent for a while, and Amos thought perhaps she was falling asleep.

"He is a little rough, and very young," she said, surprising her husband. "But I think we can trust him to look out for our best interests."

Amos nodded, though his wife could not see the silent affirmation.

"I think that's true," he said.

The bedrolls were uncomfortable, not at all what Amos and Martha Cummings and their children were accustomed to sleeping on. But all of them worked so hard during the days and walked so far, that by the time they bedded down in the evening they would have been able to sleep on a bed of nails.

-8-

At sunup, Rab Sinclair had already rounded up his two horses and also the mules and oxen of the wagon party.

"We could have managed that," Amos said, seeing Rab leading the last two mules into the rope corral.

"Yes, sir," Rab said. "It wasn't difficult at all. None of them strayed far. But I appreciate you doing what I asked of you."

Martha Cummings called over to Rab. "Mr. Sinclair, would you care for a cup of coffee?"

"I'd be obliged, ma'am," Rab said.

Rab had already noticed that Martha Cummings was wearing a pair of her oldest son's trousers and one of his cotton shirts. All of the women this morning had dressed in men's clothing and wore men's hats with wide brims that covered their faces from the sun.

"I have nothing but honey to sweeten it," she said.

"Honey is good for much more than puttin' in

71

your coffee, ma'am," Rab said. "I'll be happy to take mine with nothing in it if it means saving the honey."

"What other purposes would you put honey to?" Stuart Bancroft asked.

"Good for sealing and healing wounds," Rab said. "You get a big wound, a knife wound or falling on a sharp rock or something severe like that, and the Indians all pack it full of honey. Tends to heal it up good as new."

"That will be good to remember," Stuart said. "Honey goes in a wound."

Martha Cummings, for a woman old enough to be his mother, was very attractive. She had soft blonde hair and pretty green eyes. Her eyes were very green. Her face was a bit thin, and it showed her age some, but the wrinkles were in the right places to suggest she'd done a lot of smiling in her life. She had a pretty smile with white teeth.

"I hope you won't mind me saying, but your new outfit ain't nearly as fetching as what you was wearing before," Rab told her. "But I think it'll add quite a bit to your comfort."

Though her cheeks were plenty pink from the sun the last few days, Rab was sure he saw her blush.

"I don't mind you saying so at all, Mr. Sinclair," Martha said. "Tell me, did you know your mother at all?"

"Not to remember her. She died, or left, when I was just a pup, so I never did know her to remember."

"You have a darker complexion," Martha Cummings said. "Was your mother an Indian woman?"

"I always figured she must have been," Rab said. "Pa told me once that she was part Cherokee, so I figured she wasn't full-blooded."

He started to say something about his father's preferences, but then remembered that Martha Cummings had reprimanded him before when he was free with that kind of talk, so Rab said nothing more about it.

As he drank his coffee, Rab watched the men packing supplies and putting them back in the wagons. As they loaded the wagons, the canvas covers were pulled back, and Rab noticed that each of the wagons had heavy wooden boxes that did not look familiar to him. He stepped over to the back of one of the wagons and looked at one of the boxes. He lifted a corner and felt that it was tremendously heavy.

"What's in these boxes here, Mr. Cummings?"

"Those are books, Rab," Amos Cummings said. "The one thing a professor cannot do without is his books."

Rab lifted the corner of the box again. "Must have a million words in them books," he said. "They're mighty heavy."

"Knowledge is not gained lightly," Amos Cummings said with a smile.

"I reckon if I was to suggest to you that we leave these books, that would be something you'd be against?" Rab asked.

"I would be," Amos Cummings said, the smile dropping from his face. "I'd be very opposed to that."

Rab nodded but made no argument.

"We should be gettin' on," he said. "I smell rain coming."

They were not more than a couple of hours on the trail when Rab Sinclair rode up ahead. He'd seen clouds in the distance and wanted to see if they were now coming toward the wagon train. A small hill ahead offered an excellent vantage point. He was riding the buckskin. Cromwell was up ahead of him with the sorrel, and the sorrel was carrying the pannier.

As he hit the top of the rise, Rab saw that indeed they would soon be in the midst of a downpour, but what worried him more than the rain was what he saw when he wheeled the buckskin to ride back down and warn the wagon train of the coming rain. Off in the distance behind the wagon train Rab Sinclair saw four riders. They each had spare mounts, and they were moving quickly, closing the distance on the wagon train.

Rab's Hawken rifle was in a scabbard on the pannier. He carried on his gun belt a six-shot Colt Dragoon revolver. He had all six cylinders loaded with greased balls, but he had not put any percussion caps on the nipples.

Rab squeezed his knees against the sides of the buckskin and urged the horse at a gallop down the road to meet the wagons. As he descended from the rise down to the wagons, Rab lost sight of the riders. That meant the riders probably had not yet seen the wagons, though they had certainly seen him.

Amos Cummings was driving the lead wagon while both Martha and their daughter Rachel walked beside it.

"We'll be getting rain soon," Amos Cummings said. "It should knock down some of the trail dust, though, so it is not completely unwelcome."

"There's no reason for alarm, Mr. Cummings, but I

want you to be aware that there are four riders at a distance behind us. It would be a good idea to have the womenfolk get inside the wagons and drop down the curtains so that they cannot be seen. If you have any kind of rifle or revolver in your wagon, now would be a good time to see that it's loaded and keep it near to hand."

Rab spoke loud enough for Martha and Rachel to hear him, and neither of them hesitated in climbing up onto the wagon and crawling into the back. It happened that luckily, at that moment, none of the women were driving a wagon. Amos Cummings' sons Jeremiah and Paul were both driving a wagon each, Stuart Bancroft was driving a wagon, and Stuart and Rebecca's two sons were driving the next to last wagon. The boys were young, but they'd been eager to pitch in and learn throughout the journey from Ohio, and they were competent to manage the mule team. Graham Devalt was driving the last wagon in the line, and this worried Rab as much as anything.

Rab rode down farther along the line and gave the same warning to Stuart Bancroft.

Only Matthew Cummings was mounted on any of the horses. He was pushing the livestock up ahead of the wagon train. Rab hurried over to him next.

"Matthew, I want you to ride over beside your father's wagon and stay close to him. If any of the livestock stray, we'll get them later. Do not leave your father's wagon."

Rab looked one more time at the sorrel, his Hawken rifle in its scabbard on the horse. The Hawken was good for just one shot, but it was a powerful gun and accurate at distance. He'd have felt more comfortable having that with him if things went wrong, but there was no time to get it. Rab Sinclair's chief concern was to get to Graham Devalt in the last wagon before the four riders caught him up. So he urged the sorrel back down the line of wagons. As he went, he gave a word of caution to each of the drivers.

"We don't know who these people might be or what interest they might have in us," Rab told Amos Cummings. "It's best to slow but don't stop your wagon and let them pass as fast as possible. Let me talk to them, and other than a pleasant greeting you should say nothing."

He gave a variation of the warning to the Cummings boys and to Stuart Bancroft and the two young Bancroft boys.

But he was more stern in the warning he gave to Graham Devalt.

"I know you've got a quick wit because you're university educated," Rab said to him. As he spoke, Rab worked his revolver to put caps on all six of the nipples, and he left the gun on half cock. "But not all men on the plains can appreciate your humor. Hold your tongue with these men and allow them to pass without giving offense. Only speak a pleasant greeting to them. Do not tell them where you are from or where you are bound. I'll do all of the talking."

Graham Devalt narrowed his eyes in contempt.

"I think I'm perfectly capable of performing rudimentary communications with strangers," Graham said.

"Keep 'em rudimentary and brief," Rab warned.

And he looked over his shoulder and saw the men coming over a rise. They would catch up in just a moment. The thing that worried Rab Sinclair right away was that the men split along the trail, two coming on right side of the wagon train and two on the left side.

"Howdy friends," Rab Sinclair called to the two men riding up on the right side of the wagon.

"Howdy," one of them said, but if there was a friendly note, Rab could not detect it.

Rab tried to get a read on the men. All four were shaggy haired men with full beards. They wore the homespun clothes of men without much wealth. Their spare mounts all carried heavily laden panniers.

"Bound for Santa Fe?" Rab asked.

Three of the men rode on, and to Rab's relief they pushed their horses to a gallop to get beyond the wagon train. But one of them reined in and walked his horse next to Rab's. The man had a rifle in a scabbard and a revolver on his hip, but Rab noticed the revolver had no caps in place.

"We're bound for the gold fields in New Mexico Territory," the man said. "Come from Kentucky. Been a hell of a long journey already."

"Five more weeks, maybe a bit less, and you should be there," Rab said.

"You familiar with the trail?"

"I've made the trip before," Rab said.

"A man could get lost easy on these grassy plains," the man said. "Is the trail clear all the way to Santa Fe?"

"You should manage," Rab said. "You'll find stagecoach relay stations along the way, too. We've been passed by the stage twice already, one coming and one going."

"I reckon this is the better way to do it," the man said. "Stages get awful cramped on a long haul."

"No question," Rab said.

As they were walking, and his concerns had abated, Rab took his pipe from his pocket and lit it with a match.

"What about Indians? I've heard they can be troublesome."

"Just take a firm hand," Rab said. "Be straight with them that you ain't going to trade nothing and that you want nothing, and they'll leave you be, most times."

The man nodded once. "Obliged to you. I'd better catch up. Them boys have gold fever already, and they ain't waitin' on me."

Rab puffed on his pipe, relieved that the moment was nearly over. But that's when Graham Devalt spoke up.

"Did I hear you to say that you come from Kentucky?" Graham asked.

"That's right," the man said.

"Which way will Kentucky fall if this nonsense of secession catches hold?" Graham asked.

"Nonsense?" the Kentuckian asked, and there was a tone to his voice that Rab Sinclair did not like.

"Of course it's nonsense," Graham said. "We are Ohioans, and abolitionists."

The Kentuckian snarled and spat at the wheel of Graham's wagon. "I'll tell you this one thing, and then I'll bid you a farewell. An Ohioan ought not to try to tell a

Kentuckian how he should live. If there is trouble coming, it will be caused by the meddlesome nature of those who think it is their place to inject themselves into the affairs of others. And that's a fact."

The man spat one more time, and then he snapped his reins and pushed his horse on ahead to catch up to his three companions and the spare mounts.

Rab shook his head at Graham Devalt but said nothing. He rode on up ahead to Amos Cummings' wagon.

"We ought to stop after we get down the other side of this rise," Rab said. "It's early for a noon rest, but we can let this weather pass, and I can ride on up ahead and be sure these men have gone on."

***

Rab Sinclair unloaded his pannier from the sorrel and shifted his saddle to Cromwell. He picked the buckskin and sorrel and left the others in the wagon train to see to their own animals and to make a camp for weathering the rain.

He put his Hawken rifle in the scabbard on Cromwell, and then he rode on up ahead.

He had to ride a full mile before he caught sight of the four Kentuckians off in the distance. They were pushing their animals hard along the trail, but no harder a pace than the animals could endure. Satisfied that the Kentuckians posed no threat, Rab wheeled the blue and rode back to the wagons. His return journey saw the first of the rain, and it came down in a torrent. Though he wore a slicker, the rain seemed to easily find its way under his hat, down his neck and into his shirt. It blew up under the slicker so that his trousers were soaked.

When he returned to the wagons he found that they had been driven into an almost circle and the animals were all loose on the plains to graze during the rain. Each wagon had an oilcloth covering rigged like an awning to give everyone a place to stand and stay dry.

Rab rode Cromwell directly into the circle of wagons and dismounted when he saw Graham Devalt. He walked directly up to the young man.

"When I tell you not to speak, I expect you to not speak," Rab said.

Amos Cummings, who was standing under an oilcloth with Stuart Bancroft, correctly read Rab's anger in his posture, and both Amos and Stuart hurried over to where Rab was confronting Graham.

"I'll speak when I feel like speaking," Graham said, but some of the edge was gone from his tone. He was already cowed by Rab Sinclair's anger.

"You're a damn fool," Rab said, though he did not raise his voice or shout in anger. His words were harsh, but his tone was as even as it always was. "Engaging with men like that in talk of secession and abolition. You're lucky you didn't get yourself and every man, woman, and child of this wagon train shot dead."

"Do not call me a fool," Graham muttered.

"I call what I see by the name that fits it," Rab Sinclair said. "I don't mince my words. And I'll tell you straight, you're a damn fool."

Amos stuck a hand out to intervene, but Rab caught it and brushed it aside.

"You need to see to this fool, Mr. Cummings. He's put you and your family in jeopardy with his free mouth."

Graham Devalt balled a fist and took a swing at Rab. But the frontiersman was fast and easily dodged the blow.

In an act intended to humiliate more than harm, Rab open-hand slapped Graham Devalt across the face. When Graham raised another fist, Rab Sinclair batted it down and slapped him again.

Stuart and Amos now stepped in between the two younger men, taking hold of them and pushing them backwards a step or two.

Amos was surprised when he took Rab Sinclair by the shoulders and felt the muscles under Rab's coat and shirt. For just a moment, Amos had a feel for the difficulty of life beyond the East's civilization. Hard work and activity had made this young man like a stone sculpture.

"Mr. Sinclair, please," Amos said. "Surely there's no need to offer insults."

Rab took a step back so that Amos Cummings was no longer touching him.

"There are troublesome men on the plains and in the mountains, men who would give no thought to cutting your throat to take anything you might have that they might want," Rab said. For the first time, Amos Cummings heard a bite to his tone, though Rab did not raise his voice. "And if they have to cut my throat to get at your throat, they'll cut me, too. I'm talking about men who are thieves, but at least a man can understand what motivates them. So if you have something of value that a thief might want, you keep it out of sight. Whether it's a good gun or a bag of gold coins or a pretty woman.

"But there are also troublesome men out here on the frontier who will cut your throat because they don't like the way you look, or they don't like how noisy you are when you chew your chow or take a breath. Or they'll fire a bullet into you to see whether or not you jerk when you're hit. They's all kinds out here. And you can't tell when you look at a man what kind he might be. You can't tell if he's gentle like a gelding or ornery like a bronco. If you want to survive this trail, you give every man the same respect you would give a grizzly bear. You step wide of 'em, and you don't provoke 'em."

Now Rab raised up a finger and poked it toward Graham Devalt, and he held it rigid, accusatory, as he spoke.

"But this fool here, he provokes. He wears his opinions like a chip on his shoulder, and challenges a man to knock off that chip. Yet from what I've seen, there's no man west of the Mississippi who would not gladly and with ease knock his chip. Your assistant is a weak man with an active mouth. And your problem is that if he flaps his jaw at the wrong man, that man will shut it for him and then come after you and me and everyone else with this man."

Amos Cummings glanced at Graham Devalt.

"What did you say to those men?" Amos asked.

"I only said that we were abolitionists," Graham muttered.

"Had those men drawn knives or guns, what choice would I have had but to intervene?" Rab asked. "For your mouth, I might have had to kill those men. That's not a chore I'll willingly accept. I'll not gun down other men to protect Mr. Devalt's ability to flap his jaw."

"Nor would we ask you to," Amos Cummings said. "I'll speak to Graham, and in the future we will all be more careful about how we address strangers."

Rab Sinclair nodded his head and walked away, the rain lashing against the brim of his hat.

He chanced a tip of his hat to look up at the sky. Off in the far distance he could see light beyond the darkness of the clouds. The storm would pass soon enough. Oilcloths had been pulled out from all the wagons, and Rab now walked to the far one where no one was seeking shelter. He stepped under the awning and leaned against the wagon, and he lit his pipe, puffing on it some and trying not to think about Graham Devalt.

"What was said to those men?" Amos Cummings demanded, turning on Graham Devalt.

"I merely asked which way Kentucky would go if there was secession," Graham said. "I stated that we were Ohioans and abolitionists. If the man took offense, it is not my fault that he is overly angry about the issue."

Amos shook his head. "Mr. Sinclair is correct. We do not know the men who inhabit this part of the country, nor do we know how easily they might be provoked. We must conduct ourselves in a way that gives offense to no man. You were lucky that those men rode on. If we cannot think of our own safety, we should think of the women and children and the things we must do to keep them safe."

Graham Devalt nodded his agreement, but he was hurt and angry. He did not like the change that had come over Amos Cummings since they had left Ohio. A once passionate and vocal advocate for abolition, he now ordered Graham to keep quiet on the subject about which no man of conscience should ever be compelled to hold his tongue.

-9-

Pawnee Bill picked through the supplies in the back of the wagon. There were large bags of flour and cornmeal. There was a barrel full of salt. There was cloth for making clothes. Lots of common supplies that would be found in any farmhouse.

"If we had a cabin, we could get through the winter on these supplies, I suppose, but this ain't the sort of wagon load a man would need for making the trip to New Mexico," Bill announced. "There's flour enough and beans and rice, but there ain't no dried fruits, no cured meats."

"Is there powder and ball?" Mickey Hogg asked.

"Some."

"Farmer planned to hunt his meat for the winter," Mickey Hogg said. "We should dump the things we know we do not want and cannot trade with the Indians. We can take three days or four to hunt some buffalo and cure some meat. The real problem is that we have only the two bottles of whiskey. This will be a long and unpleasant journey if we cannot secure more whiskey."

"Maybe get whiskey at one of the stagecoach stations," Dick Derugy suggested.

"Don't dump any of the supplies until we know if we can trade some of it at a station," Chess Bowman said.

"We just need to keep going," Pawnee Bill said.

The group of men had started out from Abner Spears' hollow as soon as the sun rose, and they had made little progress. The horses wandered off every which way and could not be driven, so they had to be led. Within an hour of leaving the hollow, they mired the wagon in mud trying to cross a creek, and none of the men were skilled drivers or knew how best to work the wagon out. When they were finally back on the trail, a torrential rain blew over, and they stopped to wait it out. None of them wore good slickers, though Mickey Hogg had a slicker full of tears, and when the sun finally reappeared, they continued to not move while they hung their clothes on lines to dry. Then, at last, they began to go through the wagon to see what supplies they had.

"We haven't even got to the trail yet, and already everything's wrong," Chess Bowman said. "Maybe we ought to point ourselves east and go for a town somewhere."

"No, now, this is what we decided on," Pawnee Bill said. "We said we would ride for Santa Fe, and we ain't going to let one rain storm and some missing supplies change our plans. You're forgetting that if we need supplies we can always just take. There will be plenty of other wagons out on the trail, and they'll have the right provisions. As long as we've got caps, powder, and balls, we can get anything else we need."

"Then let's get on our clothes and start for the trail. The sooner we get there, the sooner we can start procuring the supplies we do need," Mickey Hogg said.

The men dressed into still sodden clothes and started off. Dick Derugy drove the wagon and the others rode horses, leading the spares behind them. Dick had his mount on a lead tied to the back of the wagon.

Through the afternoon they stayed in a generally southwest direction, going the way they knew the trail would be. They did not know where they might hit it, but so long as they intersected with the trail – and could recognize it for what it was – they knew they would be all right.

Through the afternoon, they traveled over what seemed to be an endless sea of green hills. The sun had come out and burned off the rain, and now the day was just hot with the sun beating down on them. It did, though, dry out their clothes.

Late in the afternoon, when there was some discussion of stopping for the day, Dick Derugy in the seat of the wagon spotted several horses far out on the horizon.

"They's something up ahead," Dick called to the others, who had outpaced him.

Pawnee Bill turned in his saddle and reined in his horse. "How's that?" he called back.

"They's something up ahead," Dick repeated. "Looks like horses out on a hill."

The riders now whipped their horses into a gallop and closed the distance. As they neared the horses Dick had seen, they saw four tents set up near the visible path of the Santa Fe Trail. Outside of the tents, four men were cooking supper around a campfire.

The mounted men slowed their horses, and Mickey Hogg and Chess Bowman backed off some while Pawnee Bill approached the four encamped men.

"Howdy!" Pawnee Bill called to them.

"Howdy, friend," one of the strangers camped by the side of the road said, standing up from the campfire. The other three men turned to face Bill but did not step up.

"This might sound like a dumb question, but can you tell me if this is the Santa Fe Trail?" Pawnee Bill asked.

"We hope that it is," one of the men said. "We've been following it for a couple of days now, and if it turns out not to be the Santa Fe Trail, we'll be well disappointed."

Bill laughed. "I am glad to hear that," he said. "We've been coming from north and liked to never find this damn road. Y'all bound for Santa Fe?"

"Headed to the gold fields in the territory," the man standing by the fire said.

"Well, good luck to you for that," Bill said. "Where y'all from?"

"We come from Kentucky," the man said.

"You've come a long ways," Bill said.

"Most of it by steamboat. Down the Ohio, up the Missouri. We disembarked there at Independence and then started on the trail."

Bill glanced back at the eight horses grazing on the hill nearby. "Y'all packin' the trail?"

"That's our plan," the man said. The other three around the campfire sat quietly, only watching and listening.

"We've got a wagon, but he's having a hell of a time trying to keep pace," Bill said. "He's back there somewhere, if the Indians ain't got him."

Pawnee Bill laughed at his own joke, but the four Kentuckians did not.

Bill was just making idle talk. He was looking for two things. First, he was looking to size up the other men. He wanted to make a decision now whether or not he thought these men might be easy to take. They looked stout enough, like they could probably fight, and they seemed on their guard about having strangers approach them. Nothing about these men made them seem easy. The other question Pawnee Bill wanted answered was whether or not the Kentuckians would invite them into their camp. If they could share a camp, Pawnee Bill and his three men could jump the four Kentuckians in their sleep.

"Run into a stagecoach yet?" Bill asked them.

"Haven't seen it. Might be coming through tomorrow. Tough for us to judge how quick they'll catch us."

"How about other travelers? Seen many of them?"

"We passed a wagon train earlier today. They're probably a couple of hours behind us now. We were moving a good bit faster than they were. Another train started out about the same time we did, maybe a day ahead of us, but we passed them a long time ago."

Pawnee Bill nodded. Still no invitation, not even to coffee.

"Coffee sure smells good," Bill said.

The Kentuckian said nothing. Bill shrugged his shoulders and nodded his head, agreeing with his unspoken thoughts.

These four men from Kentucky knew better than to share their provisions – supplies that by the end of the trail would be running dangerously low. They also knew better than to invite strangers into their camp. Whatever Pawnee Bill and his companions were going to steal on the trail, they would not be stealing it from these men.

"Well, I guess we'll ride on," Pawnee Bill. "We'll find a good place to camp on up ahead. I imagine with that wagon slowing us down, we'll be seeing you again tomorrow when you pass us by."

"I imagine we'll see you tomorrow," the Kentuckian replied.

Pawnee Bill waved his hand and pointed down the trail, and he and the other two mounted riders started west down the trail. Dick Derugy turned the wagon, cutting across the open prairie to intersect the trail farther down.

The Kentuckian who did the talking sat back down and checked his biscuits. He was making up enough for his supper tonight, breakfast in the morning, and his noon meal.

"Glad to see them ride on," one of the men at the campfire said.

"I'll be more pleased about it when we pass them and leave them behind," the other man said. "I had a bad feeling about them boys."

-10-

Graham Devalt and Rachel Cummings were walking together and collecting branches from the ground down near the creek.

It was early in the afternoon to stop, but Rab Sinclair liked having some trees and fresh water near the camp, so they'd halted the wagon train here at the creek. They had plenty of wood for the night's fire, but Rab encouraged Amos Cummings to collect more wood to put in the possum bellies under the wagons.

"I'll be glad when we put this journey behind us and are in California," Graham Devalt confided to Rachel. "I have despised every step we have taken since we left Independence."

Graham was convinced that Rachel would one day be his wife. It only made sense. They were near enough in age, Rachel was only a couple of years younger than him. He had known her for several years, had watched her grow from an awkward and embarrassed girl into a young woman. She was the daughter of his mentor, a mentor he was now following all the way across the continent. He believed that they would not be long in California before he and Rachel would marry.

Graham also knew that Amos approved of the match. The battle was more than half won.

Rachel, though, was not yet won over. She had an independence of spirit that made her difficult to court. Her parents had raised her in such a way. They had brought her up to think for herself and to question conventions. If she spurned him, Graham believed that she would live to be an old maid, single and unloved.

"It hasn't been so bad," Rachel said. "It is an extraordinary adventure, though I will grant you that the countryside is growing painfully monotonous."

"And the company is atrocious," Graham said.

"I do not know how to take that," Rachel said.

"Oh, not you!" Graham quickly corrected himself. "It's that Sinclair fellow. He is a boor. He is contemptuous of us all, and I cannot stand the disrespect he shows to your father."

Rachel glanced at Graham. "I would agree that his is boorish, but I have not seen him speak disrespectfully to my father."

Graham snorted. "He bosses your father around in a way that is unseemly. Your father is his employer, yet Sinclair speaks to him in the most rude ways. There is no instruction your father has given to your brothers that Sinclair has not countermanded. I cannot stand him, and I am eager to get to Santa Fe so that we can be done with him. I hope for the second half of our trip we are able to find a guide who knows his place."

"What happened between the two of you earlier after those men overtook us?"

"I conversed with them," Graham said. "There was nothing more to it than that, and Sinclair took offense because he thought it was his place to do the talking."

Rachel did not say anything for a moment while she added dead branches to the stack in her arm.

"It is hard to know what to make of him," she said.

"Not for me," Graham said. "I know exactly what to make of him. He is an illiterate bumpkin who thinks, because we are in his element, that he has some authority over us. He's younger than I am, yet he bosses me around as if I was a dumb schoolboy."

Rachel, who was also younger than Graham, wrinkled her nose. "What does age have anything to do with it?"

"His youth is a good indication that he does not know as much as he thinks he knows," Graham said.

"Maybe he is not illiterate," Rachel said.

"Of course he is," Graham responded.

"He does seem a bit simple," Rachel said.

"A bit?" Graham was incredulous. "He is nothing but a simpleton."

Rachel laughed at a recollection. "At the noon stop yesterday I witnessed him eating his jerky and then picking his teeth with the point of that enormous knife he wears on his belt."

Graham laughed with her at the thought of it. "No

wonder all of these mountain men are missing so many teeth."

"We should watch for the moment he encounters a particularly brutal string of jerky and cuts a tooth from his head in order to remove the gristle." Rachel felt a touch of remorse over the petty joking, but the thought of Rab Sinclair plucking out a tooth to get at some gristle amused her too much. "He wears that buckskin coat, and he is an absolute caricature. If he were old enough to have a beard, he would be too much to believe."

"We should not laugh," she said. "Were it not for him, we might still be stuck in Missouri. Father might lose his new position, and then where would we be?"

"I think we could have made it just fine without him," Graham Devalt said. "The trail is clearly defined. We were able to make it from Ohio to Missouri without his help. It's not as if he has done anything extraordinary."

"Maybe so," Rachel Cummings agreed.

Graham liked her very much. She was a lovely girl, a younger version of her mother. She was full of laughter, and her wit was slicing. In fact, her jests cut so finely that they could border on cruel. Her independent streak often gave way to a mischievous streak. She would grow out of that, Graham knew, and would make a very fine wife one day.

"What do you look forward to about being in California?" Graham asked. For him, the answer was plain – he most looked forward to growing closer to Rachel Cummings, a closeness that would lead to marriage.

"Oh, I don't know," Rachel said dreamily. "I'm excited to see the ocean. I have never seen the ocean before, and how extraordinary that the first ocean I see should be the Pacific. Beyond that, I am just curious to see what life will be like. I imagine in a town it will not be so different from what it was in Ohio. It is not as if father plans to build a sod house on the plains and farm. We will be near the university and should expect to enjoy all the trappings of a modern city, I should think."

"Yes," Graham agreed, a bit disappointed that she did not mention him in the things she was most looking forward to. "It should not be so different from what we are accustomed to. It just takes a very long time to get there."

***

Amos Cummings waited until the sun was down to seek out Rab Sinclair in his camp.

Since the encounter earlier with Graham Devalt, Rab Sinclair had avoided talking to the rest of the party. He did not come over when they stopped to make camp to ensure that everyone was going through the afternoon ritual properly. He did come to the campfire for coffee. Even when Martha Cummings called to him to see if he would have coffee, Rab merely waved a hand of acknowledgment but never joined them. He had taken to Martha, but younger men often did. Graham Devalt had been no different when he was just a promising student who sometimes had Sunday supper with the Cummings family.

Martha was an attractive woman – not just attractive for her age, and not just physically attractive. Martha Cummings was a forthright woman. She spoke her mind freely, and when she did she always left people with the impression that she was intelligent. She seemed to wear a constant smile, and had a pleasant and kind way about her. These were qualities that attracted most anyone to her, but young men especially seemed to appreciate a kindness from a pretty, older woman.

Amos knew and understood the way other men were attracted to his wife. It did not concern him – he had no doubts about her Christian virtue or her loyalty as his wife. She was thoroughly dedicated to their family.

But when Rab Sinclair declined even the invitation from Martha, Amos decided he had to try to make amends with the young guide.

"I am sorry about the trouble earlier," Amos said. He carried a lantern and found Rab reclined against his saddle, smoking his pipe. The blue was not on a picket but still stood near Rab's camp. The buckskin and sorrel both were also nearby. All three of the horses seemed satisfied that Rab Sinclair was the leader of the herd, and they did not stray far from him.

"Wasn't your doing," Rab said. "No reason for you to apologize."

"Mr. Devalt is a very intelligent young man. One of the best students I have ever had. But he does not always think, if you understand the difference."

Rab blew out a long cloud of smoke.

"It ain't an easy place, Mr. Cummings," Rab said. "They's all kinds of dangers out here, but one of the worst dangers you'll encounter is another man. Best always to keep to yourself as much as you can. If you see a man who needs help, help him. Make your friends neighbors when you can, and when you can't, make your neighbors friends. But until a stranger is either a friend or a neighbor, give him a wide berth. Let him alone so that he'll let you alone."

"Do you mind if I sit?" Amos asked.

"Ground don't belong to me," Rab said.

"You spoke awfully free about killing those men if it came to it," Amos Cummings said.

"I did," Rab said. "I reckon I wouldn't like it, but if they'd gone for their guns or knives, I suppose I'd have had to."

"Do you believe you could have killed all four of them?" Amos Cummings asked.

"There's not but one way to find out a thing like that," Rab said. "But the best thing to do is behave in a way that you don't have to find out."

"Have you ever killed a man?" Amos Cummings asked.

"I have," Rab said. "My father died four years ago when I still had growing to do. Some men think a young man like that on his own would be easy. I've had thieves try to take my hawss. I've had scalawags try to take my money. And I've had cutthroats try to take my scalp. They's been times, for sure, that I found it necessary to do hard things."

Amos Cummings stiffened.

"I am a peaceable man," he said.

Rab puffed on his pipe a couple of times. Amos watched him puzzling over the word.

"Is that what they call someone bound for the Pacific?" Rab asked.

Amos chuckled. "No. No, that's what they call someone who does not believe that violent actions are the solution to problems. I do not believe in aggressive, violent action, Mr. Sinclair. I believe that problems between men can be settled through words rather than swords, with courts or government intervention. As a Christian man, I believe in the Biblical teachings of Jesus, who taught us to turn the other cheek."

Rab puffed on his pipe a couple of times.

"I reckon if you had a Bowie knife held to your hairline you might become a believer in some of the Old Testament teachings," Rab said. "Who was the fellow? Joshua, if I remember right. Yes sir, they's many similarities between the Western territories and Canaan."

"Maybe so," Amos Cummings conceded. "But as someone who abhors violence and lives by peaceable principles, I do not want you committing violence on my behalf."

"I'll bear that in mind," Rab said. "And we'll both hope it don't come to a situation where violence is needed."

"I would extend that, too, to Mr. Devalt," Cummings said. "You struck him twice in my presence today."

"He deserved more than that," Rab said.

"Perhaps, but I would ask you not to strike him again," Cummings said.

Rab puffed his pipe and it glowed orange for just a moment, lighting up the end of his nose and eyes.

"I reckon I'll do my best not to strike Mr. Devalt again," Rab said.

"That's all I can ask for," Cummings said.

Amos did not immediately get up and walk away. He held his place on the ground and watched Rab Sinclair smoke his pipe.

"I imagine it must have been very difficult, at such a young age, to find yourself on your own."

Rab shrugged.

"It was what it was," he said. "Nothing to be done about it."

With nothing left to add, Amos Cummings sat quietly. Rab knocked he tobacco from his pipe and blew through the stem to know out any last bits.

"We did a short trip today with the rain," Rab said. "We stopped early, too. We should plan to make it up tomorrow."

Amos didn't know why, but he felt an urge to seek approval from the young man, or at least offer some further explanation. "You must think I'm a terrible coward, what with my talk of peaceful principles."

"I didn't think one way or another about it," Rab said. "But I reckon if a man leaves the states and comes out her to this trail planning to not defend himself with violence, that must take a certain amount of courage. Or he's a damn fool. And you certainly strike me as an educated man."

Amos Cummings got to his feet. He was stiff and sore, with so many hours over so many days walking so many miles. He envied Rab Sinclair and Graham Devalt for their youth and limber joints.

"It is late, and as you said, we should get an early start in the morning. I hope tomorrow evening you will join us in our camp. I know Mrs. Cummings would be grateful for you company and to know we have not offended you so that you cannot stand to be among us."

"I'll be happy to join you tomorrow," Rab said.

-11-

"They's a creek up ahead," Pawnee Bill said. "You can see the trees down there. See 'em?"

Mickey Hogg craned his neck and stood in his stirrups. "I see 'em."

In almost every direction, the sky touched the grass on the distant horizon, but up ahead, just along the trail, the row of low trees showed the place where a creek cut a path through the prairie. It would be a low spot, and the trees would provide some cover.

"We won't have long before they're caught up to us," Dick Derugy noted. Today Dick was mounted and Chester Bowman was driving the wagon. "Chess had better get moving and find a spot to hide that wagon. As far as a man can see out here, those Kentucky boys will be within sight in no time."

"He's right, Chess. You'd best get moving," Pawnee Bill said.

It was Bill's idea to find some travelers to ambush so that the men could get some provisions that would better meet their purpose than those they had taken with Ted Gibson's wagon. But it was Mickey Hogg who urged the others to ambush the four riders they'd encountered the day before.

No one liked the idea. For one, it made no sense to take supplies from a group of packers. Their provisions would last a while, but would not last long enough for men driving a wagon. For another, the four Kentuckians seemed like rough men who would not be easily ambushed.

But Mickey Hogg was certain sure that he'd seen a bottle of whiskey at the campsite, and he was feeling mighty thirsty.

"It could be days before we see another group with wagons. Unless we plan to rob a stagecoach, we might not see travelers with wagons for three or four days. But we know these Kentuckians are coming up on us sometime today. If we wait for 'em in a good spot, they'll be easy enough to take from."

Pawnee Bill didn't like the idea, but he did like Mickey Hogg.

"Wasn't they armed? Didn't they have pistols on their belts?" Dick asked.

"They did, but they wouldn't be riding with them pistols capped," Mickey said. "It's the surprise that'll get 'em."

Chess Bowman didn't like this any better than he liked what Pawnee Bill and Dick Derugy did to the sod buster family. At least there were no women in this, but it wasn't even reasonable to go after the Kentucky boys. Their supplies would be insufficient. And being from Kentucky, likely as not, they were pro-slavery.

Abolitionists and Yankees was one thing, but killing pro-slavers was like killing your own. And Chess Bowman did not like the idea of killing his own.

But he also would not speak up in protest against the move. There was no way he would be accused of playing the coward, and Chess knew that would be the immediate accusation if he said they should leave the men from Kentucky alone. So he drove the wagon quickly out across the plain.

The other three men sat their horses for a moment.

"It don't matter if we shoot their horses," Pawnee Bill said. "We don't need more horses, anyway. So when they get up near us, we'll ride out from cover, and just shoot the whole way. We'll take them by surprise like that, show them a real cavalry charge, and we'll put them on the ground. Shoot the horses out from under them, and then we can ride 'em down, use our knives if we have to. Chess is a good shot with a long rifle. I figure we can all give him our rifles and let him fire the opening volley, see if we can put one of 'em down right at the very beginning."

"So just the three of us attacking?" Dick asked.

Like Chess Bowman, Dick Derugy had misgivings about the planned attack on the Kentuckians. His misgivings did not take into account the right or wrong of the thing or the political inclinations of the men they would be killing. Dick Derugy didn't like anything that seemed like a fair fight. Being outnumbered was fine if it was women and children or unarmed men, but in this situation it was a fair fight. The only advantage Dick and the others would have was surprise, and he was not convinced that surprise alone was enough of an advantage.

But like Chess Bowman, Dick knew they would say he was playing the coward if he made some effort to talk them out of it.

When Chess was near the creek and trees, the other men galloped after him, and in a few minutes they were picking their way over a crossing at the creek and riding in behind some trees for cover.

Pawnee Bill was the last of the four to get behind the trees. As his horse slid in some mud, Bill peered through the branches of a cottonwood and saw that in the distance the four riders were now visible.

"Damnation," Bill said. "Does anyone know if they saw us?"

"They had to have seen us," Chess said. "As soon as I got back here with the wagon situated, I looked through the trees and saw them back behind us. All three of you was still riding when I saw them in plain sight."

"Look, they've stopped now," Mickey Hogg said.

"I can't tell what they're doing," Pawnee Bill said, though he thought he could see that they had their rifles out.

"Loading their rifles is what it looks like to me," Mickey Hogg said.

"Is that what it looks like?" Dick asked. His eyesight was not so good, and while he could make out shapes at a distance and knew the men were there, he was too far away to get any detail of them.

"Maybe we should sit this one out," Pawnee Bill said. "Maybe we ought to just let them pass. We'll come to someone else sooner or later."

Mickey Hogg rubbed his chin. "I sure would like to have that bottle of whiskey," Mickey said.

The Kentucky men drove their spare mounts with the panniers out in front of them, but while Pawnee Bill watched, the men spread out. One of them rode up ahead of the spare mounts. One rode off to the left of the spares, while another rode to the right. And one of them stayed at the back.

"What are they doing?" Pawnee Bill asked.

"Riding escort on their spares," Mickey said. "They's smarter than I thought they'd be. They've spread out. It makes them harder targets now."

The Kentuckians were getting closer now. The first one was near enough that they could see details of him, and the first detail they saw was that he'd drawn his long rifle from its scabbard and was riding with it across his saddle.

Neither Mickey nor Pawnee Bill nor Dick made any move to ride out and ambush the men.

"They know what we're up to," Mickey Hogg said.

And then the lead Kentuckian called out in a booming voice.

"I don't know what you're playing at, but be aware if you come out from behind those trees we will commence to shooting."

Mickey and Pawnee Bill both looked at each other and shrugged.

"Get off your horses, fast," Bill said. "Chess come down off of that wagon. Let your horses wander. Be subtle about it, but act like we're just here for a nooning."

While the other men did as they were told,

Pawnee Bill spurred his horse forward. Holding his reins with plenty of slack, Bill put his hands in the air and rode forward. The first of the Kentuckians was coming even with the creek now. Bill rode out into plain sight, keeping his hands up.

"Howdy, friend," Pawnee Bill called to him. "Not sure what's got you agitated so, but we ain't playin' at nothing. We just stopped here for our nooning. Cool water and shade trees. Stop and rest with us if you like."

The Kentuckians, who were now all in plain view, kept their rifles pointed toward Pawnee Bill and the others down around the wagon.

"You just keep your hands where we can see them while we pass," the lead Kentuckian said.

This was not the same man who spoke at the campfire the previous evening. Pawnee Bill recognized him as the one in the back.

"There sure ain't cause to be so hostile," Bill said. "We're just inviting you to join us down in the shade by the creek here. It's a good spot for your noon rest."

"It ain't noon yet," said the Kentuckian riding along the near side of the spare mounts.

Pawnee Bill noticed that while the three riders in the front merely had their rifles crossed over their saddles, the one in the back actually had his rifle leveled, one-handed, and pointing pretty near to where Pawnee Bill was sitting his horse. The Kentuckian rode like that, his barrel almost a perfect circle in Pawnee Bill's line of sight. The Kansas ruffian had to wonder what kind of strength it took to hold, one-handed, one of those long guns steady like that. It was best that he decided to abandon the plans of ambush. These men would not be willing victims.

As the last of the Kentuckians rode even with Pawnee Bill, that long rifle still pointing right at him, Bill waved a hand.

"Y'all have a good ride down the trail," Bill said. "Maybe after a while we'll catch up to you."

"Be best for you if you did not," the Kentuckian said.

As they rode on, the Kentuckians all slid their rifles down into their scabbards and kicked up the pace, galloping away from Pawnee Bill and the creek.

Bill wheeled his horse and rode back over to where his companions were milling about near the creek.

"Better just fill your canteen with some water from the creek, there," Pawnee Bill said to Mickey Hogg. I don't think them Kentucky boys had any whiskey anyway."

-12-

Each day seemed to offer a new rotation on the Cummings' wagons, with a steady change of drivers and passengers. Often as not, drivers rode alone on the wagon while the others walked alongside the wagon or rode one of the saddle horses. Some days Rachel Cummings found herself assigned to Graham Devalt's wagon, which was not so bad because Graham could be charming and amusing. Other days she drive with one of her younger brothers riding along with her. Some days she rode with her father or her mother.

Amos Cummings dictated who should ride on which wagon every morning. He did not share his method with anyone else in the group, but he made his assignments with a view to breaking up the monotony of the days by mixing the people in the group. Just as often, those who were assigned to specific wagons in the morning were no longer on them by the time the wagon train stopped for supper, but Amos felt he had done his part if no two people started on a wagon together two days in a row.

Today, Rachel was with her mother on the lead wagon, though this was not how she started out. She started on the second wagon with brother Jeremiah driving. But at noon she contrived to get up into the first wagon to sit beside her mother, though it was not her mother who held her interest.

Rachel Cummings' attention was on the rough guide in the buckskin coat.

For no reason that she could name, Rachel's interest in Rab Sinclair had increased. She found that quite suddenly she was very curious about him. With some guilt, she wondered if it was because of the way he had treated Graham the day before.

"What do you think of him?" Rachel asked her mother.

Martha Cummings, who'd been lost in her own thoughts, raised her eyebrows into a question. "What do I think of whom?"

"Our guide, mother. Mr. Sinclair."

Rachel was leaned forward, her elbow resting on her crossed knee and her chin on her hand.

"I think he makes me very sad," Martha Cummings said.

"Sad?" Rachel asked, surprised. She did not connect Rab Sinclair with sadness.

"Of course. No mother, except for a series of Indian women that his father apparently took up with. It's scandalous, to be sure, but it is also very sad to me. What kind of life is it for a boy who grows up without a mother to love him?"

"I think he is interesting," Rachel said, and there

was some lost and dreamy note to her voice that made her mother start.

"Oh, Rachel," her mother said, her tone a mixture of sympathy and foreboding.

"What?" Rachel asked, throwing in a note of innocence. "I do think he is interesting. He's certainly like nothing we've ever met before."

Martha Cummings looked at the casual slouch of the man on the horse in front of them, the easy way he sat in the saddle. She wouldn't admit it – not to her husband or her daughter or anyone – but she felt very drawn to the young man and his rough ways. "He is a curiosity," Martha said. "I will grant you that."

"Graham does not like him," Rachel said.

"I've noticed," Martha said. "You should be very careful. You know your father thinks highly of Graham and would very much like to see the two of you engaged after we have arrived in California. But if you were to encourage Mr. Sinclair, either purposefully or accidentally, it could create even more animosity with Graham. It would be good to remember that Mr. Sinclair will be with us only as far as Santa Fe, but Graham will be with us in California for a very long time."

"I will be careful, mother," Rachel said. "I know father's thoughts about Graham. I am not so sure that I share them. But I can assure you, I have no thoughts of Mr. Sinclair in that respect."

Rachel's face cracked into a smile even as she thought of it.

"The notion is preposterous," she told her mother, and she covered her face as she laughed aloud.

"Don't snort, Rachel," Martha said. "It is not becoming."

Even as Rachel's face fell from the reprimand from her mother, the wagon lurched to a stop. Martha snapped the whip – something she had gotten exceedingly good at in the last few weeks since first leaving Ohio – but the mules could not pull the wagon.

"We've gotten mired," Martha proclaimed, looking at the wheels stuck in a low, muddy spot. Talking with her daughter, she did not even see it coming.

"What's the problem?" Amos called from the next wagon back.

Martha leaned out and shouted back to him, "We are stuck in the mud!"

The wagons all halted behind the lead wagon, and Rab Sinclair turned the two horses he was leading to go back to see what the hold up was.

Jeremiah Cummings, the oldest son, was mounted on one of the saddle horses and leading the stock. He allowed them to wander and graze, but if they strayed too far he turned them back to the group.

Rab dismounted and picketed all three horses. Usually a ground tie was all he ever did with Cromwell, but experience told him that one problem usually leads to the next. A wagon getting stuck in mud is the sort of problem that leads to a horse wandering off and no one noticing until the thing is a speck on the horizon. When he was finished with the horses, he looked at the wheels.

"Mired good," he told Amos Cummings who was standing over him and looking down at the wheels.

"We'll need to unload the wagon as much as we

can. If we've got a spare board or some of the firewood you've collected, we can push that up under the wheels to try to give it something firm to catch hold to. Once we've got the weight out of the back of the wagon we should be able to get it rolling again."

The men began unloading. Water casks. Tents. Sacks of flour and salt. Boxes of provisions. Bedrolls. Spare wheels. Boxes of clothes and personal items. Even heirlooms Amos and Martha had decided to bring with them to California.

When they reached the boxes of books at the bottom of the wagon, Rab Sinclair was appalled at the weight of the things. They were in heavy wooden crates, and the books themselves were surprisingly heavy.

"Ain't they got bookstores in California?" Rab asked. "These would be best left right here. It's a cruelty to the animals and an imposition on our time to load these books back into the wagon."

"These books are exceedingly valuable," Amos Cummings said. "Beyond that, they are necessary to me for my profession. I would sooner leave some portion of the flour than I would these books."

Rab assumed he was joking, but when he looked at the professor's face he realized there was no jest.

With the wagon unloaded, they were able to lever the wheels out of the mud with a spare board, and they left branches in the low spot so that the wheels would have something to roll over.

Once the wagon was back on firm soil, the men loaded it back. Rab refused to pick up a box of books, and so Amos, Stuart, and Graham got the books while Rab loaded supplies that made sense to him.

The process was a lengthy one, and at least three-quarters of an hour were expended on the unloading and reloading of the wagon.

Rab stood by and supervised each of the wagons going across the small bridge of branches they had made. Most of the branches snapped under the weight of the wagons, but they were sufficient to give the wagons something firm to cross.

"You should collect all those branches from the mud," Rab told Paul, the youngest of the Cummings sons. "They won't be good for burning now, but when the mud dries we can knock it off and those sticks will still be good for fire."

Rab let the horses gallop for a bit. He caught up to and passed the first of the wagons with the two Cummings women, and he was soon far out in front of the wagon train.

Today he was on the sorrel and the buckskin had the pannier so that Cromwell was unburdened. He tried not to favor the blue, but he knew that Cromwell was not doing his part with the pannier. Though he preferred riding the young roan, Cromwell found that he could talk just as freely with either the sorrel or the buckskin as he did with Cromwell, and neither offered any more argument than Cromwell ever did.

"Old sorrel hawss, I will tell you that I ain't never seen nothing like these university people," Rab said. "They'd sooner starve than give up them books, knowing that it is an imposition on me and a danger to the entire expedition. And it's a damn shame to over burden them animals in that way. All for books. I cannot understand it."

The books in the wagons were like a bur under

the saddle to him. Those books stung Rab Sinclair in a way that he could not fully understand.

"I know I shouldn't let it bother me so," he said to the horse. "But those books are a stain on my conscience. I shouldn't allow them to force those mules and oxen to drag around such an unnecessarily heavy load."

***

The sun sank low on the horizon faster than Rab Sinclair would have liked. He pushed on as long as he dared, and then finally turned his horses, rode back to the train and told them they should make camp.

Remembering his promise to Amos Cummings and thinking of his own diminishing provisions, Rab took his supper that evening with the others. He helped with setting up camp and seeing to the livestock, and in that way he did not feel bad about sharing in the food and coffee. Most often in wagon trains, families and small parties separated themselves out when it came time for victuals, and in that way they made certain to preserve their own stores for the remainder of the journey. But the Cummings group all ate communally, and Rab wondered if they were keeping a good watch on their supplies.

They lit lanterns and sat around a small fire just large enough for cooking.

When supper was finished, the attention of the party seemed to turn universally toward Rab Sinclair. The Cummings and Bancrofts and Graham Devalt, after all, had been all together at supper for many weeks now, and the introduction of a new person naturally drew the interest of all the others.

They questioned him about any number of things about growing up in the wilds and among the Indians, and Rab did his best to answer them without committing to too much conversation.

"I am surprised, Mr. Sinclair, that we have not encountered any Indians on the prairie," Martha Cummings said. "I believed that they were as numerous here as the grass."

"Not so numerous as that," Rab said. "But there is no doubt whether or not they are out there. The Arapaho are west of us, nearer the mountains, but they sometimes will come this away. The Lakota and the Cheyenne are north of here, but we could encounter them. The Pawnee, too."

"If we were to encounter them, how should we proceed?" Stuart Bancroft asked.

"If they have women and children with them, they will let you alone. They might want to trade. We'll make them know we have no interest in trade. They might want to beg. It's best not to give them anything, unless we think they are truly hungry. If they are truly hungry, they will leave their women and children and come take what they want. So if they truly have no food, it's best to give them a little something – even if it might be more difficult on you later. You don't have to give them much."

"What if we encounter only men?" Stuart asked.

"Don't talk to them," Rab said, and he looked meaningfully at Graham Devalt. "Don't engage them, don't rile them. If we see only men, we'll do our best to make a circle out of the wagons and keep the livestock in the circle. We'll greet 'em with guns, and if they come near we'll have to shoot one of them. If they keep coming, we'll have to shoot all of them."

"We will not shoot another man, not even an Indian," Amos Cummings said.

"Then they'll take everything you've got, and if they leave you alive it will be a surprise to me."

"Are they all so vicious?" Rachel Cummings asked.

"I wouldn't say they are vicious," Rab said. "If a man's family is starving and he takes food, is that viciousness?"

"Theft is vicious," Rachel said.

Rab shrugged. "I reckon the Indians wouldn't see it as theft. They would see it more as survival."

"If you do not think they are vicious, then what do you think of them?" Rachel asked.

Rab lit his pipe and thought for a moment about the question.

"The Indians are an interesting people," Rab said evenly. "They are wild and beautiful, and of course each tribe is as different from one another as the English are different from the Germans and the Germans from the French, and the French from the Spanish. They have their own languages and their own traditions. But on the whole, most of 'em are a might too superstitious for me."

"How do you mean?" Rachel asked. "Why do you say they are superstitious?"

"A might too religious, I reckon," Rab said. "Them Injuns, they put a heap of stock into the spirits of their ancestors. A bird ain't never just a bird, but it's an omen that can speak of the future, and such. They take the buzzard as being a sacred beast because it cleans the land. Buzzards are a nasty bird, and I would not eat one even if I had been days without food."

Rab looked to the sky, but there were no buzzards to be seen in the dwindling light.

"They are not so different from some folks from back East that I've known," he added. "The religion is different, but it's all superstition."

Whether he meant it as such, Rachel Cummings took the last remark as a jibe intended personally against her.

"How are Easterners superstitious?" she asked.

"Too much churchin'."

Rachel's reaction was beyond her ability to control. She snorted as she laughed, then put a hand up to her face.

Her tone was now incredulous. "Do you not believe in God, Mr. Sinclair?"

"I reckon I do, ma'am," Rab said. "But I don't find much use in preachers."

"Was your father not a preacher?" Rachel asked. "You gave us to understand that he was a preacher."

"I reckon I did call him that," Rab said. "Folks called him a preacher, that's true enough, but he was never as much of a preacher as they claimed he was. He sought to teach the tribes about Jesus, that's true. But I think mostly my old pa liked the ways of the Indian people and better preferred associatin' with them than he did with white folks. And as I mentioned to you before, he was partial to squaws. My mother was part Cherokee herself."

Martha Cummings cut in.

"Please, Mr. Sinclair. In front of my children, can we not discuss 'squaws'?"

Rab gave her a smile. "Yes, ma'am," he said. "You've asked me not to do that, and I am sorry. I did not mean any disrespect to you or your children."

But Rachel Cummings was not through with him.

"Do you believe that Jesus was the Son of God, Mr. Sinclair?" Stephanie asked.

"I've had opportunity to hear some of what he said, when pa was reading from the Saint James. I reckon I don't dispute none of it. If'n he said he was the Son of God, it ain't for me to say he warn't."

Martha did not know if she was bemused or horrified at the apparent ignorance of the man.

"Do you not read the Bible yourself?" she asked, though she thought she had caught on to the answer already.

"I've had parts of it read to me," Sinclair said. "I know some of the stories well enough."

Rachel's feelings toward Rab Sinclair turned ugly, and she could not herself explain why. Perhaps she was thinking of her conversation with Graham from the previous day. Or maybe she felt hurt by the apparent insult about people from back East. Or maybe she was angry because her mother, again, had to ask Rab to watch how he spoke. Or maybe, if she was honest with herself, she felt jealous at the talk of "squaws."

Either way, Rachel's suspicions of Rab Sinclair's illiteracy were now confirmed, and she felt an opportunity to get the upper hand on this man who had been rude and demanding, lording over them for so long his knowledge of the land and the customs of its people, its dangers and its advantages.

There was an edge to her voice as she asked, "Do you know how to read, Mr. Sinclair?"

"I ain't never learned how to read letters, if that's what you mean."

Rachel Cummings smirked at him. "Mr. Sinclair, if not letters, then what you have learned to read?"

"You see them clouds yonder, Miss Miles?" Rab said, pointing to a distant cloud bank, just a darker shade against the darkening sky.

"I do."

"I learned to read them clouds, to know if they threaten a bad storm. I learned to read the signs of a track, and I can judge if there's deer or bear, wolves or lions. I can look at a print in the dirt and read whether Injuns or white men are around. So I reckon I've learned to read some things, but letters ain't one of them. The things I've learned to read serve me out here better than letters would. I notice, for instance, when y'all went looking for a guide who could get you from one place to another, you did not seek out a scholastic man with a university degree to help you. You had one of them already.

"And if we run into trouble, I reckon you'll be glad enough to have me here."

Rachel Cummings offered no retort, and Rab Sinclair was indifferent as to whether or not he'd backed down her contempt.

Rab Sinclair left Miss Cummings and the others at the campfire near the wagons and he walked over to where he had set up his small tent. He looked at the darkening sky, at the clouds blowing in, and judged that indeed they would bring a storm before morning.

"Y'all better pack up anything you don't want to blow away or get wet," Sinclair called to the others at the camp. With a grin, he added, "Especially your books."

-13-

The small caravan of wagons appeared on the distant horizon to the east, riding toward them.

"That ain't the stagecoach," Mickey Hogg said. "That's five or six wagons."

"Let 'em catch us up," Pawnee Bill said.

While they waited for the wagon train, they dismounted and picketed their horses. Dick Derugy, Pawnee Bill, and Chess Bowman lounged in the grass, but Mickey Hogg sat on the back of the wagon and watched the train coming toward them. More than anything, he hoped they were drinkers. He'd been too long without a drop of whiskey, and it made him feel worse when he didn't drink.

As the wagon train grew nearer, Mickey could see better what he was dealing with. A single horseman led the group. He was pushing two horses out in front of him. Another horseman, who was riding out through the prairie at an easy gait, was pushing ten or twelve head of cattle as well as some spare mules and oxen. There were six wagons, some pulled by mules and some by oxen.

The lone horseman at the front was riding well ahead. He was not far from Mickey and the wagon when Mickey realized that a woman was driving the lead wagon.

"Hey, Bill," Mickey called. "Take a look'ee at what's coming in that lead wagon."

Every man had his vice. For Mickey Hogg, women came along often enough, but a day without liquor was a sad day, indeed. Though he'd been with Pawnee Bill and the others only a short time, Mickey already had Bill figured out. Women served as Pawnee Bill's vice. Dick liked women himself, but he was different from Bill. Bill had a lust for hurting women.

Pawnee Bill, reclining on his elbow in the tall grass, craned his neck and tried to see for himself. But now the lone rider at the front of the wagon train was riding up to the men.

"Howdy," Mickey Hogg called out. "That's a good looking horse, there."

The man nodded. He was riding a blue roan with a black face, about as blue as Mickey Hogg had ever seen.

"He gets me from one place to the other pretty well," the man said.

"Bound for Santa Fe?" Mickey asked, conversationally.

"We are," the man said. "Y'all?"

"Yep. Headed to New Mexico Territory to see if we can't dig some gold out of the ground."

The man on the horse was younger than Mickey would have expected.

"You traveling with your family?" Mickey asked.

"I'm a hired guide."

"Kind of young for a guide, ain't you?"

"I've got a surprising amount of experience," the guide said, a grin on his face. "Mind if I step down?"

"You're welcome," Mickey said.

The guide swung easily from the saddle. Mickey watched the way he moved. He was agile, and quick. His movements seemed smooth and careless, but Mickey realized right the man was careful and precise. He dropped the reins on the ground and the horse stood in place, munching some of the grass. The guide slid a tobacco pouch from one pocket and a pipe from the other. He filled the pipe and lit it, puffing on the pipe to get the tobacco going.

"My name's Mickey Hogg."

"Rab Sinclair," the guide said. "Y'all been traveling long?"

"We started near here," Mickey Hogg said. "We were living down in a little town. I guess folks call it Spears Hollow, if you've heard of it."

"Never have," Rab admitted.

The guide eyed the buckboard wagon. "Think that'll make it all the way to New Mexico Territory?"

Mickey Hogg laughed. "Well, we hope it does, anyway. You're the guide, what do you think?"

Rab looked at the mule team and the wagon and shook his head. "I ain't real sure where Spears Hollow is, but I reckon y'all have done well to make it this far. You've got plenty of hawsses, though. You might decide to give up the wagon and mules and pack it to Santa Fe."

Rab glanced over his shoulder as Martha Cummings' wagon rolled up behind him. He turned and walked over to the mules drawing the wagon and gave the lead mule a pat on the rump.

"Keep it moving, Mrs. Cummings," Rab said. "Still too far to go to stop for a chat."

Martha offered the men reclining in the glass a nod and said hello, but she did not talk beyond that. As each wagon came along, Rab repeated his instructions to keep moving. He tried to give Amos Cummings a meaningful look, a look that spoke a silent warning, but he wasn't sure if his meaning was taken. He offered no look of warning to Graham Devalt, but was pleasantly surprised when Graham did not begin a conversation with the strangers.

When the wagons had all passed and Matthew Cummings was beyond the strangers with the livestock, Rab turned back to Mickey Hogg.

"Y'all see them boys from Kentucky come through? Maybe yesterday or early this morning they would have caught up with you."

"We did," Mickey Hogg said. "We surely did. They caught up and passed us yesterday in the afternoon. Kentucky boys, you say? I don't recollect if they mentioned being from Kentucky. Nice fellows, though."

"Most folks you encounter on the trail are nice folks," Rab said. "Everybody just making their own way to a better life, minding their own business, mostly."

"That's right," Mickey said. "That's what we're doing. Heading for treasures and better days. Minding our own business."

Rab knocked the tobacco from his pipe and was careful to grind it into the ground with the heel of his boot. He stuck the pipe back in his pocket.

"Well, Santa Fe ain't gettin' any closer with me standing here," Rab said. "Good luck to you folks."

"Good luck," Mickey Hogg said.

Rab swung himself back into his saddle and started off after the wagons. The buckskin and sorrel had both wandered a bit, and he had to go and collect them before he could get moving.

Between the strangers and the wagons, Rab spoke to his horse.

"I did not like the look of those men, Cromwell. I'll be relieved to put them behind us."

But relief was not in sight.

Immediately after Rab rode off, Mickey Hogg turned to his companions.

"Six wagons loaded with all sorts of supplies," Mickey said. "If they ain't got everything we need, ain't nobody in all of Kansas got everything we need."

"You see that woman driving the first wagon?" Pawnee Bill said. "She was a fine piece of woman flesh. I didn't get a look at the younger one walking on the other side of the wagons. How'd she look to you Mickey?"

Hogg shrugged his shoulders. "I didn't get a good look at her. Must have been the first one's daughter, so I would reckon she ain't bad."

"Let's saddle up and get after them," Mickey Hogg said. "This is what we've been waiting on. Did you get a look at the men with the wagon train? Boys and old, soft men. These ain't hard men. These are men who'll probably give us what we want if we just ask for it from behind a six-shooter."

"What about that guide?" Dick Derugy asked. "He was young, but he didn't look soft to me. Boy had sand to ride up to a group like us and dismount and smoke his pipe like that. He wasn't a bit scared of us."

Pawnee Bill had to agree.

"I'll say this about him, too. He knew who we are. You could tell by the way he watched us, the way he kept them wagons moving. He sized us up in a hurry. And like Dick said, he wasn't scared a bit."

"Maybe not," Mickey conceded. "But like you said, Dick, he was just a boy. What kind of men are we if the four of us can't deal with one boy? We kill him and the rest of 'em will all fall in line and do as they told."

-14-

Every time Rab turned in his saddle to look at his back trail, the four men with the buckboard wagon were back there.

Rab knew that the wagon train had moved too long into the day without stopping. The livestock was accustomed to a nooning. The people were, too. Sore legs, tired from walking, had driven all of the people onto wagons so that no one was walking and the animals harnessed to the wagons were having to work that much harder. Matthew Cummings, the middle son, was again riding one of the saddle horses and driving the livestock. Matthew had picked up the knack for it and enjoyed the work, and he most often worked the livestock rather than driving one of the wagons.

But the men following them made Rab uncomfortable so that he did not want to stop.

Rab rode Cromwell over beside the wagon Amos Cummings was driving, and there he dismounted from the blue and walked along beside the wagon.

"We have some trouble, Mr. Cummings," Rab said. "Them men we encountered a ways back, have you noticed that they are following us?"

"There's only one trail cutting through here, and there's not but two ways to go on the trail. Are you surprised they are following us?" Amos Cummings asked.

"It's a common practice that groups spread out on the trail," Rab said. "That away, livestock ain't competing for grazing, and come morning time you don't have to worry about your cattle and horses being mixed up with someone else's cattle and horses. It's good practice, but it's also good manners. It gives folks who don't know other folks a sense of security, if you see what I mean."

"So you think these men lack manners?" Amos Cummings asked.

"I think they could intend to do harm to us."

"Harm to us?" Amos Cummings asked, a note of surprise in his voice. "I hardly think that the men who travel this trail are the sorts who would seek to do us harm, Mr. Sinclair. The men who make this journey are ambitious, enterprising men – not thieves and scoundrels."

"Not every man is peaceful, Mr. Cummings," Rab said. "Not every man shares your thoughts about how to treat other men."

"And you gathered all of this from less than ten minutes of talking to those men?" Amos Cummings asked.

"I gathered all this from less than ten seconds of looking at them," Rab Sinclair said.

"So what do you want me to do about this, Mr. Sinclair?" Amos asked. "What do you expect me to do?"

"We need to plan to guard the camp tonight. We should do what we can to circle these wagons and keep the livestock inside them," Rab said. "We should plan to have guards with guns ready to defend the camp."

"Defend the camp?" Amos almost laughed.

"These men may be real trouble, Mr. Cummings," Rab said again. "We should be prepared for them."

"I did not set out on this journey because I am a man who lives by fear," Amos Cummings said. "And I've told you my feelings on violence."

Rab chewed his bottom lip. "Yes, sir," he said. "You've told me your feelings on violence. But if you won't give thought to protecting yourself, you should give some thought to your sons and in particular to your wife and your daughter."

"What does that mean?" Cummings asked. "What do you mean my wife and daughter?"

Rab looked back over his shoulder and saw the wagon and the three riders in the distance. "Those men back there are the kinds of men who want very specific things, Mr. Cummings. They want the kinds of things that ain't in abundance out here. There ain't a lot of women in abundance out here."

"That's enough of that sort of talk," Amos Cummings said. "I won't hear of it. How do you know these are not just men who are seeking a better life in the west – just like everyone else who travels this trail?"

"They're on a buckboard wagon," Rab said. "That's a farmer's wagon, used for going to town to pick up supplies. And the supplies in the back of it are farmer supplies – flour enough to get them through the winter. Those mules pulling the wagon, those are not mules accustomed to nor prepared for a long journey. If I had to guess, I'd say that wagon, those supplies, and those mules are all stolen. I'd hate to hear of the shape of the farmer who had them a few days ago."

"You're accusing those men of being thieves?" Amos Cummings asked.

"I'm accusing them of worse than that," Rab said. "And I believe they intend to do worse again."

"What can be done about it?" Amos Cumming asked. "What are you proposing?"

Rab Sinclair knew what he wanted to do. He'd taken the measure of the men now following them, and what he wanted to do was put a rifle in every man's hand, allow the four men behind them to catch up, and then ambush them. Such things were done among the tribes. Pleasantries and courtesies and customs such as those followed by the white men were foreign and absurd to the people among the tribes. If an Apache's enemies were following him, he would not wait for them to prove they were enemies. He would turn and face his enemy.

But Rab knew, too, that Amos Cummings, a man of peace, would never tolerate talk of such a plan.

"I want you to understand that if you and your family are going to survive, you might have to be prepared to defend yourselves," Rab said.

"I'll not use violence against these men," Amos Cummings said.

"All right, Mr. Cummings," Rab said. "I'll not argue with you about it. But if that's the case, then I will expect you to do everything I tell you to do, when I tell you to do it, and make sure your people do it, too."

"And what are you going to tell us to do?" Amos asked.

Rab looked up at the sky. The sun was still overhead. There was plenty of daylight left and many more miles to be made. Rab despised the idea of losing more time – so much had been lost already just through the slow pace of the oxen, the lengthy delays every morning. Even so, Rab's idea was to get his wagon train out ahead of those men, but to manage it he needed the wagons to stop now.

"Stop here and make camp," Rab said.

"It's too early to stop," Amos said.

"Yes it is," Rab agreed. "It's much too early in the day to stop. But we cannot simply go on down the trail, stopping and camping as we normally would, and take no precautions at all."

Amos Cummings chewed on it for a minute. He looked at the sun still high in the sky.

"Mr. Sinclair, stopping now would be a mistake. You're the one who has stressed to us over and over the necessity of speed and not wasting a moment. What if we were to run into real trouble? A broken axle on one of the wagons, for instance. That could set us back a day. Or if some or all of the animals run off at night when we've turned them out. These are serious issues that could delay us by days, and both are very real possibilities. Yet here you are, asking me to voluntarily give up an entire afternoon of progress for no reason beyond your fears. I'll not do it."

Rab took up the reins on Cromwell and, without

breaking stride, hopped back into the saddle.

"Then I'll bid you farewell here, Mr. Cummings. I wish you well."

"You can't leave!" Amos said.

"Those men intend to kill you and everyone with this wagon train, Mr. Cummings. You won't defend yourself with guns and you won't give me the ability to save you without 'em. So I'm going to ride on. I reckon I can outdistance these men without much trouble. And you can figure your own way, since you won't listen to mine."

Rab started to ride away, but Amos called to him.

"Very well, Mr. Sinclair! You've made your point. We'll stop now."

Amos called to his middle son Matthew, who was mounted on one of the saddle horses. Matthew rode over to his father's wagon.

"Pass the word to the rest of the wagons," Amos said. "We'll stop for the day up ahead."

Rab rode ahead to help direct the wagons over to a flat space where they could make a decent camp for the night, and he moved the wagons into something of a circle, although with only six wagons they did not make an enclosed circle as a larger wagon train would have. But Rab wanted the wagons to form up as much of a circle as possible to create a small paddock for the animals. Tonight, he did not want them to get too far away from camp.

While the others all started the work of getting camp set up, Rab helped Matthew to roundup the loose livestock. The other Cummings boys, Jeremiah and Paul, used rope to tie off a temporary paddock inside the half-circle made by the wagons.

While they rounded up the livestock, Rab kept his eye on the wagon and three riders in the distance. As he thought they would, Mickey Hogg and the others stopped when they saw the wagon train stop.

As Rab pushed in the last of the mules, he wheeled Cromwell over to where Amos Cummings was trying to explain to Stuart Bancroft and Graham Devalt why they had stopped so early in the day.

"I'm going to ride over to those men back there," Rab said. "When I get to them, I want you to hitch up one of the wagons and move it – move it over yonder there. As best as you can, make it look like you're doing it for some purpose. Set up the campfire near it and prepare your supper on the back of it. But when you move it, make as much noise as you can. Bang your pots and pans together, get the mules worked up so they're baying, shout at each other. As much noise as you can scare up."

"We will not participate in foolish games," Graham Devalt said.

"Mr. Cummings?" Rab asked, ignoring Devalt.

Amos nodded. "I don't understand the purpose of all of this, Mr. Sinclair. But I'm willing to go along with it for some ways."

Now Rab turned and rode his back trail, back to where Mickey Hogg and the other three men had stopped.

He rode up near the camp and reined in his horse.

"Howdy," Rab said.

"We're getting to be like old traveling

companions," Mickey Hogg said with a laugh.

All four of the men eyed Rab suspiciously. They'd done nothing, really, to make camp.

"Surprised to see y'all stop back here," Rab said. "Quite a bit of daytime left for moving on."

"You stopped," Dick Derugy said.

"We pushed on pretty hard yesterday," Rab said. "We thought it would be best to stop early today and give the livestock some rest."

"That's what we're doing, too," Mickey Hogg said.

"Mind if I join you for a spell?" Rab asked.

"Oh, sure," Mickey said. "I guess we should have invited you. Forgot our manners."

Rab swung himself down out of his saddle. "So y'all have decided to stop for the day, too?"

"That's right," Mickey Hogg said. "All this traveling and not feeling like you're getting anywhere can wear on a man."

Rab looked out to the west and back to the east.

"Scenery don't change much," he said. "Most of the time, just from courtesy, folks don't stop so close to someone else's camp. On the Trail here, folks tend to spread out more than this."

"We making you nervous?" Mickey Hogg asked with a smirk.

Rab lit his pipe and smoked it in silence for a few moments. Then he shook his head.

"Not making me nervous, no," he said thoughtfully. "There's a reason for it."

He held the bowl of his pipe and he used the tip to point.

"There's all this grass out here, plenty of grass for grazing, but you know how livestock is. They'll munch a bit here and then wander a ways and munch a bit there. Next thing you know, our hawsses is all intermingled with your hawsses, our cows is intermingled with your cows. If we're planning to move out before sunup – which we are – then it makes it awful challenging to get the right hawsses and the right cows in the dark. And oftentimes, this late in the season, the good grazing along the trail is all eat up. If you look around with a big sweeping view, looks to be plenty of good grass through here. But if you get to walking around and really start looking, what you see is that the grass really ain't as plentiful as it first appears. So folks traveling on the trail tend not to camp within sight of each other. That away, their stock don't get all mingled up and if the grazing is pretty well eat over, there still ought to be plenty."

Rab held his tone level and his manners easy. He showed these four men that he was plenty comfortable coming into their camp and advising them, even if he was younger than they were.

"It makes good sense for us, and it makes good sense for you, too."

Mickey Hogg's face showed anger. Mickey wasn't a man accustomed to being told what to do by anyone.

"So are you trying to tell us that we should move on?" Mickey asked, a challenge in his tone.

"Not at all," Rab said evenly. "No, sir. I don't see that it causes any harm for you to be here and us to be there, not for one night. We're going to corral up our livestock, so there won't be any worries about intermingling, and we've got some boys in our train who can collect grass for the animals. No, one night won't make a difference. I just thought I'd mention it to you for the future. I know y'all said you ain't been on the trail before, and you're bound to encounter others, too. Some folks won't be as friendly about it as we are. So it's just a word of caution to you."

Mickey backed down his temper a bit.

Pawnee Bill watched Mickey close, curious how the man would deal with the young guide. Pawnee Bill half hoped Mickey would gut shoot him right there in the camp and then the four men could make a charge against the pioneers down at the wagon train. He was eager to get at them women.

"I guess it's good of you to tell us," Mickey said.

"I find it's always helpful to learn from folks who have done a thing before," Rab said. "For instance, I'm sure you boys have experience that I ain't familiar with, and there's probably a thing or two you could teach me. What line of work y'all been in?"

Mickey looked casually back at the others and laughed.

"Pawnee Bill, what's your line?"

"Killing abolitionists, mostly," Pawnee Bill said. "You ever heard of the raid on Lawrence, boy?"

"I have," Rab said.

"Well, I was in that raid. A fair few others, too. And I've killed some free-staters."

"See," Rab Sinclair said with a smile. "That's exactly what I'm talking about. I've never once killed a free-stater or burned a town to the ground. So right there is something you could probably teach me all about."

"You ever taken an Injun's scalp?" Pawnee Bill asked. "Cause I done that, too. Injun scalps pay better than beaver pelts."

"I can't say that I've done that either," Rab said, and he puffed some on his pipe. "Don't it worry you to be toting Injun scalps?"

"I don't have any now," Bill said.

"But I mean, after you take 'em," Rab said. "Before you sell 'em. I reckon you're riding some distance with them on your person. A party of Cheyenne Dog Warriors comes up on you and you've got black hairs hanging from your saddle, I would reckon them Cheyenne would get a might upset about such a thing."

Pawnee Bill laughed. "I'd take their scalps, too. I ain't scared o' no Injun. Best thing to do with Injuns is shoot 'em before they get close enough to see what you've got hanging on your saddle."

"I reckon that's true," Rab said. "What about you, Mr. Hogg? What line were you in before you took to the Trail?"

"Gambling and drinking, mostly," Mickey Hogg said, laughing. "Never did find work to be too appealing."

Rab glanced down at the campsite and saw that Amos Cummings was in the process of moving one of the wagons. He puffed on his pipe, allowing a moment for the conversation with Mickey Hogg and the others to fall silent. Now he listened hard. He thought he could just barely make out sounds of the wagon moving, but not really. He could see one of the young Bancroft boys banging together two cooking pans, but he could not hear any noise from it.

"I'm sorry," Rab said, looking at Chess Bowman. "I guess I've forgotten your name."

"Chester," Chess said. "Folks call me Chess."

"What about you, Chess?" Rab asked. "Did you work before you hit the Trail?"

"Some of this and some of that," Chess said.

"I was mostly a horse thief," Dick Derugy said. "Me and Chess was pretty good at stealing horses."

Rab puffed his pipe, not troubled at all by the admission.

"We've all got to be good at something," Rab said with an easy grin.

"You ain't bothered that we was horse thieves?" Dick asked. Dick offered the information as a test. He wanted to get a reaction out of the young guide. He was disappointed.

"Not at all. That's how everyone gets along. Some men are good at ranching or sod busting, for instance. And those men who are good at those jobs, well, they need hawsses. And that's a good thing, because some men, such as yourselves, are good at stealing hawsses. And because some men have 'em, you can go and take 'em. And some men are good at bein' deputies and sheriff's and marshals and whatnot. And since y'all are off takin' other people's hawsses, those lawmen get to be good at what they do. My pa used to always say that folks is different, but that's good on account of it takes all kinds."

Dick Derugy didn't know what to think of the talk about lawmen. He wasn't sure if it was a veiled threat at turning him in to the law.

"What kind of rifle is that in your scabbard there?" Mickey Hogg asked.

"That's a Hawken," Rab said proudly. "Made in St. Louis, Missouri."

"Fifty caliber?" Mickey asked.

"That's right," Rab said.

"That's a big gun for a little boy. Can you hit anything with it?"

Rab smiled at the insult. Men like this, he knew, liked to provoke others by riling them up. It would take a heap more than an insult to rile Rab Sinclair.

"I've hit some whitetails. Dropped a couple of buffalo. But you ain't lyin' about it being a big gun. You learn in a hurry not to miss because you don't want to add to the bruise the first shot puts on your shoulder."

Mickey Hogg laughed. He liked an opponent who was tough. It made the game more fun. "What about in your holster there, what is that?"

"It's a Colt Dragoon six-shooter," Rab said. "It's a big gun to try to manage with just the one hand."

"Have a hard time with it?" Mickey asked, at last finding a place where he could get at Rab Sinclair.

"I've found it to be troublesome to heft it and get a good aim on anything that ain't right in front of me," Rab said.

Mickey reached down to his thigh, and in a swift motion he jerked up the double-barrel scattergun, cocking back both hammers.

"I ain't one of them six-shooters, so I rigged up this scatter gun to use in a jiffy."

Rab looked at the cocked hammers of the shotgun.

"That's handy," he said. "I imagine there wouldn't be much beating that. Unless, of course, you were the third man."

"The third man?" Mickey Hogg said.

"You've got a barrel for the first man. He's done for. You've got a barrel for the second man. He's done for. So I guess the trick is making sure you're the third man."

Mickey Hogg laughed at that and let down the hammers on the scattergun.

"By golly, you're right about that, ain't you, boy? You are right about that. I guess my trick is to never pick a fight with a group no bigger than two."

Rab smiled pleasantly at Mickey Hogg. He'd learned what he came to learn.

"I should be getting back," Rab said. "Who knows what them greenhorns will get up to when I'm not there to keep 'em straight? It would appear that in my absence they have decided to move one of the wagons out of the circle. How are we supposed to keep the livestock corralled when they open up the corral?"

All four of the drifters jerked their heads and looked to see what Rab was talking about. He was not the only one who had not heard the wagon move.

He hopped back into the saddle and raised an arm up in farewell.

"Obliged for your hospitality, gentlemen," Rab called as he rode the blue back down toward the camp.

***

"Did you learn anything useful?" Amos Cummings asked when Rab dismounted back at camp.

"They are camped so far back that they cannot hear our wagons move," Rab Sinclair answered. "That is useful to know."

The women were cooking supper. The boys were reaping grass and bringing it in bundles to the animals in the makeshift corral. Amos, Stuart, and Graham were standing with Rab at the center of the camp.

"I'll also mention to you, just so you understand what sorts of men are following us, without any fear of a hangman's rope, two of them admitted to me that they are hawss thieves. One of them told me he'd been involved in the burning of Lawrence. The other has a shotgun rigged on his belt for a fast draw. These men are cutthroat killers."

Rab walked over to the campfire and took a thin, burning stick and used it to light his pipe. He lingered a moment while Amos, Stuart, and Graham talked about the information Rab brought back with him. He wanted the Ohioans to begin to grasp the nature of the men following them.

"I'm going through my matches too fast," he said to Martha Cummings. "Not many places out here to replace them if I run out."

He did not speak to nor even acknowledge Rachel Cummings. Rab Sinclair wasn't sure what to make of her, and he wasn't sure what to make of his feelings towards her. She was uncommonly beautiful, and because of that he found himself drawn to her. She also had an adventurous spirit that appealed to him. But she was rude and cruel. Rab knew among these people the ability to read and write was prized more highly than an ability to track a deer, shoot it, skin it, and make use of almost every bit of the thing. The one served as a means of learning and the other as a means of survival, and though Rab knew that the Ohioans were closer to needing the knowledge of survival than they realized, he also knew that book learning was still more important to them.

In her own society back home, Rachel Cummings would have cut Rab Sinclair to the bone with her taunts about reading, and he knew that was her intent. Out here on the plains, where Rab Sinclair cared nothing for the admiration of these travelers, her taunts bore little sting. Except that he was attracted to her. He liked the free way that she laughed, so free that her mother sometimes chided her. He liked the color of her eyes and the softness of her lips. He liked the sound of her voice. It had a musical quality to it. He liked those traits in her that reminded him of her mother. Martha Cummings was a special woman. Rab could see that. She had a courage within her that her husband lacked. She had passed that courage on to her children, too.

Rebekah Bancroft yelped and jerked her hand away from the fire.

"I've set the coffee pot too close to the fire," she said.

Rab wrapped his bandanna into a ball and used it to grab hold to the handle of the pot and lift it away from the fire.

"Always turn that handle away from the flames," he said.

"Yes, I wasn't paying attention," Rebekah said. And then in a low tone she said, "Mr. Sinclair, are those men behind us on the trail a danger to us?"

"I believe they are, ma'am," Rab said.

Rebekah and Martha exchanged a look.

"Are you talking to our husbands about this matter?" Martha asked.

"I am, yes," Rab said.

"Do you have any objection to us joining the conversation?"

"No, ma'am, Mrs. Cummings. I think it would be a fine idea for you to join the conversation."

With the two women in tow, Rab walked back over to the men.

Stuart Bancroft turned his attention to Rab. "Do you believe these men will attack us?"

Rab nodded thoughtfully, holding his pipe to his mouth. "I do, Mr. Bancroft."

He glanced at the two women who had followed him over from the campfire.

"I'll tell it to you plain, because you need to understand what you're facing. I think them men over there will try to sneak into the camp after dark. I think they'll cut your throat, and Mr. Cummings' and Mr. Devalt's. I think they'll kill your children. And I think they'll violate your women. That's what I think they're intending to do."

The men all bristled at the rough talk.

"You do not need to use such language," Graham Devalt chided.

"I think I do," Rab said. "Y'all packed up your

wagons and made certain sure to include among your belongings your sophistication and your civilization. But you came out here to a place where them things ain't real. What's real out here is that every moment you're standing right next to disaster. Whether it's a flood or a fire or a rattlesnake or sickness or Dog Soldiers on a rampage or low-life scoundrels hunting up easy pickings – death and disaster live out here and thrive. From the plains to the deserts, stronger men better equipped than you have starved to death or died of thirst. You've come into a rough land, looking to smooth it over with genteel ways. But ain't nobody out here living by your genteel ways. And those men yonder, they take whatever they see that they want. And there are things in this camp that they want."

"I do not know why you are so determined, Mr. Sinclair, to shake me from my principles," Amos Cummings said. "I abhor violence, and I'll not use it against another man."

"That's fine, Mr. Cummings," Rab said. "I'll not shake you from that. But those men there, they don't abhor violence. They love it. And they love using it. It don't matter whether or not you believe in killing. What matters is that they believe in killing. But I don't propose to teach you no different."

"What do you propose to do?" Martha Cummings asked. "You did not stop us in the early afternoon without having some thing in mind."

Matthew Cummings, the middle son, came nearby with an armload of grass for the horses, and he was also listening to the conversation. Matthew, above all others in the group, had taken a liking to Rab. He often followed Rab around, helping with chores, or sought advice on tending to the animals. Matthew had almost entirely taken over the work of driving the livestock, and in this duty frequently rode alongside Rab and peppered him with questions about living on the plains and among the tribes.

"It ain't for me to decide what to do," Rab said. "I was paid to guide you to Santa Fe. Mr. Cummings here, he's in charge of this wagon train."

Amos Cummings sighed heavily as everyone turned to him.

"Perhaps I should go up there and talk to those men myself," he said. "Mr. Sinclair has given me his opinion of them, but it might be best if I formed my own opinion."

"I wouldn't go up there alone if I were you," Rab said.

"You went up there alone," Amos shot back angrily.

"I ain't you," Rab said.

"I will go with you," Graham Devalt said.

"I will also go," Stuart Bancroft said.

The three men saddled three horses and rode back down the trail to the camp off in the distance behind them.

Rab and the two women and Matthew Cummings all stood by and watched them.

"Will those men try anything against our husbands?" Rebekah Bancroft asked.

"I can't answer that," Rab said. "They ought to have taken their rifles, even if they don't intend to use them."

Martha Cummings studied Rab Sinclair's face as he watched the three men ride off.

"You're glad to let us make our own mistakes," she said.

"It ain't for me to intervene," Rab said. "Your husband has a strong will and is determined to do things his own way. I'll offer what advice I can, but he makes the decisions for your group."

"I said to you before that you did not stop so early in the afternoon without some thought of what to do," Martha said. "Will you tell me what you have in mind?"

"We've got about three hours of daylight left," Rab said, looking up at the sun's position in the sky. "Maybe a little more if you include dusk before the sky is full dark. But come full dark, we should leave this camp."

"And travel by night?" Rebekah Bancroft asked.

"Yes, ma'am," Rab said.

"But there is almost no moon tonight. It will be almost completely black out."

"Yes, ma'am. And with it being so dark, them men up yonder won't see us leave."

Matthew Cummings, listening to the conversation, caught on right away.

"That's why you went up there," Matthew said. "And why you had us move the wagon. You wanted to see if they would hear us moving the wagons after dark."

Rab nodded and smiled at Matthew. "That was part of the reason. I also wanted to see if there was any chance they'd be moving on. And I wanted to talk to them for a bit, satisfy myself that my first impression of them was right."

"And you are satisfied?" Martha Cummings asked.

"I am, ma'am. Those men are dangerous. They as much as confessed to me the dirty dealing they've done. Boasted of it."

"Do you think we can break camp and sneak out of here without them knowing?" Martha Cummings asked.

"I reckon we can, ma'am," Rab said. "We'll have to be smart about it. The livestock should be separated before dark – those that will be harnessed to wagons and those that are to walk free. We'll have to tether the livestock that ain't harnessed. If we drive them, they'll wander too far. But tethered, Matthew and Paul can set out with them first. Once they've gone down the trail, we'll send the wagons out one at a time."

"I do not like the idea of sending my sons alone with the animals," Martha Cummings said.

"Even in the dark they'll be able to follow the trail well enough," Rab said. "Ain't no danger in it. The wagons will catch them up fast enough. But if we get them going they'll be out of the way, and it'll be easier on us to get the wagons moving. We should start making arrangements. Pack up the things we can pack up without making it look like we're packing. Matthew, get your brothers to help you separate out the animals. Only mules should be harnessed to the wagons tonight, if you can help it, and you boys lead the oxen. You'll not be able to harness animals yet, but you can get them separated out in the corral."

"What will you propose to do if my husband returns and believes those men pose no threat to us?" Martha Cummings asked.

"Ma'am, if your husband comes down after meeting them men and declares they ain't a threat, then you would do well to saddle a hawss and ride on out of here with me, because that man will get you killed."

Martha Cummings blushed. "I will stay with my husband, Mr. Sinclair."

"Then you'd better hope he comes away from his meeting with them fellows with a proper sense of how dangerous they are," Rab said. "At some point tonight those men are going to leave their camp and come down to our camp here. They're coming with the intention of doing bad things. If they come too soon after dark, they'll hear the wagons moving out, and that could turn sour for us. My guess is that they'll come in the early morning. Maybe around three or four o'clock. If we want to see the sunrise, we should plan to do it far down this trail from here."

-15-

Mickey Hogg was dozing in the grass when Pawnee Bill jabbed him in the ribs with the toe of his boot.

"Got company coming to the camp," Pawnee Bill said.

"It that boy again?" Hogg asked, not stirring from the grass. His hat was over his face to block out the sun while he tried to sleep.

"Nope," Pawnee Bill said. "Three other men from the camp."

Mickey Hogg stretched and sat up. He blocked the sun with his hat and looked out across the open plains between the two camps at the three men approaching them.

"This ought to be interesting," Mickey Hogg said. "What do you reckon they want coming to our camp like this?"

"Maybe they're looking to make a stand," Dick

Derugy said. "Maybe that other one sniffed us out as trouble, and they're coming to try to settle us now."

Mickey Hogg chewed on it for a moment, then shook his head. "They wouldn't come up without the other one. He's got sand. He wouldn't have let them come without him. He'd want to be involved in this. Unless he's circling around behind us somehow – and I don't know where he'd manage to do that without us seeing him – then I reckon this is a fishing party here."

"A fishing party?" Chess Bowman asked.

"Fishing for information," Mickey Hogg said "They're trying to figure out who we are and what we want. I'll do the talking. Wake me up when they get to the camp."

Mickey Hogg laid back in the grass and put his hat back over his face.

"I'm hungry," Chess Bowman announced, and he began rummaging through the buckboard wagon looking for something. "We don't even have enough wood to make a fire to cook on."

"Quit your griping," Pawnee Bill said. "They'll be up here soon. I've got some jerky in my saddle bag there. Gnaw on that for a bit. By dawn we'll have all the grub we can want."

Bill watched the approaching men, taking notice that not a man among them was armed with either rifle or revolver.

"They's unarmed," Bill hissed at Mickey Hogg.

In a few moments the men were close enough that Amos Cummings called out to the camp. "Hello, gentlemen! Mind if we step into your camp for a visit?"

"Come on in," Pawnee Bill said. Then he reached out with the toe of his boot and pressed it against Mickey Hogg. "We got company Mickey. Wake up and be polite."

Mickey Hogg made a great production out of rising from his slumber. He stretched and yawned, and then he put on a smile and walked out to Amos Cummings and the others, stretching out a hand in warm greeting.

"I'm Mickey Hogg," he said. "That there is Pawnee Bill, and that's Chess Bowman, and that one over there is Dick Derugy."

Amos Cummings shook hands with Mickey Hogg.

"I'm Amos Cummings, and this is my brother-in-law Stuart Bancroft and my assistant Graham Devalt."

"You the wagon master?" Mickey Hogg asked, leading the men back to the camp.

"Not exactly the wagon master, no. We missed the wagon train we were supposed to join to California. It was going along the Oregon Trail. So we've struck out on our own with Mr. Sinclair as our guide. I believe you've had occasion to meet Mr. Sinclair."

"He ain't much more than a boy," Mickey said. "Surprised you'd trust your family to a man so young."

"He seems to know his way," Amos said. "We've not lost the trail, yet."

"A lot of dangers on the trail besides just losing it," Mickey Hogg said, licking his lips. "Say, Cummings, you traveling with whiskey?"

Amos was caught off guard by the question. "We have some, yes."

"It's too bad you ain't brought it over here with

you," Mickey Hogg said. "It's been some days since I've had a drink of whiskey. We should have provisioned ourselves better."

"I should have thought to bring it," Amos said.

"Would have been better if you did," Mickey Hogg said, laughing and turning to look at the others. "Wouldn't it, boys, be better if he'd brought some whiskey?"

"Would have been better if you'd brought them womenfolk, too," Pawnee Bill said.

Amos was caught off guard by the manners of the men. He made an effort at getting the conversation back on track.

"Considering that we're camping so near to each other, we thought it would be neighborly to pay you a visit," Amos said.

"Would have been more neighborly to bring some whiskey," Mickey Hogg said.

"And them women," Pawnee Bill added.

"We ain't interested in being neighborly," Dick Derugy said, and he stood up and casually picked up his rifle leaning against the buckboard wagon. "We're interested in whiskey and women. If you ain't got none to share, then you wasted your time in coming here to talk to us. We ain't on this trail to make friends."

Mickey and Bill and Dick all laughed and slapped their knees as Amos, Stuart, and Graham turned around to walk back to their own camp. The Ohioans were surprised at the behavior of the other men.

"Next time you feel like being neighborly, put on a dance and we'll come join you!" Pawnee Bill shouted, and

Dick and Mickey Hogg both joined in shouting taunts at the other men.

Only Chester Bowman refrained from the taunting. Chess Bowman knew what Mickey Hogg and Pawnee Bill were planning to do later, and he had no taste for it. He didn't enjoy the taunting, because he knew it was only a prelude to the worse that was coming.

"They sure did leave in a hurry," Mickey Hogg said. "I guess they didn't feel like being neighborly after all."

"When do you want to go down there and get to business?" Pawnee Bill asked. "I say the sooner the better. Just after dusk when it's good and dark and they don't see us coming."

"No," Mickey Hogg said thoughtfully. "We'll wait until later into the night. Let them all get good and asleep. We'll go in with knives. Don't use a gun unless you got to. I don't want to wake anyone up."

"Don't kill the women," Pawnee Bill said, and he looked deliberately at Dick Derugy. "Especially that young one. I want to get a look at her good and proper. We might even take her with us when we leave. Keep her around for a while."

-16-

The small wagon train drove on through the black night, each of the wagons spread out so that none was visible to the other.

Matthew Cummings stayed near to his younger brother Paul to be sure they did not get separated. Each of them trailed a line of animals, tethered together. The animals moved without much argument, finding the cool of the night easier going than they did the heat of the day.

Rab Sinclair had instructed the boys to keep moving and to not wait for the wagons to catch up. They could all come together again in the morning when the sun was up. As Rab had told them, the boys rode about a mile down the trail before they lit a lantern, and then they were able to move a little faster because in the lantern light the trail showed clearly.

Martha Cummings drove the first wagon to leave. Her daughter Rachel rode with her in the wagon, and Rachel waited until they had made some distance before lighting a lantern. That lantern made it easy to see the trail and to keep on the right path, but they could not see the boys with the animals in front of them.

Rebekah Bancroft followed her in the next wagon. Rebekah's three children rode with her in that wagon.

Jeremiah Cummings, the oldest of the Cummings boys, drove the next wagon, and he rode alone.

Stuart Bancroft was in the next wagon, and he was followed by Graham Devalt.

Amos Cummings drove the last wagon out of the campsite, leaving almost two hours after the boys left out with the animals.

Rab Sinclair spaced them out at such distances in the hopes that by leaving the camp one at a time it would lessen the risk that Mickey Hogg and the others might hear the wagons moving out or in some way become alerted to the flight of the Cummings party.

Rab's sorrel horse was tied to the back of Jeremiah's wagon. The buckskin was tied to Amos's wagon. Rab put his pannier inside Stuart's wagon, deciding to lighten the load on the two horses.

He kept Cromwell with him.

"Your father was unnerved when he returned to camp after visiting those men," Martha Cummings told her daughter when they were well down the trail. "I do not say this to alarm you, but I want you to know that I think those men are very dangerous. By leaving we have spared ourselves any trouble from them tonight, but I am afraid they will catch back up to us."

"What will we do?" Rachel asked.

She was trying to keep a brave face, but she had never known terror like this in her life. They were running from these other men. They were fleeing for their lives.

"We will trust your father to think of some way of dealing with this," Martha Cummings said, though she had her doubts. She, too, was very afraid. "But if it comes to it, I want you to stay very close to Mr. Sinclair."

"Mr. Sinclair?" Rachel asked.

"Of course, Rachel," Martha Cummings said.

Stuart Bancroft, driving his wagon along in the loneliness of the night, had begun to wonder about his brother-in-law's principles against violence. He had seen these men up close, and he did not like them. They were dirty and crass, and Stuart was convinced the men were dangerous. He had brought with him two rifles for hunting, and when he returned from his visit to the camp, the first thing he did was load both rifles. He gave one to Rebekah, who knew how to use it, and he kept the other in his wagon.

"A one shot rifle will not be much, but if you wait and shoot it when they are very close, it might be enough," he told his wife. "If you must use it, make sure that you hit what you are shooting at."

Amos Cummings was not questioning his beliefs about violence, but he was contemplating how a man who opposes the use of violence can get by in a world where others do not share the same principles.

Stuart Devalt, for his part, was wishing he had never come west.

Through the night, those in the wagons caught themselves drifting off to sleep with increasing frequency as the night wore on. Their eyes would shut, their minds would drift, and they would wake with a start, realizing they were driving a wagon down the Santa Fe Trail. For each of them, it happened many times.

Both Matthew and Paul dozed in their saddles.

When dawn finally came and the sun rose at their backs, the younger Cummings boys led their animals off of the trail and down behind a stand of trees at a creek. Matthew and Paul picketed the animals at intervals so they would have room to graze.

Matthew, doing as Rab Sinclair had taught him, rode back down the trail to make sure that the livestock would not be seen by anyone approaching from the east.

Then they took turns watching.

One by one, the wagons came into view, and when the boys were certain of who was driving them, they came out from behind the stand of trees and led each of the wagons to where the livestock were hidden.

"I do not understand why Mr. Sinclair has not caught up to us," Martha Cummings said when Amos climbed down from his wagon, the last to arrive.

"He never caught me during the night," Amos said. "A single rider on a horse, he should have easily overtaken me."

Matthew spoke up.

"He told me he might not catch us," Matthew said.

"What else did he tell you?" Amos Cummings asked, finding himself suddenly very worried.

"Well, he told me that when dawn came I should find a stand of trees near a creek and picket the animals behind it, like I've done. He said we should make a camp for just a couple of hours for everyone to sleep a bit, and then we should keep moving. He said so long as we stay on the trail we'll come to a stagecoach stop and an army fort before we stop."

"He said all of that?" Amos Cummings asked.

"Yes, sir. He said if he wasn't here after we'd been in camp for a couple of hours, that we should go on without him."

Martha walked over to her husband and, taking him by the arm, led him away from the others.

"Amos, you don't think Mr. Sinclair has abandoned us, do you?" she asked in a hushed tone.

"Of course not," Amos said. "He's left his two spare horses and the pannier with us. He could not survive out here without his supplies."

Martha Cummings was not so sure.

"If he has not abandoned us, then where is he?" she asked.

Amos had a thought, but he did not want to say it out loud to his wife. The last he had seen Rab Sinclair, the man was sitting astride his blue roan with his Hawken rifle across his lap and the Colt Dragoon in his holster.

"We should sleep for a couple of hours, and then we should get moving," Amos said. "Those were his instructions to Matthew. Obviously he thought there was some chance he might be delayed, or he would not have left explicit instructions for us to leave without him. He will catch back up to us."

***

The six wagons of the Cummings party left out of their campsite shortly before noon. The people were all exhausted, though the animals were holding up well. Because they had relied on mules to pull the wagons through the night, they were now going forward with oxen harnessed to each wagon and so they made very slow progress.

Matthew Cummings was riding on Rab Sinclair's buckskin horse. Whenever he came to a hill, he would sit atop his horse for a long while, watching the back trail as the wagons passed. He was watching for a lone rider or three riders and a buckboard. Nothing appeared on the horizon to the east.

Every member of the wagon train was going forward with some sort of fear. Stuart Bancroft now drove the last wagon. He had decided he would act as a kind of rearguard.

Amos Cummings drove the first wagon, leading the train. As they set out in the late morning, Amos said he would keep moving until they arrived at the stagecoach relay station that Rab had told Matthew about, and he warned the other travelers that he might continue well into the night if they had to. What he hoped was that Rab Sinclair would catch up to the wagon train and give advice on how to proceed. But if Rab Sinclair did not show up, the stage station was not a bad bet. Somewhere nearby the stage station was a fort – Amos could not remember the name of it. But a fort meant cavalry and safety. He could report the men who'd been following them – Mickey Hogg and the others – at the fort. Perhaps they might even get an escort to ride a ways with them.

But late in the afternoon, a new salvation presented itself.

With the afternoon sun in his eyes, Amos was

able to see something up ahead that broke the monotony of the plains. At first he thought it was just a small stand of trees, but as it grew larger on the horizon he realized it was something else. He sent Matthew ahead on the buckskin to investigate, and after about thirty minutes the boy returned.

"It's the stage station!" Matthew said, and the relief in his son's voice matched his own relief.

If nothing else, a stagecoach relay station manager could offer advice on what to do.

Amos called loudly to the oxen and cracked his whip over their backs to try to speed the beasts along a little faster. The stagecoach station, out here in the middle of nowhere, gave him a sudden sense of hope.

"Ride back and let the others know we will pass by the station and go on to the fort," Amos said.

The station was run by two men, Silas Carver and Danny Beck. Folks all called Danny by his initials.

D.B. met the wagon train out on the road near the station. Danny Beck was about Amos's age, early- to mid-forties. He had a growth of beard on his face that suggested he'd not shaved in a number of days, but not so much of a beard that it looked intentional. He was powerfully built from years of hard work, but he had one of the friendliest, most genuine smiles that Amos Cummings had ever seen.

"There's good grazing if you'll go past the station about a hundred yards," D.B. called to Amos Cummings. "Y'all get that rain a couple days back? First good rain we've had in a long time. Looks like maybe two years of drought is going to finally come to an end."

As Amos came up close to him, D.B. walked along

beside the wagon.

"This your wagon train?" D.B. asked.

"I suppose it is. I'm Amos Cummings, come from Ohio."

"I'm Danny Beck. Folks call me D.B. I'm a hand at the relay station here."

D.B. looked down along the wagon train and at the boys leading the livestock.

"You're a brave man taking this trail without a guide," he said.

"We have a guide," Amos said. "He stayed back yesterday and has not caught us up yet."

"Who's your guide?" D.B. asked.

"Rab Sinclair. Do you know him?"

D.B. laughed and clapped his hands together. "Rabbie Sinclair? Of course I know him. Knew his pa from years back. Just about watched that boy grow up. I come to Topeka in '54 with the first wave of settlers. Rabbie and his pa were living with the Osages then, but they spent the winter in Topeka. How long ago did y'all leave out?"

"Not yet three weeks from Independence," Amos said. "We've been on the trail eighteen days."

"You've made good time," D.B. said. "You're three hundred miles along the Trail. You've got about five hundred miles to go to get to Santa Fe. You must be making about fifteen mile a day. That's good. Of course, with Rabbie Sinclair leading you, I'd expect you to be to Santa Fe last week!"

D.B. laughed at his own joke. "That's a boy who

knows his way around. From the Missouri to the Sierra Nevada, there ain't many blades of grass Rabbie Sinclair ain't trod upon or trees he ain't leaned against or streams he ain't dipped his canteen into. One time when Kit Carson was lost he sought out Rabbie Sinclair to be his guide."

Amos Cummings looked at D.B. with some surprise but saw that the man was grinning. "You're joking," Amos said.

"It's a joke," D.B. admitted, "but it ain't far from the truth."

"But he's just a boy," Amos said. "I understand that he's had vast experiences in the West, but he's not old enough to have traveled so much."

"When you live among the Injuns, you don't stay in one place too long. He grew up with the Osages and the Sioux and the Utes and some tribes out toward California, too. They all thought his daddy was touched in the head because he used to hold services and read from the Bible to Indians who couldn't speak a word of English. So they let him come and go as he pleased and didn't bother him much. They gave him squaw wives because they worried he might have big medicine. But whatever they thought of his pa, them Injuns treated Rab like he was full-blooded. Now, where did you say Rab was?"

"Rab said there was a fort nearby," Amos said. "How far to the fort? I would like to camp there if it is practical."

"It ain't but three miles farther," D.B. said. "Used to be Camp Alert when it was closer, just down by the Pawnee River there, but when they moved in the spring they named it Fort Larned."

"Three miles?" Amos said.

"That's right. You'll get there after dark, but you won't have trouble finding it. It's just off the trail to the south, along a big stand of trees that follows the Pawnee Fork River. They's a ford there for crossing the Pawnee, and you can find it in the dark, no problem."

"I would like to speak to the commander of the Fort. It's a matter of urgency," Amos said. He suspected he could trust D.B., but he did not know for sure and did not want to risk making a mistake by telling him about the men following.

"Oh, well, the commander ain't there. Did you see any Injuns on the way in?"

"We did not," Amos said. "Who is in command at the fort in the commander's absence?"

"Well, nobody," D.B. said. "Word came in a few days ago about depredations back east a ways. Ain't but fifty cavalrymen at the fort anyway, and half of them were gone off on a scout to the north. When word came in about the Indian attacks, those that was left set tracks to the east."

D.B. leaned toward Amos on the wagon, squinted his eyes and said in a hushed, meaningful way, "Dog Soldiers, prob'ly."

"Where did this happen?" Amos asked.

"Back near Council Grove."

"We came through there a few days ago. Maybe a week ago. We ate at the Hays House. Rab said it was one of the last tastes of civilization we would have until we reach Santa Fe."

"Hays House is good eating," D.B. said. "I like to

162

get over there every couple of months for a bite, myself. Spend a day or two at Council Grove."

"Tell me about these Indian attacks," Amos said.

"A whole family was butchered. It happened not far from Six Mile Station, which I'm sure you passed. Terrible thing. They say them Injun bastards violated a young woman and her mama. Terrible thing. And then they killed a farmer and took his wagon."

"Took his wagon?" Amos asked. "Like a buckboard wagon?"

"Well, I reckon it could be like a buckboard wagon. It was Ted Gibson, a sod buster from out that way. He was on his way home after getting supplies and never made it home. His wife knew the route, and she found his body. But the wagon was gone. When word came in of Ted Gibson's murder and that other family, what was left of the cavalry all left out of Fort Larned and headed east."

Amos Cummings had a sick feeling. If D.B. had only mentioned the family that was killed, he might not have suspected anything. But something about a farmer's wagon made his stomach clench. Was it possible that the men following them with the wagon were responsible for that murder, at least?

"Do they know for sure that it was Indians?" he asked. "Were there witnesses?"

"They found a knife at the farm that's definitely a Cheyenne knife. That's why they think it's Dog Soldiers. I don't mind telling you, we've been on alert here. If renegade Indians are raiding as far east as Council Grove, there's no reason to think they won't come here and do it, too. But if they think the fort is occupied they won't dare come near us."

"If the fort is vacant, then perhaps it would be best for us to stop here for tonight," Amos said.

"Sure," D.B. said happily. "Right up there. That's where you want to camp. Best grazing we've got left around the station, just now. It's been so dry these last two years that there ain't much for good grazing anyway, and now it's well chewed over."

Amos drove his wagon into the area that D.B. indicated, and the station hand walked the entire way with the wagon train, glad to have strangers to chat with. He walked from Amos's wagon all the way along to the last one driven by Stuart Bancroft, greeting each of the drivers and introducing himself.

He made faces to Stuart and Rebekah's young children, he took his hat off for Martha and Rachel, and he chatted a bit with Stuart about Indian depredations.

When at last all the wagons were in place and driven into a half circle, D.B. stayed to help spread out the livestock and picket them.

When that work was done, D.B. invited the group to come to the station for supper.

"We've got the biggest pot of stew you've ever seen cooking on the fire. We're expecting a coach to come in later this evening, but there's plenty for you, too."

"Thank you," Amos said. "We're obliged. We'll take you up on the offer. Just let us get things settled here."

When D.B. walked off, Amos took Stuart away from the camp and told him about the Indian attacks.

"You think those men who were following us

might have killed the farmer?" Stuart asked.

"I think it's possible," Amos said, noting that Stuart reached the same conclusion without him saying it.

"If they killed the farmer, they might also have killed the family," Stuart said.

"Might have," Amos agreed.

"Where is Rab Sinclair?" Stuart asked.

Amos ignored the question. "I am uncomfortable leaving the camp unattended and going to supper at the station house. It's light now, but we would be coming back to camp after dark. Those men could be in our camp waiting for us."

"You and the women and children go on up to supper," Stuart suggested. "I'll stay here and keep a watch on the camp. Leave Jeremiah and Graham with me. When you come back, the three of us will walk up to the station house for supper."

"Do we have an obligation to go and look for Rab?" Amos asked.

Stuart shrugged his shoulders. "I honestly don't know."

The station consisted of a large wooden barn and a fenced paddock for spare horses. The station house was a flat, adobe building with rooms for the station manager and his hand, a large kitchen, a store with a few supplies, and a great room with two large tables for feeding travelers.

Silas Carver, the station manager, sat next to Amos Cummings as they ate.

"D.B. says that Rab Sinclair is your guide, but that

he ain't with you," Silas said. "Seems an odd way to guide a wagon train."

"We ran into some trouble," Amos said. "We had four men following us. Three were mounted and one drove a buckboard wagon. Mr. Sinclair had some reservations about these men. And so yesterday afternoon we stopped as if to make camp, but after sundown we left the camp and drove the wagons through the night."

Silas was older than D.B., and his round belly told the tale of which one of the two did all the manual labor at the stagecoach station. When it came time to harness and hitch up a new horse team, it was D.B. doing that work. Silas, while he might have been handy when he was younger, had reached an age where managing the station and doing the cooking was the extent of what he could offer. His beard was the color of ash, and his smallish eyes were quick. D.B.'s naturally friendly attitude might have made him seem a bit oafish, but Amos was certain that Silas Carver missed nothing.

"That doesn't explain what happened to Rabbie," Silas said.

"I was the last wagon to leave the camp. He told me drive on and not wait for him. He said he was going to stay back for a bit." Amos paused, not sure if he should say any more. But Silas was looking at him in a way that made him say the rest of what he had on his mind. "We're not sure if he confronted the men who were following us or if he has abandoned us."

Silas nodded thoughtfully and looked at D.B.

"You know him better than I do. My impression was that he was an honest man. What do you think, D.B.? Would Rab Sinclair agree to guide these folks to Santa Fe and leave them?"

"I don't hardly think so," D.B. said. "You don't think he went after them fellows and had trouble, do you?"

Silas took a drink of water from his metal cup and then breathed heavily through his large nose.

"Hard to say what might have happened."

The conversation at the table fell silent. Even the young Bancroft children seemed to understand that something serious was being discussed, and they kept their talk to their mother to a whisper.

It was Matthew Cummings who broke the silence.

"I think Mr. Sinclair is fine," he said.

"Course he is," D.B. agreed. "Rabbie's just a little bit young, but he knows how to survive. You don't grow up among the Osage and the Cheyenne without learning a thing a two."

"Do you think these men who followed us could have been responsible for the murder of that farmer?" Amos asked, directing the question to Silas.

Again, Silas took a long time to answer, chewing on a piece of meat from the stew.

"Could be," he said. "I hate to think of white folks doing such things."

From somewhere off in the distance, those at the table heard a horn blow.

"That'll be the coach," D.B. said, getting up from the table.

He took up a horn at the door of the station and walked outside and blew a response. "I'm going to get the horses ready," he called back into the station house, and then walked off to the paddock.

"I reckon it's time for me to earn my wages. Appreciate the company, and you folks is welcome to stay or go as you please. Send them others up for supper whenever you get back to your camp."

Amos sent Matthew and Paul to the camp with the women and children and told them to send Stuart, Jeremiah, and Graham to the station house for supper, but Amos lingered a bit to have a word with the coach driver.

"Jehu, on your way in did you pass any other travelers today?" Amos asked.

"I don't recall that we did," the jehu answered. He and the shotgun rider were both young men who enjoyed the freedom of their work.

The other travelers looked to be in some misery, complaining about being bumped and jostled for thirty miles and cramped in the coach with too many bags of mail. They all stretched their legs and paced about inside the station house, no one too eager to sit down to the meal.

"A lone rider on a blue roan?" Amos asked, looking also at the shotgun rider.

"Nope," the jehu said. "Nothing like it. That would have caught my eye for sure. I don't recall the last time I saw a lone man on this trail."

"What about four men with a buckboard wagon? Three of them mounted. Driving some spare mounts."

"Nope," the jehu said. "We didn't pass nobody on the trail today. Nor yesterday, neither. In fact, it's been four or five days since we last encountered anyone."

Amos thanked them and went back to the camp. He passed Stuart, Graham, and Jeremiah on their way up to the station house.

"I take it Mr. Sinclair did not come into the camp?" he asked.

"No," Stuart said. "No sign of anyone other than the stagecoach. Did you ask if they passed him?"

"They said they did not see him," Amos said.

"He's been frightened and run off," Graham Devalt said. "We're on our own now, for sure."

***

No one in camp, except the children, slept particularly well.

The stagecoach left out of the station before the party bedded down, and watching it bounce over the trail in the dim lantern light from the camp, Amos Cummings did not envy the human beings inside it. They might arrive in Santa Fe weeks ahead of his wagon train, but he had to wonder what condition the passengers would be in when they finally reached the end of their journey.

By the time they got into their bedrolls, everyone in the party was aware that the stagecoach driver had seen nothing of Rab Sinclair on the ride in. A general sense that something terrible might have happened to their guide pervaded the Cummings party, and Graham Devalt was the only one who did not regret it. But even Graham did not sleep well, because the adults all seemed to understand, without saying it aloud, that there was a strong possibility that Mickey Hogg and the men with him had committed murder.

"We'll have to keep a watch through the night," Amos Cummings said. "Martha, I want you to take the first watch. You wake me at midnight, and I'll take the second watch. Jeremiah, I'll wake you at three o'clock in the morning to take the third watch. Tomorrow we will pass the watch to others so that no one is overly fatigued."

All of the bedrolls were laid out inside the half circle of wagons, and the livestock were picketed nearby. They hung lanterns on the outskirts of the camp to give light away from where they were sleeping. Martha Cummings sat in a chair with a rifle across her lap.

After everyone had gotten inside their bedrolls, Rachel decided she could not sleep and pulled a chair up beside her mother.

"You should sleep while you can," Martha whispered to her daughter.

"I know I should, but I am too upset," Rachel said.

"We're all scared, but we must not let our fears overcome us," Martha said.

"It's not that," Rachel said. "I'm scared, surely, but it's not fear that's preventing me from sleeping. Oh, mother, I feel just terrible. I should never have teased Mr. Sinclair the way I did. He has done nothing but help us through this entire journey. And I tried to humiliate him because he was never taught to read."

Rachel twisted at the tail of her shirt, one borrowed from her brother.

"Think of how foolish we would have been out here if we'd kept wearing our dresses," she said. "A person is a dress is useless in a wagon train. I thought Mr. Sinclair was the rudest, most unsophisticated man in the world for suggesting that we should wear trousers – but of course he was right! And every other thing he has told us to do was just as right. But we argued and fought with him, and I ridiculed him."

Tears welled up in the young woman's eyes. "Do you think they have killed him?"

"Oh, Rachel, you mustn't even talk like that," Martha said, and she reached out a hand to pat her daughter's head. "I do not know what has delayed Mr. Sinclair, but you heard how those men in the station house talked about him. Surely a man who has that kind of reputation at his age can handle himself."

"But what if they are four killers?" Rachel asked. "What if these men did kill that farmer and take his wagon?"

"We don't know that that's what happened," Martha Cummings said.

Rachel wiped her eyes. She sighed heavily.

"I think I'm in love," she whispered.

"Oh," Martha said, a grin crossing her face. "That might explain why you treated Mr. Sinclair so cruelly. It's sometimes difficult, when we feel very deeply for someone, to express it. And then it comes out as a muddled mess."

"You did not think I was referring to Graham?" Rachel asked.

"Of course not," Martha said. "Mr. Sinclair is very dashing with his long hair and tan skin and buckskin coat. And he grew up among the Indian tribes and he seems a little wild and intriguing. It is perfectly natural and absolutely to be expected that a young woman would be drawn to such a man. And he is very handsome. Of course I knew to whom you referred."

"Mother, the way you talk about him, I would almost think you have taken a fancy to him as well."

Martha laughed, and she was glad that no nearby lanterns gave away the fact that she was blushing. "I think my affections for Mr. Sinclair are limited to those that a woman of my age feels toward a young, motherless man. Sympathy, I suppose, and motherly love, perhaps."

"What should I do?" Rachel asked, and there was a hint of desperation in her voice.

"Oh, Rachel," Martha Cummings sighed. "You should realize that you could never live the kind of life that he would offer you, and he could never be constrained to the kind of life you could live. And you should get into your bedroll and pray as hard as you can that Mr. Sinclair is safe and well, and that we will be, too."

For the next hour Martha did her best to stay awake, though she was entirely exhausted. She knew why her husband had put the onus of the first night's watch on his own family, but she deeply regretted that her brother did not step forward to take her watch. She was so tired, and she did not even know what she was watching for, or how to keep a watch. The thing that kept her awake more than anything was fear that she would miss something – some sound in the dark, some movement of shadow in the distance.

When the moment of danger came, Martha Cummings was awake, but she caught no warning – neither sound nor shadow. She missed entirely the meaning when the horses picketed nearby blew an alert.

Mickey Hogg had snuck into camp, squeezing between a couple of the wagons, and had come at Martha Cumming from behind. Soundlessly, he reached one hand around her – that hand clutching a large knife – and put the knife at her throat. His other hand clutched roughly at her mouth, covering it so that she did not let loose a scream.

Martha's eyes grew wide with fright. She could hear and then feel Mickey Hogg's breath against the side of her face. He whispered harshly, "If you make a sound, woman, we'll cut the throat of every man, woman, and child in this camp. Now you just set that rabbit gun on the ground, easy and quiet, and then you stand up and come with me. You make any noise, any noise at all, and we'll set in among these folks and kill all of them while you watch."

Her mother's instinct was to obey.

Martha set the rifle down on the ground, and with Mickey Hogg still holding a knife at her throat and a hand over her mouth, she stood from her seat. Slowly, he backed her along the length of the wagons, and when they'd reached the edge of the camp he turned her and started walking her toward the livestock. He took his hand away from her mouth, but clutched her shoulder so tightly that it hurt.

He hissed at her in a hushed whisper.

"I've got a saddled horse over here for you. You make any move to get away from me, and I'll come back here and gut your children," Mickey Hogg said. "You don't want to see your children's insides strewed all over the ground, do you?"

"No," Martha whispered.

Another man was waiting near their own livestock, standing with three horses.

"Damn, Mickey, I can't believe you did it," he said, almost too loud.

"Hush up now," Mickey Hogg hissed at Dick Derugy.

Hogg pushed Martha Cummings into the saddle of one of the horses, but he took the reins. He climbed onto his own horse, and leading her, started to ride away. Dick Derugy followed behind Martha.

They walked the horses quietly in a wide arc that took them well away from the station house. Even in the dark, Martha was certain they were not coming back toward the trail but instead were riding off into the deserted plains.

In his exhaustion, Amos Cummings slept well past midnight when his wife was supposed to wake him so he could take the next watch.

-17-

Martha Cummings did not speak to complain or argue. She made no effort to flee. She simply rode in the saddle, her hands tight to the pommel, and her chin held high in what she hoped was a posture of defiance.

She did not try to think of what these men intended to do with her, though she had suspicions. Had she not heard her husband say that the women murdered at the farm back east were violated? But she was not the sort of woman to weep or despair. She prayed silently for deliverance and clung to some hope that somewhere, somehow, the Lord would intervene.

"We're lost," Dick Derugy complained.

It did seem to Martha Cummings that they were riding aimlessly. The light from the camp was disappeared now. She did not know if they had ridden two miles or five. In the blackness of night, she had no concept of space or time, and her fear and her exhaustion prevented her from having any kind of intuition about time or distance.

"We ain't lost," Mickey Hogg snapped, though they were not at a standstill, and Mickey was standing up in his stirrups looking for any sign of which way to go. "I should have brought Bill. Didn't he say before Lawrence he'd been down here along the Pawnee River? Ain't that where he gets his name? He could have found the way back, sure."

"You can't trust Bill around no woman," Dick Derugy said. "He'd have already had at her as soon as you got away from that camp and the station house. I'll tell you another thing, too, about Bill. If you don't want her all beat up in the face, you'd better take her first. Bill can't enjoy a woman proper if he ain't hittin' her. That's why all the whores in Topeka won't touch him."

"Is that what you men intend for me?" Martha Cummings asked, suddenly finding her voice and her courage. "To take turns violating a married woman and then hand me over to a man who will beat me?"

"You keep your jaw shut," Mickey Hogg snarled. "Married or no, you're still a woman."

Dick Derugy laughed, but it was an uncomfortable laugh. In his discomfort, Martha Cummings found a grain of hope.

And then she had an idea. She would shame these men.

"'Be strong and of good courage,'" she said loudly, enunciating each word clearly. "'Fear not, nor be afraid of them: For the Lord thy God, he it is that doth go with thee; He will not fail thee, nor forsake thee.'"

"What is that?" Mickey Hogg asked, his voice a curse. "Is you preaching?"

"It is Deuteronomy," Martha Cummings said.

"Well, stop it," Mickey Hogg said. "I ain't get you out here to listen to no sermonizing."

But Martha found strength in the words, and she spoke again, louder this time. "'Fear thou not, for I am with thee!'" Martha said. "'Be not dismayed, for I am thy God: I will strengthen thee, yea, I will help thee; yea, I will uphold thee with the right hand of my righteousness.'"

"I told you to stop that," Mickey Hogg said.

"That is Isaiah," Martha Cummings said. "These are promises of protection from God, and so long as I carry these promises I will not be afraid of you."

"You shut your mouth, or I'll shut your mouth," Mickey Hogg said.

"'Deliver me from my enemies, O God; be my fortress against those who are attacking me!'" Martha shouted the words now, defiantly, at Mickey Hogg, and the man wheeled his horse and tried to reach out at her, but Martha's horse became startled and started to dance away from Mickey Hogg.

"Enough of that, I said!" Mickey yelled at her, reaching for her and missing.

"'Thou shalt stretch forth thine hand against the wrath of mine enemies,'" Martha shouted, swatting at Mickey Hogg's outstretched hand as her horse continued to dance in circles. "'And thy right hand shall save me!'"

Mickey lunged, clutching at Martha, but he went too far and began to fall from his saddle. All the same, he'd caught hold of her arm, and with his full weight dragging her, Mickey Hogg and Martha Cummings both crashed to the ground. The nervous horses stamped hooves all around them, and one of them kicked Mickey hard in the sides.

He let loose a string of expletives as he got to his feet, pushing against the horses. Then he dragged Martha Cummings to her feet and slapped her hard across the face.

"You want to see what shouting Bible verses gets you out here?" Mickey Hogg asked, and his voice was vicious and cruel. He slapped her again and ripped her shirt from the neck to the navel. "You're about to find out what damn good yourn Bible verses is out here!"

There was not much light, but Dick Derugy licked his lips as he watched Mickey slap the woman again. He wished he could see better. He knew her shirt was torn, and he ached to see better.

"Get her, Mickey!" Dick Derugy said, excitement filling him and all his attention on Mickey Hogg as he brutalized the woman. "Come on and get her stripped! We'll both have her."

Dick Derugy's pulse was racing and he was in such a state that he never saw the butt of the Hawken rifle swinging toward the side of his head. The Hawken impacted with a harsh thud, and Dick Derugy's entire world went black as he fell from the saddle.

Rab Sinclair slung the barrel around fast so that his right hand was gripping the stock and his finger on the trigger as he thumbed back the hammer on the long rifle.

"Turn loose of that woman," Rab said.

But Mickey Hogg was in as much a state of excitement as Dick Derugy had been. He didn't hear Rab Sinclair's soft, easy voice. He was now clutching Martha Cummings by the shoulders as she tried to wrestle free from his grip.

Rab twitched his lips in frustration and took three, quick steps closer to where Mickey Hogg had hold of Martha Cummings.

Mickey may not have heard Rab's easy voice, but Martha Cummings heard it, and the cool night air finding its way through the vent in her shirt sent a chill up her spine and down her arms, and suddenly she felt embraced by the coolness. And she smiled.

It was the smile that made him stop. Black as the night was, Mickey Hogg saw the smile cross her face, and the peace that came with the smile, and he was dumbfounded.

"What in hell are you smiling about?" he asked.

"'He is my shield, and the horn of my salvation,'" Martha Cummings said.

A rage flew through Mickey Hogg, and he raised up his arm high above his head with the intention of smashing his fist into her face, but that's when Rab Sinclair jabbed the barrel of the Hawken into Mickey Hogg's armpit.

"You done made a bad mistake," Rab said, and though his voice was still easy, it was loud, and Mickey Hogg heard it well. "You keep that hand up there where it is, and you turn loose of that woman and put the other hand up with it."

Mickey Hogg released his grip on Martha's shoulder. Martha Cummings grabbed at the torn shirt and pulled it over her chest, but the smile on her face had not left.

"Mrs. Cummings, if you'd be so good as to undo his gun belt and take that scattergun off of him, I'd be obliged."

She made to reach for the belt, but she could not unbuckle it with just one hand.

"My shirt is torn, Mr. Sinclair," she said.

"Yes, ma'am," Rab said. "But that don't matter near as much as taking that scattergun away from him. Sooner you do that, sooner we can deal with your shirt."

"Of course," Martha said, and she released the shirt, though she tried to keep herself bent so that it would hang in front of her and keep her covered as she took off the gun belt.

"Just to remind you," Rab said to Mickey Hogg. "This is a fifty-caliber Hawken that's jabbed into your armpit. I pull this trigger, and I reckon it'll pop your head right off your neck. So you might want to ask Mrs. Cummings if she's got any Bible verses that'll rid a man of the sneezes, 'cause I've got an itchy nose, and if I sneeze I don't see no way this trigger don't get pulled."

Mickey Hogg clenched his jaw but did not say a word.

"Mrs. Cummings, do you know any Bible verses related to sneezes?" Rab asked.

"Not off the top of my head, Mr. Sinclair," Martha said, finally getting the buckle undone. She stepped away from Mickey Hogg, his gun belt and scattergun in one hand, and the other back to her shirt.

Rab glanced at Martha Cummings to be sure she had stepped far enough away.

"Now just toss that gun down behind you there in the grass. It'll be well out of his reach there. Then step over to that fellow I knocked off his horse. You needn't worry about him. He'll not be waking up anytime soon.

Slide his gun out of its holster and toss it with the other one."

Martha did as Rab asked her.

"If you step over there to Cromwell, you'll find my coat laid across my saddle. You can put that on and button it up."

"Thank you, Mr. Sinclair. You're very kind."

Mickey Hogg's arms were getting tired, but he did not move. It was not just the Hawken shoved into his armpit, but it was also that this boy had somehow found them out in the middle of the prairie with nary a bit of light to see by. Mickey knew where he was going and he was lost, yet somehow this boy had discovered them in the middle of nowhere.

And that frightened him.

"Now, ma'am, if you'd take them three hawsses there and lead them off in that direction a ways, I'd be obliged. Probably be best if you keep your back to us."

"Why is that, Mr. Sinclair?" Martha Cummings asked, her tone harsh.

"Ma'am, I intend to shoot these two fellow, and I guess I'd rather not do that in front of you," Rab said.

"You can't!" Mickey Hogg screeched. "That's murder. I'm unarmed."

"I reckon it is murder," Rab agreed, "but I don't expect anyone's going to care."

"I would care, Mr. Sinclair," Martha Cummings said.

"Ma'am?" Rab asked.

"I strenuously object, Mr. Sinclair," Martha said.

"You cannot murder these men."

Rab Sinclair twitched his lips and shook his head.

"Mrs. Cummings, this here fellow punched you and threatened to do worse. And I promise you, his intention was to kill you when he was done. And then I reckon he intended to go with them others and kill the rest of your friends and family. Your husband, your sons, and your daughter. He's a villain, Mrs. Cummings. He's a damned snake in the garden, and the best thing we can do right now is cut off the snake's head."

Martha Cummings waited a few beats of her heart before she answered.

Mickey Hogg thought about trying to push the Hawken away and wrestle his way to freedom, but he suspected he couldn't get the gun away before he was shot through. His best bet, he knew, was with the woman.

"Mr. Sinclair, my family objects to violence, and we'll not have you perpetrate murder on our behalf. I'll not argue the matter with you. You may not kill them."

Rab jabbed the Hawken rifle deeper into Mickey Hogg's armpit until he yelped in pain.

"You don't deserve her kindness," Rab said.

He eased down the hammer on the Hawken, and as soon as it clicked home, he spun the gun so fast that Mickey Hogg still did not realize it was out of his armpit. As the barrel came around into his hands, Rab Sinclair clutched it like a club and swung it as hard as he could so that the butt of the rifle smashed Mickey Hogg square in the face.

Mickey crumpled to a pile on the ground, as unconscious as Dick Derugy.

Rab kicked his feet around in the grass for just a moment, but he did not immediately find the scattergun and Dick Derugy's pistol.

"I sure hate leaving them weapons here where they might find them in the daylight, but I reckon I can leave them with some other problems. First thing, we'll take their hawsses. Leave them saddles off those two, though. They are trashy things, and I don't want to have them around. Any man that won't take decent care of his saddle is a fool who don't deserve to ride."

Rab was agitated. He believed that leaving these men alive was a terrible mistake. But he also was unwilling to execute them over Martha Cummings' objections.

Rab now took a length of rope from one of the horses, and he lashed Dick's hands behind his back. Then he walked over and tied Mickey's hands behind his back. He dragged Mickey's limp form over to where Dick was on the ground, and then Rab took another length of rope and tied an end in a slip knot around each man's neck, leaving very little slack between them.

Rab laughed a little to himself, and he then tied Mickey's left leg to Dick's right leg.

"These two will have hell trying to get themselves untied from each other without choking one another," Rab said, his voice full of mirth. He laughed again thinking about the trouble he was putting them to. "They may wake up later and wish very much you'd have just let me shoot 'em."

He tried one more time to find where Martha Cummings had tossed the guns, kicking his feet through the tall grass, but then he gave up.

"We should get on," he said.

Rab mounted Cromwell and Martha got on the horse she'd left saddled. The other two horses followed them, as horses are wont to do, as they road back toward he stagecoach relay station and the Cummings camp.

***

Even in the pitch black of night, Rab Sinclair seemed to know his way.

They trotted a little, but mostly walked the horses out across the open plain. Rab Sinclair smoked his pipe, and the orange glow from the bowl lit up his face whenever he puffed on it.

"Are you terribly mad at me?" Martha Cummings asked, breaking what had been a long silence.

"Mad at you?" Rab asked. "What for?"

"Because I stopped you from killing those men," Martha said.

Rab puffed on the pipe, and Martha thought she saw an unfamiliar look of concern on his face.

"I'm afraid we might regret that decision," Rab said. "Them's vile men, Mrs. Cummings. You had just a taste of it. I'm worried they're like rattlers, and all we did was rile them. I dealt with them pretty easy that time because there warn't but the two of 'em and they didn't expect me. But I reckon they made it easier than it'll be the next time."

Martha Cummings wondered, briefly, if she had made a terrible mistake. Could she have maintained her principles – her husband's principles – if it was the young guide committing violence? She did not think so. Whatever way she might choose to try to justify it, the fact was that if she had allowed Rab Sinclair to murder those men, it would have been in her name. When she first saw the Hawken rifle go into Mickey Hogg's armpit, she had hoped that Rab would just pull the trigger and let the man die. But that hope was fleeting, and the moment she felt safe, it was gone.

"My husband is a chaplain, a man of the Word," Martha Cummings said. "He teaches moral philosophy at the university. And his moral philosophy tells him that it is wrong to take another man's life. If my husband, or I, permitted you to kill these men in our names, it would make a lie of everything my husband has ever taught in his classes. It would make a lie of all he believes and holds important. Can you understand why it is so important to us, Mr. Sinclair?"

"I understand," Rab said. "I just think you're husband's philosophy is dangerous."

Martha did not answer. Instead, she rode quietly for a few minutes. Then she spoke again.

"How did you find me?" she asked.

"I've been following them fellows all day," Rab said. "After y'all left out last night to drive through the night, I stayed back and waited. I hid myself not far from where the camp was, down below a little hill. Sure enough, they tried to sneak into the camp, and they were quite a bit miffed when they realized you'd left out. At dawn they hurried after you, and I followed behind. It ain't an easy thing to follow a man on these plains, I can tell you that. When a man can see forever, it's hard to stay out of his sight. But they drove their animals something cruel, and that helped because they didn't much check their back trail. Come dusk, they came within sight of the stage station and your camp, and that's when they cut out across the plains to make their own camp. When those two back there set out for your camp, I followed them. I was there when they took you, and if it had turned violent I was ready for them. But when they left the others unmolested and just took you, I kept on following."

Rab puffed his pipe some more, but it had gone dead. So he knocked it against the heel of his hand and then refilled the bowl and lit it again.

"I planned on taking them when they got back to their camp. I reckoned that would be the right time. They'd be distracted enough that I figured I could put a bullet in two or three of them pretty quick. But then I heard you saying all them Bible quotes, and I figured things were about to go bad. Men like that don't care for Bible verses being said to them. So that's when I rode on up and went to work on 'em."

"I did not know how the Lord would deliver me, but I suppose I am not surprised that you were the sword and shield he provided."

Rab chuckled. "Yes, ma'am, I reckon it wasn't likely to be anybody else out here."

In the distance, Rab could see lights glowing.

"There's your camp," he said. "It looks to me like they've discovered your absence. Quite a few lanterns are lit. And they're lit at the station house there, too."

"We've returned much faster than I expected to," Martha said.

"Yes, ma'am. When they rode out with you, they rode around in circles for quite a while."

Martha Cummings rode the rest of the way into

camp in silence, considering the last few hours. Terrible emotions – terror, as the knife came around her throat, settled into a resigned fear when Mickey Hogg and Dick Derugy led her out through the plains. And then that resigned fear gave way to a strange sense of calm confidence as reminders of where to seek her refuge began to come into her mind as if spoken directly to her by Providence: verses long forgotten by a woman who had outgrown girlish fears and had settled into adulthood with the sense of security that comes with a life in society. Then the sudden exhilaration sparked when like a wraith, Rab Sinclair appeared out of the darkness of the empty plains and delivered her.

And now all that terror had become – she struggled to put a name to it. Mirth?

Martha laughed at the thought of how Rab Sinclair had so easily unstrung her assailants. And then strung them.

She had a deep admiration for the young guide and his prowess.

But she realized that in the camp it was probably still her initial emotion of terror that still reigned. So she urged the horse forward at a trot.

D.B. and Silas Carver, the men from the stage station, were both in the camp with Martha's husband and brother. The four men were walking around with lanterns in their hands, looking at the ground for signs, evidence of what might have happened to Martha Cummings.

"I'm here!" Martha called out as she neared the camp. "Amos! I am here!"

Relief washed over Amos Cummings as he dashed

to his wife and wrapped her in her arms as she came down out of the saddle.

"Where have you been?" Amos asked. "What were you thinking leaving camp?"

He looked at the horse, and the two that followed her into the camp.

"What horses are these?" Amos asked, relieved though he was, he was equally confused. "Is that Rab Sinclair's coat?"

"Everything is fine, now," Martha said. "Let me catch my breath, and then I will tell you what happened."

Matthew took the three horses and he picketed them. As he did, he saw Rab Sinclair in the lights at the station house as Rab rode the blue roan into the stable at the station house. Matthew then unsaddled the one horse and rubbed down all three and left them in good spots for grazing. He also filled tin buckets and put them near the horses to water them.

It took him some time to deal with the horses, and when he returned to the wagons the first light of dawn was showing in the sky above.

When Matthew walked back into the camp, his mother was still wearing Rab's coat and had just finished telling of her harrowing adventure. She talked around the tearing of her shirt, though she did not spare her family and friends of the terror she felt. She gave the credit of her salvation to the recollection of the memorized verses and the one to whom those pleadings were made. "But Rab Sinclair was the sword and the shield that the Lord sent," Martha said.

"Where is Rab now?" Amos asked, and Martha and the others all looked around.

"I am sure he was right behind me, riding with me as we came back to camp," Martha said. "I thought he was here."

"He rode into the stable at the station house," Matthew said.

"I should thank him for what he did," Amos said.

D.B. and Silas Carver walked with Amos back to the station house. Most of those at the camp used their last bit of darkness to try to sleep just a little bit longer, though all three of the Cummings boys stayed awake to keep a watch on the camp.

D.B. and Silas returned to their rooms in the station house while Amos Cummings walked into the stable. He found Rab Sinclair in one of the stalls, fast asleep on a bed of hay. The blue was in the next stall, also asleep. Amos chose not to disturb them, and he returned to camp.

Though he crawled into his bedroll, Amos Cummings could not sleep. His mind was filled with visions of his wife's abduction and her torment on the plains, and he felt and overwhelming anger. He wanted to strike out against those men who had abducted his wife. He wanted to punish them. In a way he had never felt before, Amos Cummings wanted revenge.

-18-

Pawnee Bill found Mickey Hogg and Dick Derugy still on the ground where Rab Sinclair had left them tied together. Both men were conscious, though Dick Derugy was still dazed when Pawnee Bill found them.

"I thought you was just going to try to get a bottle of whiskey and one of them women," Bill said. "What happened?"

"Get us loose, dammit," Mikey Hogg said.

"Well ain't you in a foul temper," Pawnee Bill laughed. "Don't tell me you let a woman do this to you. Where's your horses?"

"Three or four of them jumped us," Mickey Hogg said while Pawnee Bill cut the ropes binding them. "They knocked Dick off his horse and took me at gunpoint. Then they cracked me with a club and tied us up. I come to a little while ago, but Dick's been unconscious until just now."

"You're lucky I even saw you," Pawnee Bill said, working on the knots on Dick's wrist. He couldn't cut that rope because it was so knotted up that he couldn't work his knife in without cutting Dick's wrists. "Tied Dick up but good. Yep, I come out looking for you at sunup, and I saw some horse tracks in the grass and followed those until I come across you. Looks from the tracks like y'all was walking in circles half the night."

"Just get us loose," Mickey said. "I'm ready to ride into that camp and kill every last one of 'em now."

"It wouldn't do to kill 'em this close to the relay station. Or the fort. They's fifty cavalrymen in a fort just down the way." Bill got the rope off of Dick's wrists and rolled him over. The side of his face was swollen and heavily bruised. "Damn, Dick, they knocked hell out of you. How many fingers am I holding up?"

"Shut up," Dick Derugy said, but his speech was slurred and his eyes seemed to drift aimlessly in their sockets. "Help me get to my feet," he said, but his words sounded like his tongue was too thick for his mouth.

Pawnee Bill sheathed his knife and held out his hands to help Dick to his feet, but once he was up, Dick was unsteady. He swayed one way and then the other, and Bill helped him to sit back down. "Maybe just set there a bit. Let me untie Mickey."

With the ropes off him, Mickey cussed a storm and stamped around. His face hurt like the devil, and Pawnee Bill said it looked like his nose was broken.

"If it ain't broke, it sure did bleed a lot," Bill said.

Mickey looked around and only saw Pawnee Bill's horse. "You didn't bring us horses?"

"Last time I saw you, you had three horses and there weren't but two of you. I didn't count on you losing the three you had. I just figured you was lost out here. So they followed you out of camp, huh?"

"That's right," Mickey said. "We thought they was all asleep when we grabbed the woman, but they must have been awake. Four of them. Maybe it was five. Like I said, they knocked Dick off his horse and he was unconscious the whole time. Then they took me at gun point and bashed me in the face. Must have tied us up and stole our horses."

"You're lucky they didn't kill you," Pawnee Bill said. "I wonder why they didn't kill you."

"They'll wish they had," Mickey said. "My head hurts terrible. Let me ride your horse back to camp."

Pawnee Bill spotted something in the grass. "Here's you shotgun Mickey. And Dick's Colt."

Mickey started toward Bill's horse.

"Hold on, now," Pawnee Bill said. "I didn't say you could ride my horse. If anybody's riding that horse besides me, it'll be Dick. Look at him, he don't have enough sense to put one foot in front of the other."

"I was hit, too," Mickey grumbled.

"But you can stand up. Take your gun and help me get Dick up on the horse. Our camp ain't far. Y'all was just lost."

The two men helped Dick Derugy up off the ground and pushed him into the saddle. He wobbled a bit but managed to stay atop the horse.

Pawnee Bill led the way, with the horse's lead in his hand, and Mickey Hogg walked alongside the horse with a hand on Dick to make sure he didn't fall off. Both men carried a saddle over a shoulder. They walked along for about thirty exhausting minutes in the morning heat when at last they saw the buckboard wagon down in a dry creek bed under some low trees. Chess Bowman was asleep in the shade when they walked up, but the noise they made woke him.

"Where you been?" Chess asked. "Damn, Mickey! What happened to your face?"

"Don't you worry about what happened to my face," Mickey Hogg said.

"Where's your horses?" Chess asked.

"They was followed when they grabbed the woman," Pawnee Bill said. "A couple of them gave Dick a good smash to the head, and they broke Mickey's nose. Come on over here and help me get Dick down off this horse."

Chess couldn't take his eyes off Mickey's shattered face.

"It was more than a couple," Mickey said. "Must have been five or six of them jumped us."

Pawnee Bill noted that the number of assailants was growing, but he did not comment on it. Bill was angry. He'd been looking forward to getting his hands on a woman, and he didn't care which one of them it was. But Mickey and Dick and managed to foul that up. On their first meeting, Bill had thought Mickey Hogg was a tough man, a real gunfighter who could handle himself. Bill let him take charge of the group. But now he was wondering if Mickey was the real thing or not. Bill wouldn't have let them follow him like that, and he wouldn't have let them sneak up on him.

"I don't understand how five or six of them followed you and you didn't know they was there," Chess Bowman said, and Pawnee Bill grinned at the question.

"It was dark," Mickey said.

"But how do five or six of them get close enough to bash you in the face and you don't even know they're coming?"

"It don't matter," Mickey Hogg snapped. "I'm tired of talking about it. I'm going to lay down, but when I get up we need to come up with a plan for how we're going to get at them people."

"Maybe we ought to leave them alone," Chester Bowman said. "They already been enough trouble for us."

"I'm going to kill them folks," Mickey Hogg said. "I'm going to kill every one of them. And I'll take whatever they have that I want, and y'all can take whatever you want that they have."

Pawnee Bill, who had spent time in this area in west Kansas and knew something of the Trail, spoke up.

"They'll either cross the Arkansas River in the next ten or eleven days and drop down the Jornada, or they'll go on up toward the mountains and cross at Bent's Old Fort. That will take them a week longer, but there's water all the way to Santa Fe."

"What's the Jornada?" Mickey Hogg asked.

"That's the shortcut to Santa Fe," Pawnee Bill said. "It takes less time, but there ain't much water. You've got the Cimarron River and everything else is just desert. And after two years of drought, there won't be much water in the Cimarron, if any. If they go on to Bent's Fort, there's water enough, but it takes longer and the going is rough in places. If they go to Bent's Old Fort to cross the Arkansas, we'll catch them for sure."

"You ever been to Santa Fe?" Mickey Hogg asked.

"I've been to Bent's Fort, before they burned it from the cholera, but I ain't never been to Santa Fe," Bill said.

"Which way is that guide going to go?" Mickey asked.

"He's old enough to remember the Fort if he was in this area," Bill said. "He might go that way if he knows it better. But he's with a bunch of greenhorns, so he might go the Cimarron cutoff because it's easier going. Except for the water."

Mickey laid out in the grass under the wagon where he would be in the shade, and he put his hat over his face to block out the sun.

"Whichever way they go is the way we go," Mickey Hogg said.

"Well then, we'd better hope they go by way of Bent's Fort, because we can't carry enough water to make the Cimarron Trail," Pawnee Bill.

Mickey snorted. "We'll take what we need from them, so we'll have plenty of water."

-19-

The morning after Martha Cummings' ordeal, everyone in the Cummings party expected to have a day of rest. But Rab Sinclair emerged from the stable after a couple of hours insisting that the teams get hitched to the wagons and the party get moving.

"We're exhausted, Mr. Sinclair," Amos Cummings argued.

"The animals are rested well enough, and they'll do most of the work," Rab said. "You being tired is better than you being dead. If we leave out of here now, we might not ever see those men again. If we leave now, push hard through the next few days, we can make the Arkansas crossing in five days. Maybe, with some luck and traveling after dark, we can make the crossing in four days. Then we're eight days, maybe ten depending on the crossing, to the Point of Rocks and the Cimarron River. At that point we're three weeks to Santa Fe. But it's rough going through a dry desert. There are a few springs along the way, but we can't rely on the river. They call it the 'Dry Cimarron' for a reason."

196

"Desert? But I thought we were taking the mountain pass," Amos Cummings said.

"If we go on to the old fort and cross the river there, those men will catch us and they will kill us," Rab Sinclair said. "I beat two of them and tied them up last night. Men like that take a beating as a serious thing. Those men will be intent on paying me back for that. But they'll pay you back, too. They'll kill you and the other men, and when you're dead, they'll have at your women. And when they've done that, then they'll be satisfied that they've washed the stain of last night's humiliation."

"Do you see what comes of violence, Mr. Sinclair?" Amos Cummings asked. "You have turned these men into mortal enemies."

Rab Sinclair shook his head in disbelief. "Ask your wife what comes of violence, Mr. Cummings. She found the Lord's salvation in the violence I committed. And I'll say this, if I'd done more violence, those men would be dead and of no threat to anyone, least of all us. Now the best we can do is push on through the desert and hope our water can last as long as we can."

Rab took his pipe and pouch from his pockets. He filled the bowl and lit the pipe.

"Mortal enemies?" Rab said. "They was mortal enemies when they took Miss Martha out of this camp."

Amos Cummings nodded.

"You're right, of course. And I thank you for what you did to save my wife. I should not chastise you for the means you took to do it. And I'll confess, I have a hatred in my heart for what those men did and what they intended to do. It's taking all I can muster to not want them punished for it."

"Christian forgiveness is a fine thing, Mr. Cummings," Rab said. "But you can forgive a man who's dead as well as you can forgive one who's alive. Give the order to your people to get them livestock harnessed and them wagon's hitched. Let's get to moving."

Amos Cummings turned without further argument and went to his sons and Graham Devalt and had them go to roundup the mules and oxen, still picketed near the camp. Then he went to talk with Stuart Bancroft.

Rab packed his pannier and put it on the buckskin, and he saddled the sorrel. While he saddled the sorrel, Martha Cummings came to see him.

"I have your coat for you, Mr. Sinclair," she said, holding it out to him.

"Thank you, ma'am," Rab said. "I hope you're recovered this morning."

"I am quite all right, thanks to you. You have my deepest gratitude."

"Your husband has a quarrel with the way in which I subdued those men. I reckon he don't care for bashing in a man's head any more than he does for shootings and stabbings."

"My husband is very committed to his beliefs," Martha Cummings said. "Recent events have tested some of his commitment."

"And you?"

Martha smiled. "I have no quarrel with the way in which you subdued those men. And you stopped short of killing them when I asked you to."

"I hope we don't come to regret that," Rab said.

A TRAIL TOO FAR

"I hope so, as well," Martha said. "And now I have another request for you."

Rab looked up into Martha's pretty face. He liked talking to her, and he couldn't see refusing a request. If Amos Cummings was looking to argue about traveling the Jornada, he could not have sent a better pleader.

"What request is that?" Rab asked, his tone full of suspicion.

"Would you mind terribly if Rachel rode along beside you today?"

"Mounted?" Rab asked.

"Yes, on one of our saddle horses, of course."

"It's a rough way to spend a whole day for those unaccustomed to it. I reckon she could get down and walk or ride on the wagon if she found it too uncomfortable. I suppose I don't see a problem with it."

"I'm making the request on Rachel's behalf," Martha said. "I believe that she feels bad about the way she treated you the other evening, and she would like to make amends. Or if not make amends, at least show you that she can be pleasant."

Rab shrugged a shoulder. "The way she treated me?" he asked. "I didn't notice nothing that would cause her to have to make amends."

Martha smiled and nodded. "No, Mr. Sinclair. I suspect it is true that you did not. You're not the sort of man who worries about words much, are you?"

"No, ma'am."

"Well, all the same, Rachel would like to ride with you today."

"She's welcome," Rab said.

As the wagons started out along the trail, Rab Sinclair with Rachel Cummings at his side rode to the station house. Rab went inside where he spoke to D.B. and Silas Carver, and Rachel went with him.

"These three horses I took from those men last night, I'm leaving them in your stable," Rab said.

"We'll put 'em to good use," D.B. said.

"Y'all want to be careful of those men," Rab said. "I reckon they're dangerous, and maybe not above causing trouble here at the station house. I'd be reluctant, if I was you, to try to take them on. They come looking for them hawsses, don't you hesitate to give them. The saddle from the hawss the woman rode in is in there, too. If they come looking for them, like I said, just give them over."

"We'll be careful," Silas said. "I expect they're more interested in you than they are in two old station masters."

"Maybe," Rab said.

"Which way are you planning to go, Rabbie?" Silas asked. "You taking the mountain pass or going across the Jornada? I'll remind you, we ain't had much for rain for two years. Long drought, the Cimarron might be running dry."

"Oh, we'll go the mountain pass," Rab said.

It was not true. Rab had already decided to take the wagon train through the desert. But he didn't mind misleading D.B. and Silas. If Mickey Hogg and his gang came into the station house looking for the Cummings party, as they likely would, Rab couldn't trust D.B. or Silas

not to mention which route he intended to take. Rab
didn't think they'd mention it out of malice, but neither
man was known for always thinking carefully. They
might get to rambling and say too much. So Rab wanted
to make sure that if they said too much, they didn't also
know too much.

"What's your opinion, Rabbie," D.B. said. "These
murders back east near Council Grove – the folks at the
farm and the farmer with the wagon – you think these
men did all that and made it look like Injuns?"

"There's no way I could know that, D.B.," Rab
said. "How do they know it was Injuns?"

"They found a Cheyenne knife at the farmhouse."

"Was it a good knife?" Rab asked.

"Well I don't know that," D.B. said. "I ain't seen it."

Rab took off his hat and scratched at his head.

"I've spent some time among the Cheyenne," he
said. "I've known them to do some awful things to their
enemies, and murder sure ain't beyond what they're
capable of. What I've never known was for one of 'em to
leave a good knife behind. When the soldiers get back to
the fort, you ask them if it was a good knife. If it was, then
you'll have your answer."

Rab replaced his hat and looked to Rachel.

"You ready to ride, Miss Cummings?" he asked.

"I am, Mr. Sinclair."

"Then let's get on with it."

"Sure is good seeing you again, Rabbie," D.B. said.
"I always think about you."

"Good to see you, too, D.B. And you, Silas. Next

time I pass this way I'll set a while."

"Good luck to you," Silas said. "That's a whole lot of hair you've got under that hat. Do your best to hang on to it."

Rab smiled and led Rachel Cummings out to the horses.

"Talking about your hair," Rachel said. "He means for you to not get scalped. Is that right?"

"That is his meaning," Rab said, hopping up into his saddle.

He and Rachel turned their horses and started at a trot to catch up to the wagons.

"Is that a fear where we are?" Rachel asked. "Getting scalped, I mean."

"That is a fear where we are," Rab said.

"But you lived among the Indians. Surely they would not hurt you."

"They mightn't, if it was people from a tribe where I lived. Or they might. You never can tell with Indian folk what they might or might not do. Growing up, there were some I bested in a wrestling match, and they might still hold a grudge. There were others who I fished with, and I caught more fish than they did. They might still remember such a thing."

"Mr. Sinclair," Rachel said, stifling a laugh. "These are not things that are worthy of murder."

"For some they're not," Rab said. "A man catches more fish than me, I probably ain't going to kill him over it. But some folks hold on to things in a way that others don't. A Cheyenne boy gets beat in a wrestling match by a white boy, the other Cheyenne aren't going to let him forget that for a long time. And so he holds on to it. It could be the sort of thing that gnaws on him for years."

"Were there many Indians you wrestled with?" Rachel asked.

"Very many," Rab said. "Wrestling or horse racing or throwing spears or shooting rifles – it don't matter what it is, most of the tribes I ever knew loved to turn a thing into a sport. So at one time or another, I was involved in a competition with almost every Indian boy I ever knew."

"And were there many of them that you bested?" Rachel asked.

"All of 'em that I can remember," Rab said, and though it sounded like a joke, Rachel was not sure whether or not to laugh because Rab's tone was even as he said it.

"You're an interesting man," Rachel said.

"I just come up different from you," Rab said. "That's all it is. I come up different, so that makes me different. And different is sometimes interesting."

They caught up to the wagons and rode across the open plain to get in front of them. Matthew was pushing the livestock along. Rab rode to the far side of the livestock and helped to keep them moving, and Rachel stayed with him.

"I owe you an apology, Mr. Sinclair. I was very rude to you at supper the other night when I teased you about your ability to read."

It was a hard admission for her to make. Rachel, who in many ways was her father's daughter, found it difficult to confess a mistake, and even harder to apologize for one.

"Did you tease me?" Rab asked. "It may be that I'm just not smart enough to have realized it."

"That's not true," Rachel said. "You know full well what I did. And you know that it was wrong of me. But you're too decent to say so."

"I reckon it's not the sort of thing I care to pursue," Rab said. "If I was bested, I didn't realize it. So I don't hold it against you, Miss Cummings."

Rachel smiled. "You were not bested."

"You have a pretty smile, Miss Cummings," Rab said. "A lot of women, as they get older, they stop smiling. Worries. Children, mostly. All the troubles that life brings. They stop smiling. It would be a real loss if you were to stop smiling. Your mother, she smiles. I hope you'll be like her."

Rachel blushed at the words.

"Will you call me Rachel?"

"I will, Rachel," Rab said.

"And what should I call you?" she asked. "The men at the station called you 'Rabbie.' Do you prefer that or do you prefer Rab?"

"Mr. Sinclair will be fine," Rab said.

Rachel's face fell as she looked at him, but Rab's face cracked into a smile. Rachel laughed. "You're teasing me, now," she said.

"I am. You can call me pretty much anything you like. I'll answer to Rab or Rabbie, either one."

Rachel wrinkled her nose. "What is it short for?"

"My name is Robert. My father, being a Scotchman, called things in his own way. He always called me Rabbie or Rab."

"So it is a pronunciation of Rob?"

"I reckon so," Rab said.

"I like it," Rachel said.

"Rabbie," she said, trying it out. "Do you mind if I call you Rabbie?"

"Not at all," Rab said.

He rode away quickly, over to one of the mules that had strayed to munch on some grass. He called to the mule and slapped his hand against his thigh, and using his horse directed it back toward the herd of livestock. Then he rode back over to where Rachel's horse was walking.

Rab's concern was water. The livestock were numerous. The wagons were heavy. There were a lot of people. And in '59 and '60 there was a long drought on the plains.

"The Cimarron could be dried up to a trickle," Rab said out loud. "We'll have to get our water at the Arkansas and make it last."

"What's that?" Rachel asked.

Rab laughed. "Oh, I'm just talking to the hawss."

"Did you say something about water?" Rachel asked.

"We're going to have some dry days in front of us," he said. "There won't be much water, and if there was any grazing to be had, we'll likely find it's all been blown away."

They pushed the livestock and the wagons throughout the rest of the day, stopping only for a short while in the late afternoon to change out the teams and water the animals as the crossed the Pawnee River.

The crossing was difficult because the drought had knocked the river down. The wagons rolled through the water easier, but the bank was too high to easily get the wagons up. Rab had to help the Cummings boys unhitch the teams and attach long chains to the wagons. Once the teams were up the bank, they attached the chains to the harnessed animals and with new leverage they were able to get the wagons up the bank.

Rab was frustrated with the length of time it took to clear the Pawnee River, but it couldn't be helped.

The whole while, Stuart Bancroft and Amos Cummings kept watch on the back trail, seeking any movement on the eastern horizon that might indicate that Mickey Hogg's gang of border ruffians had caught up to the Cummings party. But no one appeared on the horizon.

Graham Devalt took the opportunity to sit with Rachel while she stretched out on a blanket and took a light meal.

He was peevish.

"Are you enjoying your ride?" Graham asked, and Rachel could not help but catch the derision in his tone.

"I'm having quite a pleasant ride, actually," she said.

"You should not get too close to that boy," Graham said. "It's inappropriate for a young, single woman to be riding about with that bumpkin. It's bad enough that you're going around in trousers and with that ridiculous hat. But the fact that you are riding with him is just too much. What would your friends back home say if they saw you?"

Rachel felt her face get flush with anger, and she started to speak, but then she stopped herself. She thought of Rab Sinclair and the way that he answered criticisms and slights.

"If my friends back home saw me, I suppose they would say that I've adapted quite well to the necessities of traveling the open prairie," Rachel said. "I've altered my fashion to adapt to my surroundings."

Rachel grinned at her answer. She felt a certain satisfaction at her calm, easy answer.

"Quite frankly, Rachel, you look absurd."

Again, she held her temper.

"The hat keeps the sun off my face and will protect my skin from turning into a mask of leather," she said. "And the trousers allow me to ride with ease, and to move up and down the wagon at my leisure, and to walk without the grass annoying my ankles and legs. Perhaps on the streets of Philadelphia or Baltimore I might seem out of place, or even back home, but I think here in Kansas I must be the height of sensible fashion."

Graham Devalt saw through what she was doing in the way she mimicked Rab Sinclair's easy way.

"Don't make a mistake becoming too friendly with him. You will sully your reputation." Graham stood from the blanket and turned to walk away.

"All that are here to witness my friendship with Rabbie are friends and family," Rachel said. "I trust my reputation to the opinions of my family. So I can assume only that it must be my reputation among my friends that is in danger. Would that not suggest that those friends are not the friends I thought them to be?"

Graham did not respond but walked on toward the river where they were now bringing up the last of the wagons. He was having grim doubts about his decision to join the Cummings. If he had not been thinking of it before, Rachel's remark made him fully aware that when it came to friends and family, everyone else in the Cummings party was family. He was the only friend. Stuart Bancroft was Martha Cummings' brother, and so by marriage the Bancrofts and the Cummings were all related.

He did not have the means to pay for a return trip by ship, but perhaps once they were in California he would see if he could persuade Amos to buy him passage. What he knew was that he did not want to make this miserable trip across the plains again, and he was growing increasingly convinced that he would not want to stay in California.

It occurred to him, too, just how much Rachel Cummings had influenced his desire to come west. The sudden attentions she was paying to the guide had wholly disillusioned him. Now, he just wanted to go back home.

Rachel folded up her blanket and returned it to one of the wagons.

"Will you be joining me for the rest of the afternoon?" her mother asked.

"Actually, I'm quite enjoying the ride with Rabbie," Rachel said.

"Mr. Sinclair? Are you calling him 'Rabbie' now?"

"He said I could," Rachel said.

Martha Cummings, sitting on the driver's seat of the wagon, leaned forward toward her daughter. "Remember what I said to you about being careful with the attentions you pay to two young men. Their feelings could get very hurt if you are not cautious."

Rachel laughed. "Mother, I'm not sure Rabbie has any emotions at all."

"That may be," Martha said. "Though I doubt it. But Mr. Devalt has feelings, and he walked away from your picnic just now looking very much like those feelings were hurt."

Rachel dropped her eyes and nodded her head. "I should be more careful," she said.

When the sun set, the wagon party pressed on, going by lantern light.

Now Rab moved to the back of the wagon train, and he insisted that Rachel join her mother on the wagon.

He allowed the wagons to get a ways ahead of him so that he wouldn't have to chew on their dust, and he kept an easy pace going so that the wagons began to outdistance him.

His concern now was in being certain that the back trail was clear.

Rab Sinclair knew it was too much to hope that they could simply leave those boarder ruffians behind, but when he wanted to be the first to know it when Mickey Hogg and his gang reappeared on their back trail. If possible, Rab wanted to know it before Mickey Hogg.

The four men walked into the station house late in the afternoon, almost at dusk. Two of them looked as if they'd been beaten pretty bad with bruises to their faces. One of them had two blackened eyes and his nose was smashed flat. Blood was still caked around his nostrils and was staining his front teeth.

"Whiskey, old man," the one with the smashed nose said to Silas Carver.

"We're a stagecoach relay station, not a saloon," Silas said.

"We're hungry and we're thirsty," Mickey Hogg said, and he slid back a chair at the dining table and sat down. The other three men still stood just behind him. "Now you either fix us up some chuck and get over here with a bottle of whiskey, or we're going to get angry in a hurry."

D.B. chanced a glance over to Silas Carver. Both men were plenty nervous. They'd both been in their share of scrapes – Indian fights, mostly; D.B. had served in a militia company in the War with Mexico but hadn't seen any fighting. And now they were both old men. At least, they were both old enough that they knew better than to try four rough men. D.B. nodded to Silas who nodded back.

"I'll get the whiskey," D.B. said.

"I'll get some victuals fixed up," Silas said, walking into the kitchen.

D.B. got four glasses and a bottle of whiskey, and he set them down on the table in front of Mickey Hogg. Mickey ignored the glasses and picked up the bottle, thumbing the cork out of it.

Mickey took a long drink from the bottle of whiskey. When he set it back down on the table he let out a yelp of pleasure.

"That is good," he said. "Lord a' mercy, that is good. I've been too damn long without a drink."

The others sat down at the table with him.

"Where'd them emigrants get to?" Mickey asked. "They was camped right over there yesterday. I figured on them staying another day."

"They never stay more than a night," D.B. said. "Always camp and then move on. These ones moved on, too."

"I thought maybe with the trouble last night they might have decided to stay through the day," Mickey said.

"What trouble was that?" D.B. asked.

Mickey Hogg grinned at Pawnee Bill. "One of their women folk came to our camp in the middle of the night," Mickey said. "She said she was tired of them Eastern men and wanted to camp with some real men."

"Well then that must be your horses and saddle in our stable," D.B. said. "The guide for that group, he left them here for you."

Mickey poured some of the whiskey into a glass and then passed the bottle to Dick Derugy. Dick was still dazed from the hit to the head. He was dizzy and was having trouble staying awake. Even sitting up, he found himself nodding off.

"I guess that was right neighborly of him," Pawnee Bill said. "Considering he stole those horses."

"They weren't stole so much as borrowed," Silas said from the kitchen.

"Either way, a man takes another man's horse and he's liable to get hung for it," Mickey said.

Silas cut some strips of bacon that he cooked with beans. D.B. went out to the stable to saddle one horse and to put leads on the other two horses. He lingered out in the stable longer than was necessary, and was ashamed that he actually gave thought to riding out and leaving Silas alone with the four men. But eventually, D.B.'s sense of fate drove him back into the station house.

Dick Derugy was laid out on the floor, unconscious. At first D.B. thought the man was dead, but he saw his chest rise and fall with breaths.

"Your friend don't look good," D.B. said.

"That damn guide that was with them," Pawnee Bill said. "He come into our camp to get that woman back. We'd have give her if he'd just asked, but he came in swinging his long gun like a club. Bashed both these men. Calls hisself 'Rab Sinclair.' You know him?"

"I know him a little," D.B. said. "He's stopped here

afore."

Pawnee Bill rubbed his chin and studied D.B.

"Which way was they headed? The Cimarron cutoff or are they thinking about crossing the Arkansas up to where Bent's Old Fort was?"

D.B. chewed his lip, feeling some pressure under Pawnee Bill's gaze. Then D.B. had a good idea to mislead these ruffians and send them off the wrong way.

"Cimarron cut," D.B. said.

"Been awful dry to go that way," Pawnee Bill said, narrowing his eyes. "You ain't lying to me, are you?"

"No, that's what they said they was doing," D.B. said. "They said they could tote water enough, and they wanted to move on quick."

Pawnee Bill looked over at Mickey Hogg. Mickey had his glass up to his lips, the liquid inside just slipping through a little as he relished the whiskey he'd been without for too long. Mickey didn't care what the old man was saying about which route the wagon train had taken, and he'd not hardly touched the plate of food in front of him.

"Give me four bottles of whiskey," Mickey said.

"We ain't a store," Silas said. "Our supplies is all for passengers on the stagecoach."

"I don't care," Mickey said. "Give me four bottles of whiskey. In fact, give me six bottles. And do it now."

"I'll get you a case, right now," D.B. said. "That'll be eight bottles."

D.B. walked out to the storage room and got a box with eight bottles of whiskey and took it back. By the time he returned to the station house dining room, Mickey Hogg had cleaned his plate of the beans and bacon.

"Chester, you tote that out to the wagon and then come back in here and help Bill get Dick out there. Make room for him in the back of the wagon. He's too stupid to sit a horse right now."

Mickey stood up and looked at the two old men.

"Now, what do we owe you for the food and whiskey?" Mickey asked.

There was a tone to his voice when he said it that made D.B. nervous. D.B. had a gun on his belt, but he couldn't hope to outdraw these men, and even if he got his gun up before one did, the other was sure to get him. Silas kept a shotgun in the kitchen, but he wouldn't be of no use with it.

"You don't owe us nothing," D.B. said.

Mickey smiled. "That don't seem right. We want to pay our fair share. What do we owe you?"

"Nothing at all," D.B. said.

"We ain't thieves, mister," Mickey said. "We pay as we go. Now fix a price on the meals and the whiskey."

Chess Bowman came back in. "Come on, Bill. I pushed some stuff out of the way so there'll be room for Dick."

Bill was watching Mickey. Whatever tone D.B. had heard, Pawnee Bill heard it, too. He licked his lips as he watched Mickey and the old man argue.

"Hang on," Bill said to Chess.

D.B. eyed the shotgun hanging off Mickey Hogg's

belt.

Sweat was building up on D.B.'s forehead and his palms, and he felt the tension in the room.

"How about we make it fifty cent for the whole thing," D.B. said.

Mickey looked over at Pawnee Bill.

"You hear that?" Mickey asked. "Fifty cent for a plate of beans and a case of whiskey. Now that's the real robbery, ain't it though?"

Pawnee Bill grinned. "That's real robbery," he said. "Them beans wasn't worth a penny."

"Here I am, trying to be reasonable and pay my way," Mickey said. "And these old men are looking to steal from us. Now what can you do with a thief?"

Pawnee Bill laughed. "I got ideas of what you can do with a thief."

"Y'all get," Silas Carver shouted from the kitchen. Both barrels of his scattergun were leveled at Mickey Hogg, but the angle was such that he was pretty confident Pawnee Bill would get a face full from the blast, too.

"Pick up your friend, put him in your wagon, take your horses, and get," Silas said. "I'm an old man, so I don't care nothing about dying. But if you go to shoot me, I'll take you along. So if you don't want to leave here in a box, you walk out now."

Pawnee Bill started to slide his revolver from its holster, but D.B. beat him to it, drawing his revolver out.

"D.B., get your rifle and follow them out. If they ain't out of range in five minutes, you put a hole in all four of them," Silas said.

D.B. walked to the gun cabinet on the far wall, keeping his revolver on Pawnee Bill the whole time. Silas stepped closer so that Mickey and Bill would both be sure of his shot if he had to pull the trigger. He also kept stepped to where he could keep an eye on Chess Bowman.

"Now go on and leave," Silas said once D.B. had the rifle in hand.

The two old men followed the four out of the station house and watched as they dropped Dick Derugy's limp body down into the bottom of the buckboard wagon, untied their horses and mounted.

"I ain't going to forget this old man," Mickey Hogg said to Silas Carver. "I'll be back from Santa Fe one day, and I'll be looking for you."

"Ah! I'll probably be dead by the time you get back anyway," Silas said. "Now get going before I decide to shoot you."

They watched the buckboard drive away and the two riders outdistance it, riding off to the west in pursuit of Rab Sinclair and the Cummings wagon train.

"I didn't like that one bit," D.B. said. "I don't mind saying that I was nervous as hell."

Silas laughed as he pointed the shotgun into the air and pulled both triggers, only for the hammers to fall on empty chambers.

"You'd have been a might more nervous is you'd have knowed that gun was empty," Silas said, grinning. "Now you get a horse and ride up about a mile, and you keep a good watch all afternoon. If you don't see them come back by then, we can rest easy tonight."

-21-

Rab Sinclair knelt down inside the line of bent grass that stretched north across the plains. There were a dozen similar lines, about four feet wide, where the grass seemed to have been pushed over.

"Travois," Rab said.

"What is that?" Rachel asked, standing beside him.

Two days out from the station house, Rab and Rachel had ridden about a mile ahead of the rest of the party, and that's where they were when they came across the strange lines in the grass. Rab, of course, recognized them immediately.

"Travois are the wagons that most of the tribes use," Rab said. "Except they're wagons without wheels. They take a couple of long poles and harness them to a hawse. Then they'll take a buffalo pelt or something and lash that to the two poles. And they can carry supplies on it – blankets, tipi, provisions. Dragging the travois through the tall grass like that is what bends it over. Usually they'll ride single file so that you don't know how many are traveling together. Six lines probably means there must have been maybe as many as sixty travois. I would make that at probably a hundred and fifty men and women, and who knows how many children. They might be chasing the buffalo. But after two years of drought, I can promise you they're suffering."

"What tribe is it?" Rachel asked.

"Probably Cheyenne. Maybe a Sioux tribe, but I wouldn't think so."

"Would they be friendly if we encountered them?" Rachel asked.

"They'd be hungry, Rachel," Rab said. "Whether or not they're friendly would depend a lot on how hungry they are."

Rab stood back up and looked to the north, in the direction that the grass bent.

"How long ago did they come through here?" Rachel asked.

"Yesterday, I reckon," Rab said. "Not more than two days ago."

"I would like to see them," Rachel said. "They must be a wonderful sight."

"Some's more wonderful than others," Rab said. "Might be best if we didn't see them."

This was Rachel's third day riding astride a horse with Rab Sinclair. She enjoyed talking to him. He had a vast knowledge of everything that now seemed important.

Rab looked back at the approaching wagons.

"You wait for them to catch up," Rab said. "You can point out to your folks what these tracks are and impress them with your knowledge. Once your family have caught up, you keep them moving along the worn path. I'll catch you back up in an hour or less."

"Where are you going?" Rachel asked.

"I'm going to make a loop to the south a ways. We should be nearing a creek, and I'd like to see how it's flowing."

Rab got back into Cromwell's saddle and rode at a gallop down toward the south, following along in the path left by the unknown Indians. He intended to make a loop to the south, but his loop was going to take him back to the east. Some time ago they passed by a rise to the south, and Rab had noted its position. A man would be able to ride up from the south without being seen by anyone following along the Trail. And the rise was tall enough to provide a pretty ample view in all directions, but especially back to the east.

It had been two days since they'd left out of Silas Carver's stage station, and Rab Sinclair had decided that if the four ruffians with the buckboard were going to catch them, today would probably be the day for that to happen. If not this afternoon, then surely tomorrow by mid-morning.

Rab did not want to risk Mickey Hogg and Pawnee Bill and the others turning up on his back trail without knowing it. So he rode south a ways and cut back east, following along the bank of a creek where a line of brush would hide him from view of anyone in the distance. After a while he came to the back of the rise he'd seen from the Trail, and he rode up the back of it at a gallop, eager to get to the top to have a look around. Near the top, Rab dismounted and dropped the reins to ground tie Cromwell.

He squatted down on one knee in the tall grass and stayed still. He did not think anyone on the Trail could notice him. The Trail was still some distance away, not even close enough that Rab could make out any more of it than a slight depression in the land, worn down with thousands of travelers.

That was how white people moved. Someone cut a path and by the dozens and the hundreds and the thousands, all followers stayed pretty well on that path. They moved from one place to another, settling in the new spot and spreading out to grow like the web of a spider.

The tribes moved differently. They followed the buffalo from one place to another. They moved in the dozens, never taking the same exact path a second time. They left the grass bent from their travois, a trace of their movement that would disappear in a few days. And when they got to a good hunting ground and killed the buffalo they would need, they left the rest of the herd for the next hunt, in a month or in a year. They stayed for a while, maybe a season or maybe a few days, and then they moved on, leaving the land to reclaim all evidence that they had been in that place for a time.

Rab was indifferent to the ways of the whites and the ways of the Indians. He had seen enough of them all to know that there were good white men and bad, good people of the tribe and bad. No race of man had all the goodness, and neither did a race have all the badness.

There were plenty of whites who claimed the Indians were all savages and killers. There were plenty among the tribes who claimed similar about the whites – cheats who sought to steal the land from the tribes.

Rab's experience, moving freely between the two people, was that he liked some Indians and he liked some whites. There were some Indians and some whites he respected. There were plenty Indians and plenty whites he was indifferent about. And there were those among the Indians and those among the whites who, he understood, were bad men who could not be trusted to see a man's back.

Rabbie Sinclair intended to do whatever he could to be certain that these four men with the buckboard wagon never saw his back.

After a while he shifted from one knee to the other.

He looked over his shoulder a few times to be sure Cromwell had not wandered too far off. The horse was good about a ground tie, but left too long any horse would begin to stray. Cromwell was on a never ending search for clover.

"You find some clover, hawse?" Rab called over his shoulder. "You eat your clover, but stay down below the top of this hill, here."

The horse gave no answer other than to keep munching where he was.

"What do you think about that gal?" Rab asked. "She's a sight, though, ain't she? You ever seen prettier eyes? She's got her mama's eyes, that's for sure. Green like the summer prairie grass. I could set and look in them eyes for a spell, old hawse. I think she fancies me a bit, too. Two days riding beside me. I know she ain't doing it for the luxury, on account of seeing her last night in camp. Poor gal couldn't hardly walk she was so sore from riding all day."

Rab laughed at the thought of it and smiled down at the horse.

"You don't care about green eyes when you're atop a patch of clover, do you Cromwell?"

He took off his hat and wiped the sweat from his forehead. Rab knew he would soon miss the heat of the prairie when they got to the Jornada and replaced it with the heat of the desert.

He wiped his forehead one more time on his shirtsleeve. He set his hat on his knee and pushed his hair back and held it up off the back of his neck. The long hair seemed to make the sweat and the heat worse. In a moment he'd abandon his watch and catch up to the wagon train, satisfied that there was nothing on the back trail to see. He'd let Cromwell go at a gallop, and that would ease the heat a bit.

He slid his hat back on his head and started to stand, but in the far distance to the east a thing caught his attention, and so he stayed where he was, watching it. Something was out there, right about where the trail should be. It was moving too slow to be a stagecoach. Rab checked again to make certain Cromwell was not wandering. The horse was still fine, well down the slope of the hill.

Slowly, the thing on the horizon came into more focus, and Rab could see that there were a number of spare horses, a wagon, and two riders. More to the point, he could see that the wagon was a simple buckboard wagon.

"Tarnation," he whispered to himself. "That'll be them."

Unless the mounted men rode ahead with some speed, Rab doubted they would catch the wagon train before sundown. But how far would Mickey Hogg and his party go after sundown? How far could Rab push the Cummings group after dark?

Rab was tempted to ride out there and take on those four men right now, by himself.

If he came in from behind he might get one with the Hawken rifle before they knew he was there. And the fact was, he could only see one man in the wagon. It was possible, he reasoned, that the four might now be three, and that could be a fairer fight.

Amos Cummings would never know. Neither would Martha, nor Rachel.

But it felt something like murder to try such a thing unprovoked. Mickey Hogg and the other one, Dick Derugy, had provoked plenty when they abducted Martha Cummings, but if Rab was going to kill them for that then he should have done it when he disarmed them and beat them. The other two had no part in that, but Rab was sure if he tried them now he would have to kill all three of them – or four if one of them was on the wagon and Rab just could not see him.

"If I ain't going to kill 'em, then we'd better get on out ahead of 'em before they can see us," Rab said.

He crouched back down the hill to Cromwell, then he stood up and led the horse farther down the slope. When he was satisfied that he could mount and the hill would still obscure their view, Rab swung himself into the saddle and set off south, seeking out the tree line along the creek that would continue to conceal his presence.

Then he followed the creek to the west for some distance, retracing his earlier ride.

After some time he cut back up to the Trail. Cromwell enjoyed the freedom to move, and the horse kept up a pretty fair trot most of the way. Even so, it took Rab longer than he expected to catch up to the wagon train after he'd followed the Indian tracks back to the Trail.

Already the sun was beginning to drop, and dusk would be upon them in an hour or so.

Rab rode past the back wagons, giving all of the drivers a wave as he passed each one, but when he reached the front wagon, Amos Cummings was walking beside it while his youngest son Paul drove the wagon.

"See anything back there?" Amos asked.

"Saw that buckboard wagon and them men," Rab said. "I could only see three of them, but the fourth one might well have been on the wagon bench, or even in the back."

"Are you certain it was them?" Amos asked.

"I am, Mr. Cummings. We're a long way from anything out here. There's not even a stagecoach relay station for some distance. I can't believe anyone else would have a buckboard wagon out here. You need one of these prairie schoolers for making this journey. That buckboard ain't going to last going across the Arkansas, and them men are fools to try it. Unless they think they can find themselves a good wagon somewhere along the way."

"But where would they find a wagon on the way?" Amos Cummings asked, but he cut short the question when he realized what Rab meant. "What do you recommend we do?"

Rab grinned at Amos Cummings. "The only thing I know to do is the thing you've said I cannot do. We can keep trying to outrun them. We can stop up here a ways and switch out the teams and travel through the night. Hope they have to stop. Rest for a bit after daybreak and then push on again. If we stay out ahead of them far enough, maybe we get across the Arkansas and get clear of them. But Mr. Cummings, if I'm being honest with you, this thing is going to come eventually to them killing me or me killing them. I don't see a way past that."

Amos Cummings sighed heavily. "I refuse to believe there is no alternative."

"Some men are bad, Mr. Cummings. They're bad all the way to the ground. You can wish it warn't so, but it's so."

"Ride ahead and tell Matthew to bring the livestock to a halt. We'll push through the night."

Rab nodded and urged Cromwell forward to catch up to Matthew and Rachel, who were pushing the livestock ahead of them.

***

For the next three nights and two days, the party moved almost without stop, pushing on through most of the nights, spending only three or four hours sleeping just before dawn. They stopped three or four times each day to switch out the teams pulling the wagons. The animals were beginning to get irritable, and so were the people.

But Rab insisted to Amos Cummings that it was necessary to keep ahead of Mickey Hogg, and Amos Cummings insisted to the rest of the party that there was no choice.

Even Rab Sinclair, who could stand a long journey as well as any man, found himself suffering from exhaustion.

The young Bancroft children had to sleep in the

wagons. Those who walked often fell far behind the wagons, and those who drove the wagons frequently dozed while sitting upright on the driver's bench.

The morning after the third night, the sun revealed that there had been a subtle change in the terrain. The tall grass seemed shorter here. There were patches of sagebrush and swaths where sandy soil showed. When she mentioned the change in the terrain, Rab confirmed that she was seeing something different from what they'd been traveling through for the last several days.

"We're coming out of the prairie and into the high plains," Rab told Rachel. "When we cross the Arkansas we'll be in the high plains, through the Cimarron desert."

Not long after noon that day, Rab Sinclair and Rachel Cummings were riding out well ahead of the wagon train, almost out of sight. It was there that Rab saw a lonely tree sitting by itself down in an arroyo. The tree was unique with a bend in its trunk. It was squat, and all its foliage sat at the top of the tree. The unique curve of its trunk and the way it grew up in an arroyo was familiar to him, and he recognized it as a landmark.

"I know that tree," Rab said to Rachel. "We'll be at the Arkansas in just an hour or two. We'll follow the river for the afternoon and part of the night, and tomorrow we will ford the river."

"Will it be a difficult crossing?" Rachel asked.

"It should not be. There's a good ford where we are crossing, and the river is surely low with the drought," Rab said. "But we will have to fill the water casks at the river, and so it will take time. Right now, any delay is our enemy."

"But surely we've left those men behind? Surely

they have not traveled as hard and as fast as we have," Rachel said.

"That all depends on how badly those men want to catch up to us," Rab said. "If they think we have something that they want bad enough, they can catch us. If that wagon falls to pieces on them, and it will sooner or later, then they'll leave it. And when they do, they'll be able to travel quite a bit faster. I have no confidence that they won't still catch us."

"What do we have that they want?" Rachel asked.

Rab filled the bowl of his pipe and lit it. He was getting low on matches and was trying to spare the pipe, but he and Rachel had ridden their horses to a stop to allow the wagons to catch up, and now was a good opportunity to smoke. He puffed the tobacco a few times to get it lit.

"Wagons. Provisions. Money, if you have any. Your mama and Mrs. Bancroft, and I reckon you, too."

Rachel shivered at the thought.

"But once we get out on the Jornada, what they'll want is our water," Rab said. "And that's when it becomes most dangerous, because that's when it's not about what they want, but what they must have to survive."

"They are vile men, aren't they," Rachel said.

"They sure are, Miss Rachel. Vile and dangerous."

"Would you fight them to protect us?" Rachel asked.

"I reckon I would," Rab said. "I signed on as your guide to get you to Santa Fe. I'm bound to do that. If those men come after you, I'd have no choice."

"My brothers would help you," Rachel said, dropping her voice and glancing back at the wagons. "And Uncle Stuart, too. My father is opposed to violence, but Uncle Stuart was talking to my mother in camp this morning. He said to her it would be better to defend ourselves than to continue to push the animals so hard. And I know my brothers would fight."

"That's good to know," Rab said.

Rachel glanced back to the wagons again. Then she leaned forward on her horse so that she would be closer to Rab. And she spoke quietly. "You would kill those men to protect me, wouldn't you?"

Rab puffed his pipe. With the tip clenched in his teeth he said, "Miss Rachel, I reckon to protect you I'd kill just about everybody."

Rachel smiled. "I will fight, also."

"If it comes to that, you might have to," Rab said.

"We have hunting rifles in the wagons. They are old guns, but they shoot fine."

"Have you ever shot one of those rifles?" Rab asked.

Rachel laughed. "No, Rabbie, I've never shot one."

Rab reached into his saddle bag and drew out a long hunting knife in a scabbard.

"You put this on your belt," he said. "That will do you better than a hunting rifle. This is the weapon that would be most likely save your life if it came to that."

Rachel held the knife and in her hands for a long time, looking at it.

"I don't know if I could use this on a person," she

said.

Rab nodded at her, puffing on his pipe.

"It's a hard thing to take a man's life," Rab said. "It's hard to do because he's fighting to keep it. So you have to be stronger or faster or smarter than he is. So the task itself is a hard thing. But it's also hard because your heart tells you it's wrong to kill a man. But you have to push those feelings away, and you don't have time to think it through when the time comes. Because you have to be faster and smarter to win that fight. You can't wait to think about it. The only way that knife will do you any good, Rachel, is if you decide right now that your life is more valuable to you than his life. You have to decide right now that you'll do anything to stay alive. Including shoving that knife into his throat, or through his eye."

"Rabbie, don't," Rachel said, frowning in disgust. "Don't say such things."

"I am going to say such things, Rachel," Rab said.

He looked over his shoulder to see the wagons still off in the distance.

"I'm going to say such things because I want to tell you something else. Your life is important to me. I don't know how to pick out the words. Maybe this is where I could do with some book learning. Maybe if I could read poems I'd have some way of saying what I think. But you make me feel this way, and I don't know how to put a name to it. You make me feel sad and happy all at the same time. I look at you, and I just want to hold you up close to me and smell your hair. I don't even care what we're talking about, I just want to talk to you. But then it makes me sad because I realize this ain't going on forever. These last few days, riding side by side with you. I reckon I'd be happy if this trip to

Santa Fe took another hundred years, because I don't want it to end. I know how stiff and sore it makes you, riding all day. But here you are, and I think you're doing it just to ride along beside me. And I'd like to have you riding along beside me every day. Not just on this trip, but every day from now until forever. I don't want to ever be without you. That's how I feel about you, and I wish I knew a better way to say it."

Rachel blushed, and then she smiled at his sincerity. And then she wiped away a tear that had come unbidden to her eye.

"Oh, Rabbie Sinclair. I think you could teach the poets a thing or two. I feel the same way. We just ride along together and talk about everything, and you know so much about this world that I have never even guessed at. And I can't even bear to think of Santa Fe, because I know that in Santa Fe we will be leaving and you will be staying. And I just want to stay with you. And my heart hurts when I think about leaving you to go to California. It seems absurd to even say it, but I've been wondering if maybe when we get to Santa Fe the right thing wouldn't be for me to stay with you and say goodbye to my family instead of the other way round. That's what my heart wants. But Graham says it could never work because you are so different from me, but it's those differences that make me feel so drawn to you."

Rab nodded and blew out a small cloud of smoke.

"Either way, that's why I say to you the things you don't want me to say," Rab said. "The eyes or the throat. But if you can't get to the eyes or the throat, under the ribs with an upward thrust. The stomach, and you twist the knife. But you don't stab a man and turn loose of the knife. You hold onto it and you jerk it out and you give it to him again."

"Please don't say it," Rachel said.

"Over and over, until the fight is gone out of him. You stab him everywhere you can, over and over until you've taken what he fought to hold onto. And you decide now that you're strong enough to do that."

"What if he's made the same decision?" Rachel asked.

"He ain't even thought about it, because he has no qualms about killing you. He'll do it. So he's never thought about any of it. And when the time comes, he won't be thinking about it. He'll just be fighting. So you've got to meet him there and fight, too. Your life has to be more important to you than his life is to him. And if you make that decision now, you won't have to think about it when the times comes."

Rachel Cummings nodded as she slid the knife's scabbard onto her belt.

"Before the wagons get here, I'd like to say a word more about Santa Fe," Rab said. "It may be that you don't have to go on from Santa Fe. Not if you don't want to."

Before Rachel could answer, the livestock came up around them, and Matthew Cummings rode up behind the animals.

-22-

When the last of the wagons was across the Arkansas, the Cummings party set about the work of getting water. With two years of drought, the river ran no higher than Rab's thigh, and the wagons did not have to float across. But the bottom was rough and uneven, and the oxen had to be coerced to keep the wagons moving so that they were not stuck.

The chore of getting water was arduous. The wagons were stopped up beyond the low bank, so the casks had to be carried down to the water. The sand was loose and difficult to maneuver with full casks. The casks that still had water had to be combined to keep the water from the Arkansas separated from the better spring water they still had. Then the casks had to be filled in the river, hefted back up the bank and lashed to the sides of the wagons. The sun beat down on the Cummings party, and the boys and men engaged in filling the casks baked in the heat. Graham Devalt took ill and had to rest in the shade under a wagon. Jeremiah and Matthew, who both had taken readily to the hard work of the trip, several times had to sit and rest after toting each cask from the river to the wagons.

The river was low, which made for easy crossing, but it left the water smelling and tasting like soil.

"It's a shame we can't find a spring," Stuart Bancroft remarked to Amos. "Ground water always has a better taste than river water."

Rab Sinclair heard the comment.

"Mr. Bancroft, soon enough you'll be glad to get what you have and wish for more," he said.

"Is the desert route the best way for us to go?" Stuart asked. "I realize the mountain pass would take longer, and the terrain would be rougher going, but we don't have to worry about suffering from lack of water or losing the animals. They are already exhausted from how hard we have pushed these last few days, and now we are asking them to cross a desert."

While they went about the task of collecting water, the livestock was all turned out. Able to rest or roam and graze at will. Rab had concerns about how the animals would hold up. What Stuart Bancroft said was accurate – the animals had been pushed too hard, and now that the wagon train had crossed the Arkansas and would be entering the Cimarron Desert, the going would get worse for those animals. Rab had learned in his life that a man who depended on animals was wise to treat them better than he treated himself. In a bad spot, a horse would get a drink of water and a man would get only a sip.

The spare animals had been a great help to keep the wagon train moving day and night these last few days, but they would soon be a burden. Spare animals drank just as much water as those harnessed to the wagons, and a rest would not replenish a thirsty animal.

Rab chewed on Stuart Bancroft's question for a few moments. It was the same question he'd asked himself over and over for the last few days, and now the question had to be answered once and for all.

"We'll be thirsty if we drop south here and travel through the desert," Rab said. "But if we keep going on the other side of the Arkansas and try for the mountain pass, I believe we'll have to kill those men following us, or die trying. What's important for you to remember, Mr. Bancroft, even if Mr. Cummings was to relinquish his demand that we not fight those men – what's important is that those men are killers. In the last couple of months they've slaughtered a family and they've killed a farmer. Who knows what else they've done?"

"Are you sure they were the ones who did those things?" Amos asked.

"I wasn't there to see it happen, but I'm sure. I've looked at the supplies in that buckboard wagon. They've got supplies to get through the winter, not supplies to go to Santa Fe. If it was Cheyenne Dog Soldiers, we would have heard of more attacks. Dog Soldiers don't kill a family and disappear. They spread terror."

Rab looked back at the Arkansas and across it as far as he could see. Mickey Hogg and his party were not yet there, but Rab knew they soon would be.

"Those men are killers. At least a couple of them have probably killed free-staters over in Lawrence. So even if we decided to make a stand against them, what they have on their side is that they know they can kill. They know that they don't have any second thoughts or hesitation about it. Can the same be said about us? I think the wise strategy for us is to get ahead of these men in the desert. We may lose some animals taking the Cimarron cut. That's a fact. But those men can't follow us through the desert. They ain't equipped for it. They can't carry the water they need. I've seen their wagon. They have only one cask for water. And they've got a herd of stolen hawsses they'll have to water, or turn loose. They ain't smart men, but they're smart enough to see that. They will not follow us this way. But if we make for the mountain pass, they'll follow us. They'll catch us. And they'll fight us. And then we have to trust that we can kill easier and better than them."

"And we probably cannot do that," Stuart Bancroft said. "We're not those kind of people."

Rab nodded his head in solemn agreement.

Stuart looked south. Even here from the river valley, he could already see that the terrain turned more hostile in appearance. The luscious green grass of the prairie was replaced here by a shorter, drier looking grass. Patches of brown sand showed between short sagebrush. Even with a lack of rain, the prairie through which they had been traveling still was a never ending ocean of waves of grass. But south of the Arkansas, the short grass of the high plains showed the lack of rain.

"Are we those people who can manage to cross a desert?" Stuart asked.

Rab grinned at him. "There is only one way to find out, Mr. Bancroft."

Amos Cummings looked up at the sun in the sky. They had started the crossing at first light, but it was already late in the afternoon.

"Shall we make camp here tonight?" Amos asked.

"No," Rab said. "Once those casks are all full, we should get on the way."

"We've pushed so hard," Amos said. "Surely before we start across the desert we should stay by the river one more night."

"We should," Rab agreed. "But if we do, I believe we will wake with knives at our throats."

"It is too much that we should be so harassed by these men," Stuart Bancroft said. "Amos, we should make a stand."

Surprised by the suggestion, Rab looked from one man to the other, interested to hear what Amos Cummings would say.

"You know I cannot do that," Amos said.

Stuart shook his head in disgust. "Even to protect our families, you will not raise a fist?"

"Thou shalt not kill," Amos Cummings said. "How can I trust in the Lord's Word and His protection but be unwilling to submit to His commands? The Mosaic Law tells me that God's will is that I should not strike down another man. And I will not. Nor will I sanction killing in my name. Our entire purpose in this journey is to protect our children from what we both agree will be war. To keep them out of such a thing, because we both believe that such a thing is wrong. How heavy would it sit upon my conscience to be responsible for the killing of four men because I wanted to flee killing?"

"But killing to save your family?" Stuart asked, and his tone was almost a plea.

"Killing in Ohio is a sin," Amos said. "It is no less a sin just because we have crossed the Missouri River."

"These Western territories is sinful places, Mr. Cummings," Rab Sinclair said. He did not wait for an answer. He turned around to see about the filling and loading of the last casks.

When the casks were finally full and loaded, Rab etched markings into the casks still full of spring water.

"This is what we'll drink," he said, making the announcement generally to all of the travelers. "We can leave the water from the river for the animals. If we run out of the good spring water, we'll turn to the river water. Your instinct will be to drink, and to drink lots. But we will have to ration the supply we have to make it last as long as possible."

Here, going through the section of the Trail known as the Jornada, the ruts that served as a guide were harder to find. Wagon wheels did not cut so easily into dry, baked earth, and fewer travelers had come this way.

Rab and the Cummings boys all rounded up the livestock while Amos and Stuart harnessed the teams and hitched them to the wagons.

They were losing daylight, but Rab wanted to get as far from the river as possible. He was sure that if Mickey Hogg and his group did not arrive to the river by sundown they would be there at sunup.

As the wagons started to roll out and Matthew Cummings began to push the weary livestock forward, Rab, mounted on the sorrel, rode up to him.

"You lead the way through the rest of the afternoon," Rab said. "Set your path just a little south of the sun, and set a pace that won't too much labor the animals. At dusk, call for a halt and make camp."

"What are you going to do?" Matthew asked.

"I need to see to one last thing. If something happens and I do not rejoin the party, you should not try to cross the desert without me. It would be too easy to lose your way. In the morning, at sunup, break camp without me and keep traveling in the same direction you're going this afternoon. You know how to set the falling tongue of the lead wagon to be sure you start in the right direction?"

"I do, Rab," Matthew said.

"If I have not joined you by tomorrow at dusk, turn your wagons north and find the Arkansas River again. Follow it west until you find a crossing. Then cross it and go north until you find the trail. Then follow that west. There ain't any relay stations on the Cimarron cut, but you'll come to a relay station on the mountain route. There, your pa can decide if he wants to keep going or if he wants to turn around and go back east."

Matthew stared at Rab. "But what are you going to do?"

"Don't worry about that," Rab said. "I have one last chore to take care of before we can cut across this desert. If I don't show back up, you take good care of my blue hawss."

"I will," Matthew promised.

"Now, you understand what to do, right?"

"Follow the sun today. Camp at dusk. Set the falling tongue to find my direction in the morning. Follow the same direction tomorrow. If you don't catch up to us, turn north and find the river. Follow the river west. Find a crossing. Find the trail. And then go to a relay station."

Rab smiled at him. "That's it. You're the guide now, Matthew. This is no place to get lost, so don't forget any of it."

Rab started to wheel the sorrel, but Rachel Cummings came riding up to him, a big smile on her face.

"I feel better already, knowing we're across the Arkansas," she said.

"Good," Rab said. "Help your brother keep these animals moving until sundown. I'll join you again tomorrow."

"What are you going to do?" Rachel asked, her brow wrinkling to concern.

"I've got a chore to take care of," Rab said. "I want to make certain those men do not try to follow us."

"Rab, what are you going to do?" she asked again.

"Just going to watch for them and make sure they don't try to cross here," Rab said.

-23-

Mickey Hogg and Pawnee Bill stood on the sandy bank of the Arkansas River looking at the tracks cut by the six wagons.

"They crossed here for sure," Pawnee Bill said.

"It ain't much of a river," Mickey said. "I thought the Arkansas was supposed to be a big river for steamboats."

"It is farther east of here," Pawnee Bill said. He wasn't sure why, but he felt defensive about the river. He knew that Mickey considered him an authority on this part of the country, and he felt like Mickey's criticism of the river was directed at him personally.

Since they'd got the whiskey from the stagecoach station, Mickey was hard to get along with. He drank too much in the evenings and was irritable in the mornings.

Dick Derugy was still in the back of the buckboard wagon. He complained that any time he tried to stand he went dizzy, and he said he had a fog floating in front of his eyes all the time. He'd never been much of a thinker, but Pawnee Bill was certain that when Rab Sinclair hit him he must have broken something in Dick's head.

Chester Bowman had gone to complaining. He didn't like driving the wagon, and he thought they should turn around. They were all hungry and regretting that they'd not stolen some provisions from the stagecoach station. Mickey was keeping all the whiskey for himself so that Pawnee Bill and Chester had nearly been shot to no benefit.

And now they were fixing to try a desert crossing. Bill had never been on the Jornada before, but he knew that here was the place where Jedidiah Smith was killed. He'd heard stories of men being stranded in snow storms and others dying of thirst with the blazing desert sun baking them. This was no place that Pawnee Bill wanted to find himself, no matter how much he wanted to get his hands on those women.

But Mickey could not be deterred, and Bill was scared to again broach the subject of turning back.

"Let's get moving," Mickey said. "Them folks ain't gettin' any closer with us standing here looking at the river."

Chester was up on high ground away from the river bed, sitting in the shadow of the wagon. "Come on, Chess!" Bill called to him. "Let's get across. You can drive that wagon through."

Mickey and Bill drove the horses down into the water and followed them with Chester coming into the river just behind them. The buckboard wasn't made for crossing a river like this, and it didn't sit up as high as the prairie schooners the Cummings drove, so the back was going to get wet. Chess lifted the bags of flour up to his bench seat where they would stay dry. Dick Derugy, who wasn't stirring much regardless of bumps or jolts, was going to be wet in the back of the wagon. There was nothing Chester could do about that.

The spare horses came out the southern bank. Chester was poised with the front wheels just starting to get wet. Mickey and Pawnee Bill were out in the middle of the river, holding their boots aloft to keep them dry.

And that's where they all were when a thunderous boom cracked out and echoed, and a lead ball splattered into the water just between Mickey and Pawnee Bill.

The shot startled all three men, and both Mickey and Bill dropped their feet into the river.

Mickey's shotgun on its swivel rig was of no use to him mounted, but Pawnee Bill and Chester both drew their Colt Dragoons.

To make the shot, Rab Sinclair had stepped out from behind some scrub brush on the south bank of the river.

"Just wanted to make certain I had your attention," Rab said. He smiled a friendly smile, but he was reloading the Hawken rifle as he spoke. He was not concerned about the guns pointing at him. He had faith that neither Pawnee Bill nor Chess Bowman would hit him where he was standing.

"You've got our attention," Mickey said. "What fool game are you playing?"

Rab had spent a long and restless night camped south of the Arkansas and near the crossing, and it was a relief to him when the men appeared not long after sunup. He did not want to spend too much of his morning waiting for them. He was eager to get back to the Cummings party before they abandoned the journey because he had not returned.

"Mine ain't the fool's game," Rab said. "I want you men to listen close to what I say. I've been through this desert before. I'm going to tell you now, you'll never make it if you cross the river. You don't have supplies and can't carry the water you would need to stay alive."

Mickey snarled at him as Rab finished loading the Hawken. "We'll decide for ourselves whether we've got supplies enough."

"I reckon you will," Rab said. "But I'm warning you all the same. You come across that river and keep following us, and you'll never cross back over it. Either the desert will get you, or I will."

"You think you're man enough to take all three of us?" Mickey asked.

Rab looked at Chess Bowman on the bench of the wagon, then back at Mickey and Bill. "Weren't there four of you? What's happened to the other fellow?" he asked.

"He's in the wagon," Mickey said, irked because he thought Rab Sinclair was making a point. "There's still four of us."

Rab craned his neck to see past Chess, and that's when he saw Dick Derugy in the back of the buckboard.

"That man don't look to be in decent shape," Rab said. "I reckon there's only one way to find out if I'm man enough to take the three of you. Or four of you. I would recommend to you that you leave that an unanswered question."

Now Rab Sinclair backed away, keeping the

Hawken in his folded arms but knowing that he could move it quickly if he had to. "Take my advice," he said. "The desert don't care how much of a man you are. A man with sand all the way to the ground still gets thirsty. I've crossed this desert and others worse than this. I know what I'm talking about. You'll not survive it."

He reached the top of the south bank and then turned and started down the opposite side. He'd tied the sorrel to a cottonwood below the other bank where the border ruffians would not see the horse as they approached the river. He removed the percussion cap from the Hawken rifle and slid it into its scabbard, and then he mounted up on the sorrel and rode away to hurry to catch the wagon train.

"What are we going to do?" Bill asked as Rab Sinclair came out from behind the rise on the opposite side of the bank and they could see him off in the distance riding away.

"We're going to hurry up and try to catch him," Mickey said. "We've got all the provisions we could want to get us through this desert. We just have to catch up to our provisions, is all."

Mickey turned and looked at Chester. "Come on with that wagon, Chess! Get it across the river and let's keep moving."

The wagon train had only made about ten miles when Rab Sinclair caught up to it near dusk. Amos Cummings had already called for a stop for the day.

The wagons were arranged in a half circle. The livestock were picketed near the circle, all of them on long leads so that they could get to what grass there was. The Cummings boys were all engaged in washing the animals when Rab rode up.

"Don't use too much of that water," Rab cautioned them. If he'd been with them when they halted for the day, Rab would have told them to dry rub the animals and not to use water.

"Oh, Mr. Sinclair!" Martha Cummings called out when she saw him. "We were growing concerned that something had happened to you."

Amos and Stuart, Martha and Rebekah, and Graham Devalt, had all been discussing their options. Matthew had told his father about Rab's instructions for going back across the Arkansas River if he did not show up. And that was the conversation they were now having. Only Graham Devalt was not relieved when Rab rode up on the sorrel.

"You've stopped early," Rab said. "Should have gone on another hour at least."

"The animals are sore fatigued, Mr. Sinclair," Amos said.

Rab slid down out of the saddle. He removed the saddle and blanket and gave his horse over to Matthew to picket and rub down.

"It will get worse," Rab said. "You're probably going to lose some of your animals. Water is scarce, and with a drought on, the water we might have found in the Cimarron will surely not be there. We've got probably eighty miles to make the Lower Spring on the Cimarron River. That's where we'll come to the first water."

"What delayed you?" Amos asked.

"It got to gnawing on me what you said about whether or not them men would realize they could not make it across the desert," Rab said. "More I thought about it, the more I thought maybe they ain't smart enough to know that. So I waited at the river to see if they would attempt to cross it."

"And did they?" Stuart Bancroft asked.

"They thought about it," Rab said. "I attempted to persuade them. I cannot say if I was successful, but maybe I delayed them a bit longer."

Rebekah Bancroft and Rachel Cummings were both kneeling at a campfire, preparing an evening meal. In a cast iron skillet, Rachel was cooking cornbread while Rebekah was heating beans with a slab of bacon.

"We will have to keep moving and press hard," Rab Sinclair said. "If these men cannot see reason and continue to follow us, we must do all we can to stay ahead of them. Until we reach Fort Union in New Mexico, the remainder of our trip will be very difficult. From there it will not be far to Santa Fe."

In the evening, as the sun descended beyond the western horizon, Rab took his three horses and set up his own camp about a half mile to the east of the Cummings camp. He wanted to position himself between Mickey Hogg's ruffians and the Cummings family. If they were traveling at night, Rab wanted to be the first one they came to.

With the sun down, the night air grew cool, and Rab put on his buckskin jacket and wrapped himself in his bedroll. He was quickly asleep with the three horses picketed around him.

At some point in the night, Cromwell blew a warning, and Rab opened his eyes. He did not stir but listened for any sound as his hand found his Colt Dragoon beside him in the bedroll.

There was a moon tonight, and while it was not a full moon, it was enough to cast a silvery light over the terrain. Rab turned his head slightly to scan the road to the east, but he saw no movement nor shadow in the moonlight that might indicate Mickey Hogg or the others riding up.

Cromwell blew again, and this time it was more urgent. Rab heard a sound to the west and turned his head. He cocked back the hammer of the Colt when he saw a figure moving toward him, but he realized instantly that it was Rachel Cummings.

"Rabbie?" she whispered into the night. "Are you

there?"

"Miss Rachel?" Rab asked. "What are you doing? Is there a problem at the camp?"

Rachel leaned forward to peer into the darkness, and then she saw the dark spot on the ground that was Rab's bedroll. She picked her way over to it and kneeled down beside the bedroll.

"I wanted to come to see you," she said. "I missed you as we rode yesterday and today. I missed spending time with you."

Rab let down the hammer on the Colt. "Well, I missed you, too."

"It gets very chilly at night," Rachel said, shivering.

Rab sat up and swung his legs out of the bedroll, and he lifted up the heavy blanket so that Rachel could sit under it with him.

"Thank you," she said.

He did not intend to leave his arm wrapped around her, but when Rachel sat down and Rab put the blanket around her, his arm came around her shoulders. He left it there for a moment, and Rachel reached up and took hold of his hand. Then she leaned into him, snuggling her head against his shoulder, allowing his arm to wrap up her body.

"I have thought all day about what you said about not leaving when we reach Santa Fe."

Rab nodded. "I meant it."

"Are you asking me to stay there with you? Asking me to marry you?"

Rab was silent for a moment. The idea of marriage was not something he'd ever given much thought to. Among the tribes, marriage was a different sort of thing than it was among white people. So he had not grown up with the same concept of it, though he understood what it meant for white folks.

"I reckon I am," he said.

"But what would we do?" Rachel asked. "When we reach Santa Fe, how would we survive? How would you earn money?"

Rab shrugged under the blanket.

"I'd find plenty to do. I'm planning to do some prospecting when we get to New Mexico. I can guide or hunt or trap."

"What kind of life would that offer for me?" Rachel asked. "And what if we had children. Could you earn enough money to support a family?"

It was a perplexing question. Rab Sinclair had never once in his life thought about a thing like a career. If he'd ever given thought to the future, it didn't look like much of anything other than maybe a log cabin near a spring with plenty of game. And if he'd thought about having a woman, it was never a woman like Rachel Cummings.

In the flash of an instant, Rab Sinclair saw that whatever he felt for Rachel was not a thing that could last.

"These are not things I've given much thought to," Rab said. "Maybe I was too loose with my speech when I said that you could stay with me in Santa Fe."

"I want to," Rachel said. "But it frightens me to

think of what kind of life that would be. It's not a life I'm accustomed to."

"No, I reckon not," Rab said.

"I don't know that it's a life I could be happy with," Rachel said. "But then I think that if I was with you, I could be happy in any kind of life."

Rab did not know what to say, and so he said nothing.

Rachel needed to fill the silence.

"It was already so much to pick up where we were and leave to go all the way across the country to something completely new. And now you have me thinking of not even going all the way with my family, but stopping in some wild and distant territory, alone and separated from everyone else that I know. And the thought of it scares me. I don't know that I am cut out to be the wife of a frontier man."

"I would find a way to give you the kind of life you want," Rab said.

"What if I want parties and to entertain guests?" Rachel said. "What if I want to live in a town, in a big house, and have fine luxuries? I just don't know that I can live in a wild place, and I don't know that you can live in a place that is not wild."

Rab took a heavy breath and turned his face toward Rachel. He put a hand to her cheek and turned her face toward him. Rab put his lips against her lips, and he wrapped both arms around her, holding her close to him.

And in that moment Rachel gave herself over to him, wild though he was. She embraced the passion she felt. She abandoned her fears and her worries, and she allowed herself to live in the moment without a thought to what it might mean.

Later, when she fell asleep in his arms, pressed against the warmth of his body under the blanket of his bedroll, she did not worry about what it might mean or what kind of life she would have.

Graham Devalt woke in the middle of the night. The lanterns around the camp were all extinguished, but in the light of the moon he could see the others in their bedrolls.

He could see, too, that Rachel's bedroll was empty.

He knew where she must have gone, and his heart was sick over it. Not for the first time on this trip, he cursed his decision to join Amos Cummings. And he again wished he had stayed back east where he was happy.

***

The western sun seemed to fill the entire sky. It was a brutal heat bearing down on the travelers.

The Kansas prairie had been hot, but under the canvas of the covered wagon, a man could find shade and maybe a bit of a breeze that offered relief. An afternoon nap beneath a wagon could be pleasant enough. Mounted, or even on the wagon's bench, even if no wind was blowing a breeze could be got up that would make the heat sufferable. But most of the time a good wind blew out across the prairie.

Here the wind that blew seemed to carry more

heat. It certainly carried bits of sand that got in the eyes and the teeth and the nose. They were in the high plains proper now, though they might as well have been in the desert. Sage brush and buffalo grass littered the landscape in patches but left plenty of spots for the wind to whip up sand to assault the exposed places. The sun seemed to occupy at least half of the sky. It grew enormous here, and the heat it put off was like an adobe stove. The heat not only came from the sky, but it came up from the ground, too, so that a man felt cooked from top and bottom.

Rab now rode with his buckskin jacket tossed into the back of one of the wagons.

The ground was baked hard, and this was the only grace in the desert. It meant the wagons could roll easier and faster. If the animals could better stand the heat, they might make twenty miles every day from the ease with which the wagons rolled across the hard ground. But the animals had to be stopped more frequently and allowed to graze and drink from buckets filled with river water.

They were now making not much over ten miles a day, and the first good spring was still more than sixty miles away.

The wagons had stopped again to rest the animals. Rab Sinclair had ridden to check their back trail. For two nights in a row, Rachel had snuck away and joined him at his camp. Graham Devalt had been aware of it both nights. And now, with Rab away and everyone at a stop, Graham Devalt decided to play his card. Amos Cummings and Martha Cummings were sipping water. Their daughter was standing with them, waiting her turn.

"You look exhausted Rachel," Graham said.

Martha Cummings looked at her daughter. "You do look exhausted," Martha said.

"I'm sure we all look exhausted," Rachel said.

"I suppose that's true," Martha said. "This heat, it takes so much out of you."

"I feel drained all the time," Amos agreed.

Graham would not be deterred so easily.

"I suppose getting up and leaving camp in the middle of the night only adds to the exhaustion caused by the heat," Graham said.

"What's that?" Amos asked.

Rachel shot Graham a look, and she saw on his face that he knew.

Martha Cummings saw the look of terror on Rachel's face. And she immediately understood.

"Have some water, Rachel," Martha said. "Graham, you should have some water, too."

"What do you mean 'leaving camp'?" Amos Cummings asked.

Graham grimaced, as if he did not want to say any more. "I've noticed the last couple of nights Rachel has awakened in the middle of the night and left our camp."

"And gone where?" Amos demanded.

Rachel did not answer, and Graham was only too happy to provide the answer himself.

"She's been going to Mr. Sinclair's camp."

"For what purpose?" Amos asked, fury rising in his voice.

"I have only gone to visit Mr. Sinclair to talk with him and keep him company because I know he is standing watch for us," Rachel said, but her excuse sounded weak, even to her.

Amos Cummings grasped her by the wrist. "You'll not defile yourself with that man," he said. "He is no better than a savage."

"Amos," Martha said, her voice soft, and she reached out and put a hand on his arm. But Amos Cummings did not release his grip on his daughter's wrist.

"Has he touched you?" Amos asked.

Graham Devalt smiled at Rachel, and then he turned and walked away. He'd done what he wanted to do.

"I am in love with him," Rachel said.

"That's not an answer to my question," Amos said, the anger in his voice frightened his daughter. She had never heard him sound like that before.

"Yes, it is," Rachel said.

Amos Cummings did not release his grip on his daughter's wrist, but he raised up his other hand and slapped her hard across the face. Rachel fell away, but Amos jerked her wrist and brought her back to her feet.

"Amos!" Martha called out. "Stop that now!"

"Did you let him touch you?" Amos asked again. "Like a common whore?"

"Amos!" Martha Cummings shouted, trying to break her husband's madness.

But Amos Cummings raised up his hand a second

time and slapped his daughter across the face again. This time he let go his grip on her arm she fell to the ground.

"No more riding with him," Amos said. "No more riding with him, and no more leaving the camp at night. I will hogtie you in your bedroll if I have to. Do not defy me, girl."

Amos turned and walked away.

Martha dropped to her knees. Rachel was sobbing torrents of tears and she could not catch her breath.

Martha stroked her hair with one hand and held her head up off the ground with the other. She shushed her daughter.

"Ride with me in the wagon," Martha said.

Now Amos called out to the entire party. "Harness the mules. Let's get moving."

"Shouldn't we wait for Mr. Sinclair?" Stuart Bancroft asked. He had seen the altercation with Rachel, but he did not know what caused it and had heard nothing that was said.

"Mr. Sinclair can catch us," Amos said. "He is not my concern."

-25-

Chess Bowman picked up Dick Derugy's head and tried to pour a little water into his mouth. Dick chocked and spit out the water.

They were in the back of the buckboard. Already two horses had fallen out and had to be shot. The water was running perilously low. The animals were all spent. Dick looked bad. The sun had cooked his face so that it was red and blistered underneath his thick growth of whiskers. His eyes were vacant. His lips were cracked and bleeding. He didn't make sense when he tried to talk. No words formed, just grunts and moans.

Not that anyone else was faring so much better.

The three men had become disoriented, losing their way twice. They had to ride in circles on the second afternoon out from the Arkansas to find the evidence of a campsite that put them back on the right path. Wherever they could find them, they followed tracks from the Cummings wagon party, but the wind blew so hard that the tracks were often covered over, and the ground was so hard that the tracks sometimes did not exist at all. Following the sun was no use because it filled the whole of the sky, or seemed to. It was impossible to distinguish its arc and know which way was west until very late in the afternoon. There were no landmarks to judge direction or distance.

Pawnee Bill and Mickey Hogg had taken to arguing with each other. Bill was for turning around. Mickey wanted to press ahead.

"We're three days from the Arkansas," Mickey said. "We've got to be closer to them emigrants than we is to the river," Mickey argued. "If we leave the wagon and just go on horse, we'll catch them by morning."

"Dick can't go on horse," Pawnee Bill noted.

"I don't care about Dick," Mickey whispered. "That man is dead already. When that boy hit him in the head, he knocked his brain aloose. There ain't nothing left to do for him 'cept leave him."

"We can't leave him," Bill hissed back.

"Sure we can. Or we can put a bullet in him. Shoot him like you would a horse with a busted leg."

"I'll not do neither," Bill said, and his tone made Chess look up. He could not hear what was passing between the two of them, but Pawnee Bill's tone was enough to let him know there was an argument.

"It's down to him or us," Mickey said. "If we don't strike fast, we'll be too weak to strike."

"What are you saying?" Chess called from the back of the buckboard. "What're you contemplating?"

Bill and Mickey both wore guilty looks. "You best come down off of that wagon and talk with us," Bill said.

Chess tried one more time with a bit of water, but it just dribbled out of the side of Dick's mouth. He capped the canteen and climbed down out of the buckboard.

There was no sky out here. It was all sun. All sun just beating down and baking all that existed below it. There was no escape, neither. The desert offered nary a tree for shade. Even under the buckboard they could find no relief.

"We're going to have to abandon the wagon so we can move faster and try to catch that wagon train," Mickey Hogg said, squinting out the sunlight as he watched Chess's face for a reaction.

"Dick can't ride a horse," Chess said. "We have to take the wagon."

"We'll have to leave Dick, too," Mickey Hogg said. "Leave Dick. Leave the wagon. We'll die out here if we don't."

Chester Bowman pleaded his case to Pawnee Bill.

"Come on, Bill," he said. "You been with us a long time. You know me and Dick have ridden together for years. You can't expect me to just leave him out here to die in this sun."

"Put a bullet in him," Mickey Hogg said.

Chester glanced at Mickey, but he continued to try to work on Pawnee Bill.

"He was at Lawrence with you, Bill," Chess said. "You can't leave a man to die who was at Lawrence with you."

Pawnee Bill dropped his eyes to the ground and shook his head. He knew that Mickey was right. If they didn't mount up on horses and overtake that wagon train now, they'd succumb to the thirst.

"We got one chance, Chess," Bill said. "Mickey's right. If you don't want Dick to suffer, you should bust a cap on him. If you can't do that, we should cover him with a tarp, leave him with a little water, and if he gets better maybe he can make it out of here on his own."

Chess Bowman looked at Mickey Hogg, but Mickey was holding his face up to the blinding sky, his eyes shut against the heat of the desert sun.

"I just can't believe the two of you would talk like this," Chess said. "Dick's our friend. He's been with us since way back."

"He ain't been with me since way back," Mickey said. "Y'all just joined up with me a month ago."

Mickey kicked the crusty soil with the toe of his boot, loosening some of it. He pushed it around with his toe.

"You joined up with us," Mickey said. "And now you're talking about leaving one of us behind. That never happened before. Did it Bill?"

Pawnee Bill looked over at Dick in the wagon. The man was unconscious. He looked like he was well on his way to a greetin' with the Devil.

"Dick's dead already," Pawnee Bill said. "It's foolishness to leave ourselves at risk for a man who's already dead. You just got to get that fixed in your mind, Chess."

Chess Bowman shook his head and walked away from the two men. The troubles all started when the stage pulled in at Six Mile Stage Station, when Pawnee Bill saw the daughter of that sod buster and set his mind to having her. It was those killings that led them to Spear's Hollow, and that's where they fell in with Mickey Hogg.

And now Chess Bowman found himself stuck in a desert with two no accounts, and poor old Dick Derugy was going to be left to cook to death, no better than if the Kiowa or the Apache had got to him.

Dick was senseless, but he was in pain. Chess knew from the way he grimaced and moaned that he was in pain. And if they left him, he'd die a sorrowful death of thirst. So Mickey fixed it in his mind, just as Pawnee Bill said he had to.

Without a word to the others, but with both of them watching, Chess walked over to the buckboard wagon. He let down the back of it and took Dick by the collar, dragging him out of the wagon and dropping him down to the ground. He fell with a thud. Chess slid the thong off his revolver and drew it from his holster. He cocked back the hammer, took a steady aim at Dick's head, and looking away, Chess pulled the trigger and ended Dick Derugy's suffering.

"Okay," Chess said. "You want to get after them folks and take what they've got, then let's go. But when we get them, you hold that guide for me. He's the one that did this to Dick, and I intend to cut him open and show him the color of his guts before he dies."

-26-

The big Hawken rifle exploded, and across the small valley of the Cimarron River all those of the Cummings party could hear its echo.

"Do you think he got something?" Martha asked.

Amos Cummings said nothing, instead he sipped on his coffee, still too hot to drink.

They were setting up camp at the base of the Point of Rocks, intending to stay here for two nights. The cottonwoods in the valley provided shade. The Middle Spring was running with good, clear water. The men and women, the children, and the animals were all at last equally refreshed.

Rab Sinclair had purposely passed by camping at the Lower Spring. They stopped for an afternoon, long enough to fill water casks and water the animals at the spring that ran through the thick buffalograss, but then Rab insisted that they keep going after dark.

"If those men followed us on the Cutoff, they'll be desperate for water," Rab told Stuart Bancroft. "They are in bad shape, if they're not dead already. They will be desperate to get to the Lower Spring. This is a place where folks usually camp for a day or two, and those men will have to. Our animals are ornery enough, but their hawsses won't leave the water. Not right away. They'd be whipped to death first. So we move on because we can. We'll camp for a couple of days at the Middle Spring. The water ain't as tasty, but it's just as wet."

Three days later the large rock outcropping on the flat plains came into view – the Point of Rocks. The next day they arrived there and made camp.

Amos Cummings had not spoken to Rab Sinclair, and the guide's instructions all had to go through Matthew or Stuart or one of the others. Amos had also forbidden his daughter from any conversation with Rab Sinclair.

When they arrived four days later at the Middle Spring, the Cummings party set up camp, planning to stay two nights at the spring.

While they set up camp, Rab went into the cottonwoods in the Cimarron valley, looking for fresh meat. Elk and sometimes buffalo were plentiful here, and it did not take him long to track a herd of elk, and firing only one shot with the Hawken he took a buck. Rab used his knife to field dress the elk and then carried it back to the camp over his shoulders.

He gave the elk to Stuart Bancroft, and showed him how to make a mountain roast of it, spearing the meat and setting it on a stake over the fire.

"Cut the meat into strips, dry it over the fire for today and tomorrow, and it will last the rest of the way to Santa Fe," Rab said.

When he was done instructing Stuart on the meat, Rab rode Cromwell up the back side of the large rock outcropping known along the Trail as the Point of Rocks. There was a second Point of Rocks, in New Mexico, between Rabbit Ears and Wagon Mound, but this Point of Rocks was the last bit of Kansas they would see. Below the large table outcropping was the Cimarron Valley, a green place full of cottonwoods fed by the spring and what water the Cimarron River could offer when it was not running dry. From this point on, though, while water was still scarce it at least existed. In places the Cimarron would have decent water. There were more springs and creeks flowing down out of the mountains of Colorado Territory.

Rab Sinclair had sat here before, when he was young. He and his father had camped at the Middle Spring with a band of Arapaho. One of the warriors had brought Rab up to the top of the Point so that Rab could see how far the cottonwoods stretched, like a giant green snake, following the Dry Cimarron. It was a beautiful sight to behold. In the distance, beyond the cottonwoods, the desert reached out in every way to touch the blue horizon. From the top of the point, it seemed that the desert was everything, and the only bit of anything that wasn't desert was the valley of cottonwoods down below.

All the beauty in the world was right there at his feet, a cottonwood forest snaking out into the desert. Around the cottonwoods, just holding the desert at bay, were the small flowers of white horsenettle and purple sage. Even the yucca seemed beautiful, a bright green to contrast with the brown grasses of the Jornada.

And all the ugly in the world was there, too. A gray and dead desert grassland that offered nothing but misery.

Rab Sinclair had found misery there in that desert grassland. Every time he saw Rachel Cummings, he felt sick in his heart and sick in his stomach. It seemed an impossible cruelty to be separated from her.

"I did not know if I would ever see this sight again," Rab said to the black faced roan. "I remember seeing it with that Arapaho so long ago. I've seen prettier places, but I've seen few as stark as this one, with all the beauty contained in a neat little strip of river valley. It's a glorious place, hawss, and I hope you'll appreciate that I've brought you here."

Rab stood up, putting a hand on the roan, and started to jump up into the saddle, but a glance out to the east gave him a new sight. He strained his eyes to be sure of what he was seeing, and then he jumped up into the saddle where he had a slightly better view.

Three riders, driving a couple of spare mounts, and pushing hard toward the cottonwoods, hard toward the Middle Spring where the Cummings party was camped.

If it was Mickey Hogg and the others, they had abandoned the wagon, some of their horses, and one of their men.

They were coming on hard toward the cottonwoods, and something about the way they rode, something about the way their horses moved, suggested to Rab Sinclair that they were suffering. It was possible that they did not stop at the Lower Spring because they did not know about it. Unlike the Middle Spring, surrounded by a valley of green trees that would tell any fool that water was nearby, the Lower Spring was more difficult to find, and the only clue to its existence was a patch of bright green buffalograss.

If they did not know to look for the Lower Spring, they would easily pass right by it.

But they would see the trees and know that here was water, even if they did not know of the Middle Spring.

Rab judged the distance and decided he could beat them to the base of the Point of Rocks, to the Cummings party's campsite – but it would be a close run.

He pulled the reins and turned Cromwell to go back down the path to the valley below, urging the horse forward with pace.

***

The Cummings party was camped inside a grassy clearing within the line of cottonwoods and not far from the Middle Spring. There was no clear road here in the hard-caked sandy soil of the desert, but the space in the trees created a natural roadway that was easy to recognize, and Mickey Hogg, Pawnee Bill, and Chess Bowman followed the space between the trees into the open clearing.

When they saw the wagons, Pawnee Bill and Chess Bowman reined in their horses. Mickey, though, had already pulled his horse to a halt. Mickey saw the big Hawken rifle in Rab Sinclair's crossed arms before he even noticed the wagon.

Rab Sinclair was in the saddle of the blue roan. He'd ridden down from the Point of Rocks and arrived at the camp just as the trio broke into the clearing through the cottonwoods.

"Y'all best move on," Rab said, his voice loud, but

still unhurried.

Amos Cummings was cutting meat from the elk. Stuart Bancroft and his sons were starting a fire. The three Cummings boys and Graham Devalt were filling casks at the spring. The women were all washing clothes – the first wash anyone's clothes had in many days.

Amos and Stuart both stood up, seeing Mickey Hogg and the other two for the first time.

"We need water," Mickey Hogg said. "We're about dead. Our horses are about dead."

"I told you not to come this way," Rab said. "Your troubles ain't my fault. If I was you, I'd head for the Lower Spring. You passed it about thirty or forty miles back."

They would find a water hole closer if they kept going west, but Rab did not want these men in front of him.

"We're here for water," Mickey Hogg said. "We're dying of thirst. Move out of our way."

Rab cocked back the hammer of the Hawken, and he slid a percussion cap onto the nipple.

Mickey's shotgun was useless at this range. He might pepper the roan, but neither the horse nor the rider would be hurt much unless the horse threw the rider. If it came to shooting, the best bet was for Bill or Chester to charge the young guide. But Mickey wondered if even this strategy would work. If Rab Sinclair could keep his cool with two men charging him, he'd get off a shot with that Hawken and only one man would be charging. And that man would be thirsty and weak. None of them were in a position to fight, but the man mounted on the blue roan looked like he was ready.

"You'll have to go back to the Lower Spring," Rab said. "There ain't water for you here."

"It's murder!" Pawnee Bill yelled out, and by the looks of him he was telling the truth. "You let us at that water, or you're killing us. Just the same as if you lifted that rifle and fired a lead ball into my chest."

Amos Cummings was walking forward. Rab could see him from the corner of his eye. But he did not look away from the three ruffians.

"Mr. Sinclair, a blind man could see that these men are suffering," Amos said. "You cannot prevent them from getting to the water."

Rab twitched his lips into a grin and shook his head slightly.

"Mr. Cummings, you'd be wise to defer to me on this matter," Rab said.

But Mickey Hogg had a loose strand, and he wasn't about to let go of it.

"That's right," Mickey said. "We are suffering. We done lost one man. Succumbed of thirst. You can't leave us all to die like that."

Amos was still walking forward, putting himself dangerously close to Mickey Hogg and the other two. The silent man sitting his horse just behind Hogg was staring hate at Rab Sinclair, and Rab noted it. The silent one, Chess they called him, was the one who'd been driving the wagon at the river, and Rab assumed he was close to the man who died. Brothers, maybe. Longtime friends, at least. Thirst may have gotten that man, but Rab Sinclair knew that it was the blow to the head from the butt of the Hawken rifle that killed him.

"We are Christians, Mr. Sinclair. Regardless of what kind of morals you learned among the savages, we are Christians and will conduct ourselves as such. It is written in Proverbs: 'If thine enemy be hungry, give him bread to eat; if he be thirsty, give him water to drink.'"

"That's right," Mickey Hogg said. "You can't turn us out and call yourselves Christian men. We'll die of thirst if you turn us out."

Rab leaned forward a bit on the horse, and Cromwell shifted beneath him.

"Mr. Cummings, I'll ask you not to take another step toward those men. If you do, you'll be within easy pistol shot of them."

Amos Cummings turned on his heel and stared lightning and fire at Rab Sinclair, but Rab's face remained impassive.

"You'll not talk to me about where to step and where not to step," Amos Cummings thundered, but he stopped all the same.

Rab took a breath.

"Mr. Bancroft, go down to the spring and move the women over behind the wagons and under the tarpaulins where they will be safe and out of the way," Rab said.

Stuart left the fire to his sons and hurried back to the spring.

"It's Mickey Hogg, right?" Rab asked, looking at the leader of the ruffians.

"That's right," Mickey said.

"You men slow and easy toss your guns and knives on the ground. When you've done that, slide out of your saddles and walk your hawsses over to the spring. I'll go along to keep a watch on you. Water your hawsses, fill your canteens. Get enough water that you can go on back east to the Lower Spring. But you won't linger here without getting shot."

Mickey Hogg looked over at Pawnee Bill and Chess Bowman. As much as he wanted to rush the young guide and do for him once and for all, Mickey knew that the three of them were weak and exhausted. Water and rest was what they needed.

"Do as he says," Mickey instructed the other two.

It took both hands for Mickey Hogg to release the scattergun from its swivel rig. He drew out his big Bowie knife and tossed it onto the ground beside the gun. Mickey didn't carry a rifle. Pawnee Bill and Chess Bowman both did, but neither of them had their rifles loaded. Bill and Chester both unbuckled their gun belts and dropped them to the ground.

Now the three men led their horses and spares forward, taking them to the spring. Rab allowed them to pass, and then he rode behind them at a slow walk. As he passed by where he could see Matthew, Rab Sinclair raised up his hat and waved it at Matthew to get his attention. Dutifully, the young man began to hurry over to where Rab was following the three men.

"There's the spring, yonder," Rab said, loud enough for the ruffians to hear. "Now go on and water them hawsses, fill your canteens. And understand this while you've got your backs to me – I'd let you die of thirst out on that desert, and I wouldn't lose a wink of sleep over it. And it ain't for the Christian conscience that you now get to drink. I won't see them hawsses be turned out in your care without first getting some water."

The horses drank – all of them. That told Rab all he needed to know about how thirsty these men and their animals were. Even in the desert some horses, if well cared for, wouldn't immediately take to the water. But these animals had been viciously used.

Matthew came up to where Rab was sitting on Cromwell, but his eyes were fixed on the three men filling their canteens.

"They tossed down their weapons back there," Rab whispered to Matthew. "Run along, and without them seeing you, disable their guns. Take the percussion caps off of them and drop them in your pocket. Be sure they don't see you, and when you've finished, go on and skedaddle out of there."

Matthew smiled and nodded and ran back to where the men had thrown their guns on the ground.

Amos Cummings had still not spoken directly to Rab Sinclair since he'd discovered his daughter's cavorting. But now he walked over to where Rab was mounted on Cromwell.

"Give off threatening these men," Amos said. He had the decency to keep his voice down and not let Mickey Hogg or the others hear the argument. "You are only riling them and making the intercourse with them more contentious than it need be."

Rab took his pipe from his pocket, along with his pouch of tobacco. He filled the bowl of the pipe slowly, keeping his eyes on the three ruffians. He struck a match and puffed the pipe a few times to get the tobacco burning.

"Mr. Cummings, the man who does all the talking for them. Mickey Hogg is his name. Do you know why his nose is smashed all to hell?"

"I suppose that is what you did to him when he abducted my wife," Amos Cummings said.

"That's exactly right," Rab said. "Our intercourse with them fellers there, it ain't going to get less contentious until he feels satisfied that he has paid me back for his busted face."

"Be that as it may, I am appalled that you intended to send them back out into the desert without a drink. You do not speak for me, nor for this wagon party."

Rab puffed on the pipe and looked up at the tip of the pointed rocks above them. The rocks were like jagged teeth climbing up to the height. It was a beautiful spot, and Rab was glad to have returned here.

"I sat on that point above us with an Arapaho warrior when I was younger," Rab said.

Amos Cummings shook his head, not understanding the point – not even sure that there was a point.

"I reckon you're sore angry with me," Rab said. "And I can appreciate your perspective. But being mad at me is no reason to get your family killed, Mr. Cummings."

"Angry at you?" Amos Cummings spat the words. "You have defiled my daughter. You have treated her like an Indian whore."

Rab blew out a cloud of gray smoke. "Are you talking to your daughter?"

"That is none of your concern," Amos Cummings said. His anger was growing fierce.

"I take that to mean you're not speaking to her any more than you're speaking to me," Rab said. "I want to encourage you to give up on that. Go on and be kind to her. The fact is, Mr. Cummings, when we reach Santa Fe and you've found a new guide, my intention is for Rachel to stay with me. It would be best for you and her both if you'd make peace with her now. You don't want to part on poor terms."

Amos Cummings slapped his hands together to give vent to his anger, and the three ruffians turned to see what made the noise. Mickey Hogg smiled and nodded when he saw Rab Sinclair watching him.

"She will not stay with you in Santa Fe," Amos Cummings hissed. "I'll see you arrested first."

"Arrested for what, Mr. Cummings?" Rab asked.

"Premarital relations," Amos said, and it pained him to even speak the words.

"There ain't a lawman in Santa Fe would arrest a man for such a thing," Rab said. "I'm trying to be fair and straight with you, Mr. Cummings – just like I was fair and straight with these men when I told them not to come into the desert. Your daughter loves me, and I love her. It would be best for her and you both if you'd accept that and realize the truth of what I'm saying. Ask her if you don't believe me."

The horses now started to leave off the water.

"Them canteens are full," Rab said. "Now get on back east to where you can camp for a day or two at good water."

"If we have passed it by once already, we'll never find it," Mickey Hogg said.

"Then keep on going until you come to the Arkansas, and you can get your drink there," Rab said.

"Your ability to find your way or get lost don't make a difference to me. But if you're still within ten miles of this camp at dusk, I will shoot you."

"That's enough, Mr. Sinclair," Amos Cummings said, but this time he did not have the decency to keep his objections between just the two of them. "Do not utter another threat against these men."

Rab walked the roan away from the path of Mickey Hogg and the other two. Rab noticed, though, that Mickey's eyes were darting here and there, taking account of everything he could see of the camp. He looked at the position of the wagons, the location of the animals. He even craned his neck to try to get a look at the women. After the three men passed by, Rab followed them back to where they'd left their guns. He was closer this time, much closer and in easy range of the shotgun.

"I guess we won't ask if we're invited for supper," Mickey said, grinning at Rab.

"You ain't."

Amos Cummings had followed them over and was standing near to Cromwell. Rab waited and watched as Mickey tossed a gun belt first to Chess and then to Pawnee Bill. He saw a look pass between the three men, and he knew what was coming.

Mickey bent over to pick up his shotgun, and he took a glance at Rab. Then in a swift motion, Mickey fanned back the double hammers on the scattergun and pulled both triggers.

Just as he did, both Chess Bowman and Pawnee Bill slung their revolvers from holsters and cocked and fired their guns.

Every trigger pull dropped a hammer down

where no percussion cap could fire.

But the sudden violence of it, the fear of the explosion of shot that never came, drove Amos Cummings backwards and he stumbled and fell to the ground.

Mickey Hogg laughed at the college professor sprawled on the ground, but then the smile dropped from his face as he turned his attention back to Rab Sinclair on top of the blue roan.

"I guess I didn't see you remove the percussion caps," Mickey Hogg said.

"No, I reckon you did not."

"Next time I point this gun your way and pull the trigger, there will be a cap to bust."

"Maybe," Rab said. "Or maybe we should find out right now whether or not there is a cap on this Hawken."

Rab raised up the butt of the gun and dropped down the barrel, catching it in his left hand. He sighted down the barrel right at Mickey Hogg, and Mickey must have seen death in the Hawken, for he quickly scrambled up into his saddle, wheeled his horse and rode off at a gallop. Pawnee Bill and Chester Bowman were not as quick to run, but they followed close behind.

Amos Cummings was still sitting on the ground, a horrified look on his face.

"They would have killed us," Amos said.

"Yes, sir."

"You had Matthew remove the caps?"

"I did."

"We allowed them to have water, and they would

have killed us," Amos said, and he still seemed to struggle to believe it.

"You allowed them to have water, Mr. Cummings," Rab said. "You've seen now for yourself that they will pull triggers on you. They will kill you, unprovoked. Now you have some hard decisions that you have to make, because those men will be back here after sundown."

Rab urged the blue roan forward and rode through the grove of cottonwoods to where he could see the three men riding across the desert. They would soon be out of range of the Hawken. All the same, Rab raised the gun to his shoulder again, sighted it well away from the men, and pulled the trigger. The explosion boomed across the open plain and only one of the three riders turned to see Rab Sinclair reloading the big Hawken.

-27-

"He's made a fool of us, and that's twice he's done it," Mickey Hogg complained. "And he's killed Dick. We're going to pay him back, and we're going to do it tonight."

"I'm hungry," Pawnee Bill said. "They had deer or something they was fixing to cook over that fire. I saw on a table they had onion and potato. They's fixin' to have a feast. I saw we ride back in there right now. I want that supper."

"You saw it yourself," Chess put in. "The only one of 'em that'll fight is that guide. They's three of us and one of him. Bill's right. We should go right now and take everything they've got that we want. Including that venison."

The men left out of the cottonwood grove and rode east until they were down below a hill and out of sight, only the distant table rock visible from their location.

Mickey Hogg was a killer, no doubt, but he was a close-in killer. His victims sat across a table from him, or

276

stood in a room with him. Often as not, they had their backs turned when he dropped the hammers on the scattergun. He wasn't the type of man to face another man in a stand up fight, and certainly not with rifles. He did not like his chances if they rode back at the campsite in daylight.

"We could turn around and ride back there right now, but you'd better believe that guide is standing watch with that Hawken rifle," Mickey said. "If he sees us again, he ain't foolish enough to let us ride up to their camp. He'll shoot one, maybe two of us before we ever get close. But if we wait until dark, we can sneak in there through the cottonwoods. He'll never see us coming. If we're lucky, we can catch him asleep."

Pawnee Bill was trying to find shade behind his horse, squatting down some behind its neck. He took a long drink from his canteen, more water than he'd taken at once in many days.

"I am damn glad to have that water," Bill said.

Mickey had already left off the water for the last bit of whiskey in his bottle. "I'll be damn glad if they've got whiskey in one of them wagons."

"Leave the women untouched," Pawnee Bill said. "I've been too long without a woman. They's enough of them there for all of us to have one to ourselves if we don't kill them."

Mickey spat at the ground and took another drink. He wiped his mouth on his sleeve.

"We'll get the women, don't you worry about that," Mickey said. "But if we don't kill that guide right away, it'll be a trouble for us."

"Don't you worry about him," Chess Bowman

said. "It'll be a pleasure to kill him after what he done to Dick."

"Now, when we rode out of that camp, I took a good look around. The emigrants is all camped up by their wagons. I saw bedrolls and tarpaulins hanging over by the wagons. But I also saw a pannier sitting off by itself. I'd wager good money that will be the pack that belongs to the guide. When we go in tonight, you two follow me, and I'll lead you right to him."

The three men attempted to sleep, but the baking sun and the heat made it impossible. So they dozed on the ground.

Pawnee Bill found small relief in the wind, hot though it was, but Mickey Hogg despised the wind because it kicked up sand in his eyes and teeth. For Chess Bowman, none of it mattered. He did not care about violating women. Chess Bowman was miserable, but a sense of fate had come over him ever since he shot Dick Derugy. Chester was convinced, now, that this trail would never end, that they would never reach a destination, and somehow everything left in life would have to be lived here in the desert.

-28-

Amos Cummings was frightened.

Those men that Rab Sinclair called "killers" and "ruffians" had pulled triggers and attempted murder. Amos still could not believe that after he let them get water from the spring they still would have tried to kill him and Rab Sinclair.

So he ordered that two people keep watch at all times through the night, breaking the watch up into three shifts.

He even set aside his anger at Rab and discussed the possibility of leaving in the night again. But the young guide said it was impossible.

"The animals need the rest," Rab said. "They need another day here at the springs, under the cottonwoods, with decent grass for grazing."

"And if those men come back?" Amos Cummings asked.

"We'll have to do what we can."

Amos Cummings put no more restrictions on what means could be used against the men. He armed the night watch with hunting rifles, and those who were not staying awake to keep watch got into their bedrolls, every man and woman with deep concerns.

Rab Sinclair gathered up this things and moved out into the grassy clearing where the animals were picketed. His concern was that Mickey Hogg and the others might try to drive off the oxen and mules. He laid out his bedroll near Cromwell, trusting the horse to alert him if anyone approached.

Matthew and Jeremiah took the first watch of the evening.

They set up lanterns throughout the camp to make it easy to see if someone came within the camp. Rather than sit in one place, the boys carried hunting rifles and walked around the camp. Rab Sinclair instructed them to always be sure that they could see each other, and if someone approached them the important thing was to get off a shot, even if the shot went into the ground or straight into the air. The noise of the gun, he said, was more important than striking a target because the noise of the gun would wake the rest of the camp.

Near the animals, Rab was farther away than he would have liked. If a rifle shot woke him, he would be some vital seconds getting to the camp. But protecting the livestock was as important as protecting the people. If the ruffians drove off the mules and oxen, the people would all be dead just the same. They could never walk out of this desert.

Awake and unable to sleep, Rab looked through the darkness of the cottonwoods to the lights around the camp. As he watched, he could see Matthew and Jeremiah patrolling around the campsite.

Rab was opposed to leaving lanterns lit through the night, but Amos Cummings insisted on it. The memory of his wife's capture weighed on him. Amos viewed the light as a protection and did not give thought to the way it would help their enemies. Rather than coming into the camp blind, Mickey Hogg and Pawnee Bill and Chess Bowman would have the benefit of seeing everything they needed to see.

Thirty minutes turned into an hour and an hour into two. Exhaustion overtook fear, and those in the camp who had trouble sleeping began to drift off at last.

Rab dozed, the way he did when he was in the saddle and exhaustion came over him. He was not fully asleep, but he was resting all the same.

So when Cromwell snorted, Rab was immediately awake.

He did not move, but he heard the noise of a person walking among the nearby cottonwoods. The person was taking great care to keep quiet.

Rab felt the grip of his Colt Dragoon and he slid it under his thigh to mask the sound of him thumbing back the hammer to full cock. Then he slid the heavy Colt out of the blanket so that it would not be hampered when he needed to raise and fire the gun. With his free hand, Rab found the grip of his big Bowie knife, tucked inside its scabbard beside his bedroll. He silently slid it part way out so that he could easily fling off the scabbard.

And now he waited as the soft footsteps got closer.

Cromwell blew again. One of the other horses,

Rab thought it was the buckskin, snorted and became restless.

A hoot owl somewhere among the trees let out its lonely call, and Rab eased the hammer back down on the Dragoon.

"Rachel?" Rab whispered into the night.

"How did you know?" Rachel asked, her voice barely audible. She was still trying to find her way to him, but the moonlight illuminated the shadow of the horses, and she knew Rab would be bedded down near Cromwell.

"What are you doing?" Rab asked, sitting up. "Your father will have a conniption fit if he catches you here with me."

Rachel felt her way over to Rab's bedroll, and she sat down on the blanket. She put her arms around his neck and she kissed his face.

"I had to come and see you," she whispered. "After those men came today, my mother asked me if I intended to stay in Santa Fe with you. Did you say something to my father about it?"

"I told him how it was with us," Rab said. "If you have not changed your mind."

"I have not changed my mind," Rachel said.

"I thought you father should know so that he can make peace with you before we get to Santa Fe."

"I believe he is having a softening of his opinions," Rachel said. "He said he would like to speak to me tomorrow. And then my mother came and asked me my intentions. I told her I intend to marry you in Santa Fe."

"And how did your mother take that news?" Rab

asked.

He could tell, not because he could see her so well in the moonlight, but from the sound of her voice, that Rachel was smiling. "She said she did not blame me and she is not surprised. She asked only that we might consider coming to California to be nearer to them."

"Is that what you would want?" Rab asked. "To go to California?"

There was a pause. Then she answered, "Not right away, but maybe one day."

"There is a danger that those men might come back to our camp tonight," Rab said. "It's a real danger. You should not have risked coming over here."

Rab didn't say it, but he also was concerned that Rachel's brothers were on watch, yet she was able to sneak out of the camp.

Rachel ignored him.

"Rabbie, how did you know it was me sneaking over here? How did you know it was not those men?"

"I heard an old hoot owl," Rab said. "He ain't far, just up yonder there in the cottonwoods. If it had been those men sneaking through there, that owl would have flown away. But when I heard him call, he wasn't moving. That's how I knew it was you and not them. Animals can sense what feelings people put off. If people are planning something bad, the animals can sense that. So they flee. But that old hoot owl, he knew you weren't up to no good. So he just sat his limb and called out. If it had been them ruffians, he'd have screeched and gone darting off through the woods to find a safe place. When you're in the woods at night, if you'll be quiet and listen, you can hear all these things."

They stayed together for some time, whispering to each other about the things that young lovers will talk about. Mostly they dreamed of how it would be when they were married. Rachel told Rab that she wanted to have six children.

"I want four boys and two girls," she said. "First I want a son so that he can be the head of the siblings, and he can protect the younger ones. And then two daughters so that they can help when their baby brothers are born. And we must have two girls, because a girl needs a sister."

"You ain't got a sister," Rab said.

"That is how I know that a girl needs a sister. I would very much have liked to have had a sister close to my own age while I was growing up. And once we have the two girls, then we can have the other three boys. And they'll have you and their older brother to help raise them into strong men."

"The older son won't have anybody close," Rab said. "Maybe it ought to be two boys, then two girls, and then two boys."

"Our oldest son will have you," Rachel said. "He'll go with you everywhere you go and you will teach him all the things. And then when he has little brothers, he can help you teach them. It's how it works best."

"I will trust you on that," Rab said. "And how can we ensure that we're having boys when we're supposed to have boys and girls when we're supposed to have girls?"

Rachel giggled at him. "That's all about what the moon is like at the moment of conception. A full moon is sure to be a boy. And a half moon will be a girl."

"Is that a fact?" Rab asked.

"I don't know," Rachel said. "But we can enjoy testing it."

After some time, Rachel said that she should return to the camp.

"I should go back before they switch out the watch. I told Matthew that I was coming to see you. That's how I got out of the camp so easily, and how I will get back in."

"You should stay here," Rab said.

"Oh, Rabbie, I want to, but it will only infuriate my father all over again."

"I mean it's not wise to go back now. Those men could be making a move on us. I don't want you getting caught out between here and there."

"I have to go back," Rachel said. "I will be careful."

"Then I'll go with you," Rab said.

Rachel laughed. "You're too worried. I will be fine."

She stood up and Rab started to stand with her. But Rachel put a hand on his shoulder to push him back down.

"You stay here," she said. "You have to keep a watch on the animals. I am only walking from here back to the camp, just through those trees. I can see the camp the whole way."

Rab twitched his lips. He thought it was a mistake to let her go back by herself.

"You should stay with me," he said.

"I'll be fine," Rachel said, and her voice was more than a whisper. "Besides, I still have the knife you gave me."

She touched the handle of the knife to show him that she had it on her belt.

And now Rab relented. "Go quickly, and quietly. If you hear something or see something, shout to me. Use that knife if you have to."

Rachel kissed him on the top of his head and then turned and walked back toward the camp. She went just as softly as she had come.

Rab leaned back on one of his elbows and, as far as he could see it, he watched her shadow among the cottonwoods. He felt very tired, but he knew he could not get a decent sleep. He could doze off, but if he felt himself falling asleep he would have to get up and walk around. Protecting the animals was crucial.

Rab thought the whole thing through carefully before he picked his bed. If it was him

Rachel picked her way slowly. The lights from the campsite gave her a clear view of her destination, but among the trees it was hard to see anything that was near. She had to place her feet carefully so that she did not turn an ankle on a loose branch or step into a hole.

As she got closer to the campsite she saw Matthew. He was not much more than a silhouette against the lanterns hung around the camp, and she could not see him clearly. But she recognized the way he walked. She thought how independent Matthew had become on this trip – taking charge of the animals, acting as the guide on the Trail when Rab Sinclair rode ahead to check for water crossings or dangers or rode behind to check the back trail. Matthew, even more than Jeremiah, had grown up these last few weeks. He even carried himself differently – bigger, stronger looking, more sure of himself.

She stopped and watched for a moment, admiring her brother. If she suggested it, she thought he might stay with them in Santa Fe. She smiled as she thought of how her father would respond if she made the recommendation. Her father would object, but it would be so good for Matthew. And Rabbie liked Matthew. Rab treated him like a little brother.

When she saw the other shadow, the movement in the lantern light, Rachel thought it was Jeremiah, also keeping watch with Matthew. She knew their watch would end soon and she needed to get back to the camp before anyone else was awake. It would be a humiliation if someone else – Stuart or Graham, who had the next watch – fired a rifle to waken everyone just because they heard her coming in the darkness.

Rachel realized, though, that she did not recognize the movement of the man. He was taller, lankier than Jeremiah. She tried to make the silhouette fit the frame of her Uncle Stuart, thinking maybe he was awake and ready to relieve Matthew on watch. But it was also not Uncle Stuart. Nor was it Graham Devalt.

The gleam of the knife was what gave her to know that the second silhouette she saw was danger.

The reflected light on the blade of the knife came up from behind Matthew in a flash, just as a hand grabbed him from behind, covering his mouth. The knife slid in sickening violence across her brother's throat, and Matthew dropped to his knees.

Rachel felt herself go weak. Her voice caught in

her throat as she dropped to her knees.

There was a man inside the campsite, and he had just cut Matthew's throat.

She found her voice and called out, "Rabbie!" But the sound was insufficient. Fear, a terrible terror, left her paralyzed. She couldn't make her voice louder.

She watched the silhouette move away from Matthew, searching out Jeremiah. Where was he? And then she saw him, struggling, fighting with another man. Jeremiah's rifle exploded, a flash and a boom.

Rachel found her voice and her legs all at one time. "Rab!" she screamed, and the scream cut through the cottonwoods.

She turned back toward the animals and shouted again, "Rabbie Sinclair! They are in the camp!"

Then Rachel remembered the knife on her belt. She drew it from the scabbard and started to run through the cottonwoods.

She could see up ahead that there was chaos. The rifle shot had awakened the rest of the camp.

People were screaming. Voices that Rachel recognized were shouting. A gunshot exploded, and then another, enormous sounds that made Rachel flinch even as she ran to them. She did not know if Rab Sinclair was coming behind her, but she trusted that he would be.

"Go to Matthew," Rachel shouted, hoping that if she could get someone to him that he would not die.

She ran hard, blind to everything around her except the light of the camp. Even as it came nearer, she could not see anything other than movement – lots of movement – and she realized that the camp was no clearer to her because her eyes were full of tears.

"Someone please go to Matthew," she yelled again.

Another shot from a gun, and then another. And then a loud explosion, another gunshot but so much louder than the others. And more screaming filled her ears.

The whole camp was movement and violence. People were shouting and crying out.

Rachel ran into a low branch, and it hit her in the face like a club. She staggered backwards, stunned from running into the branch, and she dropped the knife Rab had given to her.

She started to bend over to pick it up, and then decided to abandon it. She had to get to her family and try to help.

Rachel broke into the clearing, now just ten yards from the nearest wagon. She was in the light. She stopped running and wiped the tears from her eyes and tried to focus on what was happening in front of her.

A man was mounted on a horse. He had a revolver in his hand and was holding a woman sprawled over the back of the horse. He fired a shot into a crowd of people – people Rachel recognized – and then the man galloped away, following the clear trail between the trees that they had used to bring the wagons in close to the spring.

There were still two strangers inside the camp.

Jeremiah was swinging his rifle like a club, trying to bash one of the men, but he was crouched in a fighting stance, dodging the swinging rifle. The other man was trying to get his horse under control to mount up and get away.

Rachel started toward the man fighting with Jeremiah, but a heavy push from behind knocked her to the ground.

She struggled to get to her feet and realized it was Rab Sinclair. He had knocked her down to keep her from getting closer.

As she watched, the man worked a foot into the stirrup of the startled horse, and he wheeled the horse and rode hard through the campsite, kicking over a camp table as he charged past it.

Rab Sinclair leapt through the air and smashed hard into the man Jeremiah was fighting. The man, Chester Bowman, never saw Rab coming at him.

The two men went down to the ground, and Jeremiah stumbled back. That's when Rachel saw for the first time that Jeremiah's white shirt was stained red and a knife was protruding from his side.

"Jeremiah," she exclaimed, and she pushed herself from the ground and ran to her brother.

Rab was on his feet now, and the other man, too.

"Your friends have gone," Rab said. "Rode out and left you. You'd be wise to run now."

"You killed Dick when you smashed him in the face," Chess Bowman snarled. "I ain't come here to leave. I come here to kill you."

Chess Bowman had no weapon. His knife was in Jeremiah Cummings' side and his six-shooter was lost in the scuffle. Rab Sinclair had both knife and six-shooter.

"You ain't going to do that," Rab said. "Best thing

for you would be to get up on that hawss over there and ride on out of here."

Chester Bowman answered by charging at the young guide, closing the distance between the two of them and swinging a heavy fist at Rab's face. The fist caught Rab on the jaw and staggered him. He stumbled backwards and for a moment he was stunned, a deafening ringing in his ears and a senseless in his mind.

Rab stumbled a bit, and Chess saw an opportunity. He swung again, this time catching Rab in the nose. The punch landed light, not much more than a glancing blow, but it started Rab's nose bleeding furiously.

At the sight of the blood, Chess believed he had landed a heavy blow and he now looked for a weapon. All he found was a broken leg from the camp table knocked over by Mickey Hogg's horse when he made his escape. Chester leapt for the broken table leg and swooped it up in his hand, turning quickly so that he would be prepared to parry an attack.

Now Rab's senses were coming back to him. He wiped some of the blood away from his mouth, and seeing his hand covered in his own blood Rab assumed he must have been hit harder than he realized. Now Chess Bowman was coming at him again, the table leg reared back to use as a club. Rab slipped his knife from its scabbard and used it to block the club when Chess swung.

Rab stabbed at Chester and missed, and then he felt the table leg smash into his shoulder. The blow knocked him to the ground and he dropped the knife.

Chester flung the table leg at Rab, who was now sprawled on the ground. He darted for the knife, and scooping it up believed he had won. He turned to come at Rab with the knife, but the young guide slid the Colt Dragoon from its holster. Without hesitation, he raised it up, drawing back the hammer with his thumb, and shot into Chester Bowman's stomach as the border ruffian came at him with the knife.

The bullet smashed a hole into Chess's gut, but his momentum carried him onward, and Rab saw the knife aimed at him as Chester fell forward.

Rab rolled out of the way, and when Chester hit the ground, Rab rolled back, smashing his elbow into Chester's back.

The young guide got to his knees and straddled Chester, pinning him to the ground. Rab pushed his knees into Chester's arms, holding him there so that the knife was useless. Rab punched Chester hard in the back of the neck, and when the wounded man turned loose of the big Bowie knife, Rab picked it up and plunged it into Chester's right shoulder, twisting the knife to cut the shoulder and disable it. The right arm under Rab's knee went limp. Rab stabbed Chester in the other shoulder.

Chester screamed out both times, and the realization that he was dead overtook him. With foul oaths, he cursed Rab Sinclair and swore that Pawnee Bill would get revenge.

Rab Sinclair stood up, dizzy from the punches but victorious in the fight. He found a canteen and poured water on his face to try to clear his mind, and then he addressed the violence before him.

-29-

The light from the lanterns exposed the ghastly pageant of murder that had taken place in the campsite.

Matthew was dead, his throat cut in vicious fashion. His body was grotesque, crumpled to the ground and covered in his own blood. The sight of his son sent Amos Cummings into a fit of agony. The father who had come west to save his sons from war now had lost one of them, and he was inconsolable, on his knees beside Matthew's body, sobbing out a prayer and blaming himself for his son's death.

Graham Devalt's body was sprawled at the foot of one of the wagon wheels. Mickey Hogg blasted a barrel from the scattergun into Graham's back as Graham attempted to flee the carnage. The shotgun blast peppered him from the shoulders to the small of his back, and the damage to his body was significant. If he survived the initial blast, it was only for a few moments.

Stuart Bancroft attempted to make a stand to save his sister when Pawnee Bill snatched her by the arm and started dragging her toward his horse. Bill clubbed Stuart with the barrel of his Colt Dragoon, opening up a gash in his forehead that was still bleeding freely. Stuart was conscious but dazed. He was holding himself up against one of the wagons.

"Sit down, Mr. Bancroft," Rab said, taking him by the arm and helping him to the ground. Rab looked quickly for Rebekah Bancroft, but she had run for safety with the children. So Rab took his bandanna and pressed it against Stuart's bleeding head. "Hold this here now. There are others more hurt than you, and I've got to see to them."

Rab guided Stuart's hand to the bandanna. The man's eyes were matted with blood and it was running down his face.

"Lay back on the ground and hold that bandanna there," Rab said, hoping the stunned man could understand him.

Rab turned next to Jeremiah who was on the ground. Rachel was kneeling beside him, holding his head in her lap. Jeremiah was hurt, but Rab thought he would probably live.

Once, when he and his father were living among the Cheyenne, there was a fearsome battle with another tribe. Many warriors were scalped and others suffered terrible wounds from spears and knives. Rab had helped to nurse those who were wounded.

Rachel was sobbing and stroking her brother's hair. Jeremiah struggled to only take shallow breaths, the pain in his side was intense with every breath.

The knife was stuck in Jeremiah's side, but it was not so deep.

Rab used his Bowie knife to hack a small block of wood off the table leg. He hurried over to Rachel and Jeremiah with it.

"Bite down on this," Rab said.

Jeremiah shook his head slightly. "I've been stabbed," he muttered. "So much pain in my side."

"I know," Rab said. "I need you to bite down on this piece of wood."

Rab pushed the wood into Jeremiah's mouth, forcing it between his teeth.

Looking at Rachel he said, "Hold his head."

Gingerly, Rab wrapped his fingers around the grip of the knife, trying not to put any pressure on it until he was ready.

"Bite down hard, now," Rab said. Quick as he could, Rab jerked the knife from Jeremiah's side. His scream of pain was muffled some by the block of wood in his teeth, but he still shouted as the knife slid from his body.

"Hold him," Rab said to Rachel, and he poured water from the canteen into the wound. "I'll be right back."

Rab rummaged through one of the wagons until he found a jar of honey, and he took that back Jeremiah and Rachel. Rab used his own knife and cut Jeremiah's shirt away, exposing the wound. With the knife out of his side, Jeremiah was breathing easier, though he was still in terrible pain. He had already spit the wood from his mouth.

"That's at least some better," he told Rab.

"Pour some of this honey into that wound," he

said. "Pack it in there so that it gets deep. Don't cover it, or if you do, don't press down too hard on it. After some time, maybe half an hour or an hour, it's going to start to run out. That's good, and you want it to do that. When it stops coming out, you pour more honey in there. Then just let him rest. Make him comfortable. He'll be sore, but he'll survive this."

Paul, the youngest of the Cummings sons, was missing. Rab could not see him anywhere. He also did not know what happened to Rebekah Bancroft or the children. He did not think any of them had been taken, but he did not readily see them.

He checked quickly on Stuart Bancroft. He was holding the bandanna against his head and seemed to be coming around some.

"They took Martha," Stuart said.

"I'm aware," Rab told him.

Now he went to Amos Cummings.

Amos was still bent over his dead son, still talking to God and blaming himself.

Rab stepped over to him and put a hand on his shoulder. It was a firm hand. If the man needed comfort over the loss of his son, Rab Sinclair was not there to give it.

"Now ain't the time for mourning, Mr. Cummings. I know you're sore pained, but there's living folks who need you to do things now. You can mourn when those things that need doing are done. Stand up and lend me a hand."

Amos Cummings did not argue, but in a daze he struggled up to his feet. His legs felt as if he would collapse.

"Your son Paul is gone," Rab said. "I cannot find him. I also do not know what happened to Mrs. Bancroft and her children. Mr. Devalt is dead and Mr. Bancroft and Jeremiah are both hurt. I need you to take one of those lanterns and go toward the spring. I'm guessing that's where Mrs. Bancroft took her children. Call for her and bring her back here. But when you bring her back, take her around the other way so that she and the children do not see Matthew's body."

"Where is Martha?" Amos Cummings asked. "They killed our son."

"Yes, sir," Rab said. "They did. And they hurt Jeremiah, and I don't know what happened to Paul. Do you understand me?"

Amos Cummings had a blank look on his face – a mixture of shock and sorrow.

"Where is Martha?" he asked again.

"Mr. Cummings, they rode off with your wife," Rab said. "And that's why I need you to get yourself together now."

In spite of the carnage, Rab Sinclair was calm. His easy way of talking did not give way to the panic that had swept over the rest of the party. But his patience with Amos Cummings was being tested.

"I understand you're upset. I need you to get together and go find Mrs. Bancroft."

Still, Amos Cummings looked at Rab with a blank stare.

"This is my fault," Amos Cummings said. "It was my idea to come west. Matthew is dead because of me."

Rab slapped Amos Cummings across the face.

"Listen to me," Rab said, and there was anger in his voice. "You get yourself together. I know you're suffering, but them that's alive need tending to, and you're the only one I've got who can tend to them. Get the lantern like I told you and go find Mrs. Bancroft and those children. Do it now."

The slap was what got his attention and broke the spell that had taken hold of Amos. He nodded.

"I will go and find them," he said. "You think they're near the spring?"

"Go and look for them there," Rab said.

Rab put the lantern in Amos's hand and put his hand in the older man's back to prod him along, away from the body of his son. Rab found a blanket and covered the body. It disturbed him to see Matthew like that.

He took down another lantern and took one last look at his charges. He felt a weight of responsibility for them, in part because he accepted that the blame fell on his shoulders, regardless of what Amos Cummings believed.

There were two clear paths leading from the spring through the cottonwoods, paths created many years ago that allowed the wagon trains to get near to the spring. Hundreds of American emigrants and Spanish explorers had camped here, and before them many thousands of Indians. It was still a favorite spot for the tribes that Rab Sinclair knew. Not long ago, the Arapaho had fought a terrible battle in the area of the Point of Rocks, and for more than a week they celebrated their victory at the spring. White settlers had come upon them and were terrified to find them here, but the Arapaho invited the emigrants to join them in their celebrations. It was an incident still talked about up and down the Trail. But there had also been attacks on settlers here, going back to the first years that the Trail was in use.

Like so many other places, the Point of Rocks seemed to attract and hold death. A fresh spring at the edge of a desert, men came here in search of life. But some men walked with evil in their hearts. Rab Sinclair knew this was true. And evil men at a place of death will hear the call of violence from the spirits that haunt the place. They are lured by that call and made drunk in their lust for wickedness.

Pawnee Bill and Mickey Hogg were two such men, and Rab Sinclair knew what they were when he first saw them. They were possessed, both of them, with a lust for wickedness. Mickey Hogg was a cruel man who reveled in blood. He dealt death wherever he went. Pawnee Bill was no different, but the death he dealt was a means to satisfying his foul lechery.

These were all things that Rab Sinclair knew because he had judged these men at first sight and understood what they were. In judging them, he knew also what their sentences must be. And he knew that he would never reach Santa Fe without executing those sentences. Yet he had allowed himself to be restrained by Amos Cummings, by a misplaced sense of righteousness that could exist only in a place where men are civil and abide by agreed upon rules of conduct. But there was no law in this place, and righteousness belonged to the man who could walk away.

No act was immoral in a place where simply surviving was the only honorable deed.

"I should have shot them men when they was caught out crossing the Arkansas River," Rab Sinclair said to himself as he followed the path out of the cottonwoods. This was the way they had come, Rab knew because he had seen them both ride away. But by lantern light he could find no tracks, even among the cottonwoods where the ground was softer.

He walked well out into the grassland, searching for something that might show him the way. But there was nothing he could see, until at last his light fell on a crumpled form on the ground.

"Miss Cummings?" he asked out loud, and the sound of his voice made the form jump. It was Paul, the youngest of the Cummings boys.

"They took her," Paul said. "They rode off with my mother. I ran as far as I could to try to catch them."

"You come a long ways, boy," Rab said. In years, they were not so distant. Paul was about sixteen years old, maybe fifteen. Just five years younger than Rab. But somehow the boy seemed like a little child to him, and Rab felt a need to comfort him like a father would comfort a child. "Come on back now. We'll hunt for your mother at dawn. They's other work now that we need to do. We need to see about Jeremiah and your pa, and we need to bury Matthew."

The forest of cottonwoods followed the Dry Cimarron for many miles to the west, all the way into Colorado Territory and the rocky hills and valleys leading into the lower mountains. Farther to the west, the Dry Cimarron had water. If the terrain were not impassible for wagons, it would have been the better route to Santa Fe. A person could follow the Cimarron and have an abundance of water. But the rocky mesas and steep, narrow draws made it an impossible road. So the Santa Fe Trail dropped south and west through the desert where water remained scarce.

Rab Sinclair's instinct was that Pawnee Bill and Mickey Hogg, mounted on horses and lacking provisions, would stay along the edge of the cottonwoods, keeping to the river valley.

After finding Paul and taking him back to the campsite where Amos Cummings had already returned with Rebekah Bancroft and her children, Rab wrapped Matthew's body in a blanket. He put the body on a horse and took it to the top of the cliff overlooking the Dry

Cimarron valley. Here at the top of the Point of Rocks, Amos Cummings helped Rab Sinclair dig a shallow grave for his son. They buried Graham Devalt beside him, though Rab felt less about that than once when he'd buried a dog that followed him around. Rab had seen no decency in Graham Devalt, though he knew the man was outside of his place.

"Matthew was a fine man," Rab said to Amos as the first bit of morning light touched the sky above them. They had piled rocks over the grave. "He took to them animals well and cared for them in a way that earned my respect. That may not mean much in a town or at a university, but out here it's all a man can be asked to do."

"My sons are everything to me," Amos said. His voice caught in his throat, but he'd cried out all the tears he had to give. Rab Sinclair had never before seen a grown man sob so freely, and he was not sure how to think about it. But he felt sorrow for the man. "I brought them here to protect them, and now I have lost one of them."

"We need to see about your wife," Rab said, broaching the subject carefully.

"I do not know what to do," Amos said. "I must rely on you."

"Wait here at the spring," Rab said. "Tend to your wounded. Jeremiah is hurt bad and needs to rest. Mr. Bancroft is not well, either, though he'll recover soon enough. You have food and water to last you a month here. If another wagon train comes through, which is doubtful, you should join up with them and go on to Santa Fe. And then stay there and wait. I will go and find your wife, Mr. Cummings. I cannot promise what those men will do, and I cannot promise you that she will be alive. You should be prepared for that. They are vicious men."

Amos choked back a sob, staring out into the darkness of the valley below them. "You think she is dead?"

"I think those men are bad men, Mr. Cummings," Rab Sinclair said. "And there's only one way to know if she is still alive."

In the light of the lantern at their feet, Rab could see Amos Cummings working out everything in his mind.

"If you find them, you will kill those men. Won't you?"

Rab reached into his pocket and took out his tobacco and pipe. He struck a match and lit the pipe and smoked it for a moment. He had to choose his words.

"They are bad men, Mr. Cummings," Rab said. "They need to be killed. What they've done to your family they will do to others. Have done to others. I ain't a lawman and don't care to act like one. But I believe in doing what's right. I should have killed them already. There's a reason that fourth man didn't do no harm to your family last night. If I'd done for all of them, young Matthew there would be seeing to the animals about now."

"I stood in your way," Amos Cummings said. "I stopped you from doing the thing you knew you should do."

Rab blew out a stream of gray smoke that quickly mixed into the darkness and disappeared.

"I'm my own man. I make my own decisions, and I make my own mistakes. You didn't cause me to do one thing or another. If I picked the wrong path, that's not on your conscience. I'm just sorry you have to suffer. When those men were crossing the Arkansas I had them caught out in front of me. I should have shot them down there and then."

The two men took the horses that carried the bodies up to the Point of Rocks and descended back down into the valley where the wagons and the rest of the party were.

Rab gave out instructions quickly. He told Paul to care for the animals. He showed Rachel how to treat Jeremiah's wound.

"Mr. Bancroft, are you able to think right?" Rab asked.

"My head is pounding, but I can think right."

"I want you to take charge of this wagon train." He said it in front of Amos and all the others. "Mr. Cummings is suffering powerful loss, and his wife is missing. He doesn't need to be making decisions for the group. I am leaving to go and find Mrs. Cummings and bring her back here. I do not know how long it will take. Those men have a big jump on me, and they are lost and foolish. Lost and foolish men are more difficult to trail than men who know what they're doing. If you leave out of here on your own, you'll die in the desert. If you have to, you can survive the winter here, but I'll be back before that becomes necessary. Make sure the animals are always ready to go, and keep your water casks full. That way, you can pack and leave quickly if you have to.

"If another wagon train comes along, join up with them and go to Santa Fe. If you're not here when I get back I will come there looking for you. Keep your guns loaded and be prepared to defend yourselves, either against Indians or emigrants. If you encounter only men with no women and children, do not go with them and do not trust them. If you encounter a wagon train with women and children present, going with them is better than waiting for me."

Rab looked to Amos Cummings.

"Do you have any argument with doing what Mr. Bancroft tells you?"

"I'll do what he tells me," Amos Cummings said. "I am a humbled man."

"Mr. Bancroft, walk with me to my hawss," Rab said.

In private, away from the others, Rab said, "Your biggest fear in this place is that Indians will come."

From his saddlebag, Rab took out a carved pipe. It was longer and more elaborate than the pipe he usually smoked.

"If you encounter Indians, show them this pipe. There is some small chance that they will know it is mine, and it will be some protection for you. If you show them this pipe and they threaten you, stand tall and do not show any fear. If they attack you, fight back and kill them in any way that you can. Indians are quick to cut their losses. They don't fight to the last. But if you see that you will be overwhelmed, understand that what comes next will be terrible death. Some men would kill their families and themselves before allowing Indians to take them."

"I could never do any such thing," Stuart Bancroft said.

Rab Sinclair nodded. "I understand that sentiment. If they take you, you'll find that killing your wife and children and killing yourself would have been far easier than what you were left to endure. That look of fear on your face right now is the one I'm talking about. Don't show Indians that look."

Stuart Bancroft swallowed hard. "It is an unpleasant conversation."

"It could be an unpleasant conversation with them Indians, too," Rab said. "We'll hope it don't come to that. It's on you, now, to keep this camp in order. Find work for everyone to do. Especially Mr. Cummings. It's easy in a camp to start to think too much. Nobody needs to come behind me. They won't make it. Nobody needs to wander off for Santa Fe. They won't make it. If you have to, every day make everyone who can put leads on the horses and walk them around to graze them. Anything that keeps them busy. Hunt for elk. Empty the casks and refill them. Whatever jobs you can find. Just keep everyone busy."

"I'll do that," Stuart said.

"Keep that pipe on you, too. If you need it in a hurry you don't want to have to go looking for it."

Rab walked Stuart back to the others, and then he took Rachel by the hand.

"After I find your mother, I'm coming back here. I've buried my pannier. If a wagon train comes along and your uncle says you're to go with them, then go with them. Don't argue or think that you should wait for me. Take that buckskin and that sorrel with you. Ride 'em if you like. They're both good hawsses, and I need you to care for them. Wait for me in Santa Fe."

"Thank you," Rachel said.

"For what?" Rab asked.

"For going after my mother."

Rab nodded. "Look after your pa. He ain't hurt, but his head and his heart are injured. Make him understand he has three children yet to look after. Keep tending to Jeremiah and make him rest and drink water. He will be fine."

"She will be dead when you find her, won't she?"

"I cannot know that," Rab said. "And you cannot know that. But whatever I find, the living have to go on living. You have a whole life. Your father, too. Matthew would not want you to die with him, and if your mother is dead, she would not want you to die with her. Your obligation to them is to keep on with life."

Rachel put her arms around Rabbie Sinclair and held tight to him, squeezing him against her. She put her cheek against his chest. The leather tassels on the back of his buckskin jacket tickled across her arms.

"How long will you be gone?"

Rab continued to hold her. He could have stood there like this with her for the rest of his life, and a part of him wanted to.

"I hope not more than a day or two. They have a jump on me and it may take a while to find them."

"Are you going to kill them?" Rachel asked.

"I am," Rab said.

"Are you afraid?" Rachel asked.

Rab smiled and kissed her hair. He stepped back away from her and put a foot into Cromwell's stirrup. He gave a hop and bounced into the saddle.

"This is just a chore," Rab said, still smiling at her.

"There's nothing about a chore to be afraid of."

Following his instinct, Rab rode west, trailing along with the forest of cottonwoods along the valley of the Dry Cimarron. He rode fast to try to make up ground as it was pointless to look for tracks. But he saw signs along the way that made him believe he was moving in the right direction. He first came to a spot not far from the camp where stakes in the ground and clean, fresh-cut ropes showed that the three ruffians had picketed their horses before attacking the camp and then cut the ropes and led them away in a hurry. He passed by fresh horse droppings. When he saw a discarded canteen he reined in and examined it. The water was fresh and clean. The outside of the canteen was clean. Surely this was dropped in a struggle with Martha Cummings. Rab got back in the saddle and continued on.

"Cromwell, you are in a mood to run today," Rab said out loud to the horse. "A young hawss don't want to be cooped up, even in a pasture up under the cottonwoods with a clear spring nearby."

Rabbie Sinclair wasn't given much to praying for things outside of his control, but he hoped he would find Martha Cummings before nightfall.

"Them men will spend the day on the dodge," Rab told the horse. "But come nightfall they're going to hunker down somewhere. If we don't find Miss Cummings before then, they'll have had at her for sure."

He'd seen what could happen to women who were taken by tribes, beaten and used horribly. Some never got over the shock of it. Martha Cummings was a strong woman. Stronger than her husband. What Pawnee Bill and Mickey Hogg might do to her would probably not break her spirit, Rab thought. But if she fought them, they would likely take what they were after and then kill her. She might easily make herself troublesome to them.

With these concerns in mind, Rab let the horse run.

-31-

A day's ride west of the Point of Rocks there on the north bank of the Dry Cimarron there is a long, green canyon surrounded by two high bluffs that weaves its way up to a spring, and from beyond the spring the canyon continues and narrows and fans out. When the rains come and the water is high, mountain streams will run down to find those narrow channels and combine with the spring to fill the arroyo that runs through the center of the canyon. But in dry times, the spring runs but the stream gives out before it reaches to the Dry Cimarron. The spring is about two miles into the canyon, north of the Cimarron, and near the spring the canyon is thick with cottonwoods. It is a beautiful spot among the rocky foothills, and the water from the spring is fresh and clear. It is not a place where a man expects to find the ravaged and broken body of a brave and beautiful woman.

Rab Sinclair arrived at the canyon on the morning of his second day away from the campsite at the Point of Rocks. He rode throughout the day that first day, but at dusk he had to stop. He had desperately hoped he would find Martha Cummings before nightfall, but when night came he knew he could not go on. In the night, he might easily pass by some track or sign that would lead him in the right direction.

He had to force himself not to think of what sort of night Martha Cummings was enduring.

Early the next morning he mounted and began to ride again, and by mid-morning he spotted the canyon.

The opening to the canyon seemed a natural choice when Rab came upon it. Animals had cut a clear path through the cottonwoods and over the Dry Cimarron leading directly to the mouth of the canyon. The natural trail suggested to Rab that there would be water in the canyon, and knowing that Pawnee Bill and Mickey Hogg had lost a canteen, Rab suspected finding good water would be a priority for them.

He rode Cromwell over the dry riverbed and up to mouth of the canyon. There at the opening, where flood water sometimes poured out into the Cimarron, the slopes on either side were not particularly steep, nor where they very high. Cottonwoods sprang up here and there along the slopes. The canyon curved just beyond the mouth, and from there it stretched straight back for half a mile. In the middle of the canyon, in the bed where a stream sometimes ran, there was a solitary cottonwood. Rab rode toward the lone tree, keeping a watch for any movement. There were few places in the canyon to hide, no crevices in the walls nor large boulders where a man might seek shelter.

Rab rode past the cottonwood tree, and beyond it the canyon bent hard one way and then the other and disappeared around the bend. Here the walls were steeper. Rab rode slowly. The Hawken rifle stayed in its scabbard, but he slipped his Colt Dragoon from its holster and let it rest across his lap as he walked Cromwell, the reins loosely held in one hand.

He worked his way through the bends in the canyon and again came to a place where it ran straight for some distance. The canyon was wide, fifty or sixty feet wide in most places, and deeper into the canyon there was a thick stand of cottonwoods growing up out of the dry stream bed. The grass around the cottonwoods was thick. Rab knew that the vegetation proved there must be a spring at that spot, but the canyon continued on deeper past the cottonwoods. There had to be other springs farther along, or streams higher up that fed into the canyon and helped to carve it away over the centuries.

When he arrived at the running water of the spring, Rab dismounted and left Cromwell to drink.

His intention was to look for signs among the trees or in the grass that Pawnee Bill and Mickey Hogg had camped here with Martha Cummings the night before.

But he drew back in shock when he saw the body under the canopy of the trees.

She was stripped. Her face and body were bruised and bloody, showing that the two men had beaten her. Rab saw the evidence, too, that they had defiled her.

His heart sank at the sight of her.

"Ma'am, I am sorry to you that I could not catch you up in time to prevent this," Rab said.

Rab cut away the canvas from his bedroll and wrapped her body in it. He could not bury her here, in the spring canyon, because a flood would wash away the body. He would spare her one last indignity by finding a decent place to bury her.

He searched around the area for tracks that might indicate which way Pawnee Bill and Mickey Hogg had gone.

"Finding Miss Cummings was just one of our chores," Rab told the horse. "We've still got work to do to finish what we came out here for."

He found hoof prints in the damp soil near the small stream that came from the spring. The prints were a mess, indicating that the horses had been picketed here overnight. Rab counted at least four horses. After some time, he discovered tracks that convinced him Mickey Hogg and Pawnee Bill had ridden out of the canyon.

"All right old hawss, I hope you're ready for a run," Rab said to the roan, patting his black face. He took a look at the canvas wrapped body. "I'll come back for you, ma'am."

He swung himself into the saddle, and horse and rider bounded back down the canyon and out into the valley of the Dry Cimarron.

He knew the men had not gone back east, or he would have passed them, so he held the reins lightly and let Cromwell run at will off to the west, toward the rocky mesas and rough country that gave a traveler to know he was coming nearer to the great mountain range in Colorado Territory.

He rode west, following along beside the river valley, all the rest of that day and the next. He still saw occasional sign that Pawnee Bill and Mickey Hogg were somewhere ahead of him. He found their tracks at springs where he stopped. He found the remnants of a campfire and an empty can of beans.

Though he had seen the tall mesas rising on the horizon in front of him, it seemed that the landscape changed quite suddenly. He left behind the flat, wide open expanse of the desert grassland and was in among the rocky mesas they led directly to the Sangre de Cristo Mountains of Colorado Territory. By late afternoon on the second day, with the sun already dipping behind the rising mesas, Rab Sinclair rode through rough and hilly country dotted with gambel oak and large rock outcroppings.

Rab was considering stopping for the day as Cromwell picked his way along through the rocky terrain beside a tall mesa shooting straight up into the sky, but it was at that moment that Rab smelled smoke.

He pulled the reins on the horse. "Whoa, boy," Rab whispered. He took another deep breath through his nose. There was no question, he smelled smoke on the air.

Rab slid out of the saddle and tied a long lead, staking it into the ground in a place where Cromwell would have room to find both shade in the shadow of the mesa and grass to eat. He removed the horse's saddle. Cromwell was noticeably miffed that he wasn't getting rubbed down after a long day of riding.

Then he drew out his Hawken rifle from its scabbard and took up his old possibles bag with balls and gunpowder for both the Hawken rifle and the Colt.

"I'll be back, Cromwell," Rab said to the horse, stroking his neck. "I'm off to get what we've come all this way to find."

***

The mesa rose up in terraced slopes, and it was easy for Rab to climb one slope to the next until he reached the jagged, vertical outcropping that topped the tiers of the base of the mesa. He crouched low, hoping to avoid being seen, and tried to move from one scrub oak to the next to hide his movement.

As he climbed higher he lost, and then found again, the scent of the smoke. From the higher vantage point he could not see any sign of the men he was seeking, so he worked his way around to get a look at the other side of the mesa. And there, hiding themselves in a small canyon between two large rocky outcroppings, Rab found Pawnee Bill and Mickey Hogg. They were sitting beside a small campfire. They had a skinned rabbit on a spit over the campfire. They had four horses picketed outside of their campsite.

Hanging would have been his preference, but there were no good trees in the valleys between the mesas.

Rab saw no point in ceremony. There were two of them and one of him. He did not come all this way for a fair fight. He came here to kill these men. So he cocked back the hammer on the big Hawken rifle and pulled the rear trigger to set the front trigger. He picked out his target carefully. When he was sure his shot would tell, Rab gave just a touch the front trigger. The Hawken cracked its thunderous boom and a small cloud of white smoke drifted in front of Rab's eyes so that he could not clearly see. But he did not need to see to know what he'd done.

Mickey Hogg screamed in terror when the fifty-caliber lead ball smashed into his abdomen. He flung forward, knocking over the rabbit they'd intended or dinner and falling into the fire. The coals of the fire burned him, and Mickey hollered all the more. Pawnee Bill ducked down beneath a rock. Unwilling to break cover, he kicked Mickey Hogg out of the fire and onto his back. Mickey's clothes were singed and burned through in some places, and his exposed arms were burned badly.

"Bill, I'm shot!" Mickey called out. "He's done for me, Bill. I'm dying here."

Rab poured out a measure of powder into the gun and rammed another fifty-caliber ball down the barrel. He placed a percussion cap on the nipple and raised up the beavertail stock to his shoulder. Again, he pulled the rear trigger, the one that set the front trigger and made it a hair trigger pull. Then he looked down the sights for Pawnee Bill.

"Who's out there?" Pawnee Bill called from behind his rock fortress.

Mickey Hogg was roiling in pain, his hands clutching his lower abdomen where the big shot had done sickening damage. The damage was done on purpose. Having seen what they'd done to Martha Cummings, Rab intended to give both men time to consider their imminent death. He could have put that fifty-caliber ball in Mickey Hogg's chest and blown the man's heart right out his back, but Rab's sense of justice was learned from men whose justice earned them the title "savages." Mickey Hogg's wound was fatal, but it would certainly take him hours and it might take days to die of the havoc done to his intestines. Meanwhile, he would suffer the physical pain with the knowledge that the only end for it would be death.

Again Pawnee Bill hollered out from behind the rock where he was hiding. "Is that you Sinclair? Answer me!"

"It is Rab Sinclair. I've come to kill you for what you did to that woman and her family."

"I didn't have nothing to do with none of it. Every bit of it was Mickey Hogg, here, and you've done for him."

"You was there, just the same," Rab said. "I'll be killing you, too."

Mickey Hogg wasn't willing to put up an argument to Pawnee Bill's lie. He was kicking at the dirt with his heels, squirming on his back, and sobbing at the pain.

"Well, I ain't coming out from behind this rock," Pawnee Bill vowed. "Any killing you plan to do from here on you'll have to come down here and do it."

"That's fine," Rab shouted back to him. "I'll be glad to get a closer look at the both of you."

Just over the top of the rock, Rab could see the barrel of a Colt waving back and forth. Pawnee Bill had armed himself, but it would be a small miracle to hit Rab at this distance.

Rab was leaning against the rocky outcropping of the mesa, but he was not really behind it. He had no need of breastwork from his vantage. If Pawnee Bill came out from behind his rock and tried to get off a shot, Rab would have him right away.

"What are my choices here?" Pawnee Bill shouted.

"Damn few," Rab said. "If you like, you can stand up and I'll shoot you where I am. Or you can stay hiding behind that rock and I'll come down there and shoot you."

Pawnee Bill laughed in spite. "You're right. Them ain't many choices. I thought them folks didn't go for killing."

"A man's mind changes pretty fast when he sees his son's throat cut," Rab said. "No one raised an objection to my coming after you."

"Maybe a trial?" Pawnee Bill said. "I'll toss out my gun and ride back for a trial."

"You've had your trial," Rab said. "I done judged you."

"What about my partner, here? What about Mickey? He needs a doctor."

"I could get him a thousand doctors, and none of them could help him. What he needs is a box maker and a preacher. But he'll not get either of those. I intend to leave both of you for the birds and the animals."

"That's a kindness to the birds and animals, I suppose," Pawnee Bill said.

Bill was looking about for any chance of escape. But the horses were well away from the protection afforded by the rocks. He'd have to clear open ground to get to them. And none of them were saddled. Bill knew, too, that he'd never hit the young guide from this distance. A sick feeling overtook him when he realized he was trapped. Even with a gun in his hand he could not fight his way out of this.

"You can't just kill a man like this," Pawnee Bill shouted.

"Ask Mickey Hogg if I can kill a man like this."

Bill did not reply, and at that moment Rab saw that Pawnee Bill had pressed his face against the side of the rock and was inching his head up to try to get a look. Rab took careful aim, and as soon as he saw Pawnee Bill's face appear he touched the trigger on the Hawken. The gun again spit fire and thunder. The ball struck the rock right where Pawnee Bill was trying to get his look, and Bill started screaming. The ricochet of the lead ball sliced across his face, knocking his eye out of the socket.

Pawnee Bill threw down his gun and pressed both hands against his face. Now Pawnee Bill was screaming, and he fell away from the rock, landing on his knees by the campfire.

Rab set the Hawken down against the rock outcropping and hurried down the terraced slopes toward the place where Mickey Hogg and Pawnee Bill were suffering from their wounds. He drew the heavy Colt Dragoon as he went and cocked back the hammer.

He slid down the loose rock and soil of the biggest slope and then hurried down the next one. He pointed the Dragoon at Pawnee Bill in case the man went for his own six-shooter.

Just a few yards away from the rock where Bill had been hiding, Rab broke into a run and jumped out, landing on the big rock that had been Pawnee Bill's protection.

Bill, with his hands covering his eyes, heard Rab but did not see him.

"You've shot my eye out!" Bill shouted.

Rab took careful aim with the Dragoon and shot Bill in the stomach. Pawnee Bill stumbled backwards and he dropped one of his hands to the fresh wound.

319

"I've come for you Bill, to pay you back for all the evil you've done," Rab said.

He sprang from the rock and kicked Pawnee Bill in the knee, dropping the man to the ground. Rab put his own knee into Bill's throat and pulled from its sheath his heavy Bowie knife. With one hand he took Bill by the hair. Pawnee Bill began to scream, begging for mercy, but his pleas mingled with his sobbing, and whatever he said was lost.

Rab slid the knife blade into Bill's hairline and lifted away his scalp while the man sobbed and cried out.

Dying though he was, Mickey Hogg witnessed the horror of Pawnee Bill's final moments, and he began working the fastener on his scattergun, trying to get it undone from his belt so that he could get off a shot.

As the Bowie knife sliced clear and Pawnee Bill's scalp came loose, Mickey Hogg got the shotgun off its swivel rig and tried to find the strength to raise it up. He'd already bled so much and was in such pain, and he felt weak all over. But he did not want to be scalped alive.

Rab Sinclair turned on Mickey Hogg and saw the scattergun in his hand. Rather than try to clear the distance before he could get the hammers cocked and the triggers pulled, Rab kicked his boot through the fire, sending a spray of red hot coals all over Mickey Hogg's face and torso.

Now Rab stepped over the fire and closed the distance between him and Mickey. He grabbed Mickey by the wrist, turning the scattergun away, and swung his Bowie knife as hard as he could into the bend of Mickey's elbow. The knife cut deep and Mickey's arm went limp. The scattergun fell away.

Rab grabbed a handful of Mickey Hogg's hair and took a second scalp.

It was savage justice, maybe, but it was the justice of the land that had come for Mickey Hogg and Pawnee Bill. Rab Sinclair was simply the vessel in which that justice was carried.

"You've both been given what you deserved," Rab Sinclair said over their cries. "Now I'll give you mercy."

He drew the Dragoon and fired a shot into each of their heads, killing them and ending their suffering.

Rab riffled through their belongings until he found a burlap sack he could drop the scalps into. He took the leads of all four horses and walked them around the big mesa, back over to where Cromwell was picketed. Rab had no desire to stay in this place, and even though the sun was nearly set, he saddled the blue roan and pushed the four horses out in front of him. He was three days away from the Point of Rocks and the campsite. He hoped that by the time he arrived he would find the Cummings party had already joined another wagon train and would be on the way to Santa Fe.

-32-

Rab Sinclair buried Martha Cummings beside her son up on the table rock overlooking the Dry Cimarron valley. It seemed right to him that she should be laid to rest in that place.

Though he found that he longed to see Rachel, Rab felt a great relief at returning to the campsite and finding it empty. He did not want people. Not even Rachel. Not yet.

He had seen it done, but Rab Sinclair had never before taken a man's scalp. It was brutal violence to do to a man, and he now regretted having done it. He was driven by an anger he'd never felt before. He had thought if he could not bring back Martha Cummings to her husband and daughter, he could at least bring back the scalps of the men who murdered her. But he knew the gesture would not be appreciated, and he left the scalps in their burlap sack out in the desert.

He did not linger at the Point of Rocks. He camped one night to rest the horses and allow them to drink. He unburied his provisions and put the pannier on one of the horses he'd taken from Pawnee Bill and Mickey Hogg. With five horses he could ride hard for the next few days. He anticipated doing thirty miles a day, even in the heat of the grasslands, and he expected to catch the wagon train before it arrived in Santa Fe.

On his third morning out from the Point of Rocks, Rab caught sight on the distant horizon of a low mound. At first it looked like nothing more than a distant cloud in the place where the sky touched the earth, but after an hour or so its gray form took on a distinct shape, and it might have been a tree. But an hour later of moving and Rab was no closer to it. That was when he was sure that it was Rabbit Ears.

Any traveler along the Cimarron Cutoff longed to see Rabbit Ears Mountain. Emigrants allowed themselves to become convinced that the two high peaks rising out of the desert did resemble a jack rabbit, the lower mound the crouched body and the higher mound the perked ears, but in fact Rabbit Ears Mountain was not named for its appearance but for the Comanche warrior Rabbit Ears who was killed and buried in the vicinity of the mountain. But more important than what it looked like, Rabbit Ears was the landmark that meant the journey was finally ending.

Rabbit Ears meant that the long, wide expanse of the barren plains would soon be broken by mountains and, more importantly, rivers. For those harassed by Indians, Rabbit Ears meant that Fort Union was six days away, four if you had to press it. Knowing the cavalry was so near did much to hearten many a weary and harried traveler.

By the late afternoon of the third day, Rabbit Ears Mountain was in stark relief against the setting sun, and

Rab knew his journey was fast approaching an end.

On the fourth day he passed both Rabbit Ears and Round Mound, putting these first two landmarks since the Point of Rocks at his back.

On the morning of the fifth day, Rab Sinclair watered his horses in the Canadian River.

But now his provisions were all but gone. He was out of flour and coffee and had only a little of the Elk strips left in his saddlebags, and that meat was beginning to turn. It had not smoked long enough to preserve it, so he tossed the last of his food into the Canadian River.

Rather than dropping south directly to Wagon Mound, Rab diverted from the Trail and followed the Canadian River. When he found a likely spot in a valley among the tall mesas, he ran a line in the river and managed to catch a decent sized carp that became his dinner. The river valley also offered better grazing for the horses, and Rab turned them out to allow them opportunity to graze. He camped here two nights.

On the eighth day out from the Point of Rocks, Rab rode up out of the Canadian River valley and made west toward Wagon Mound, the landmark that resembled a high-topped shoe when viewed from the north. There were springs and creeks along the way here. The western horizon was broken with mountains and high ridges and mesas.

Now a sense of peace came over Rab Sinclair.

He had been two weeks without conversation except that which he had with Pawnee Bill or his horses. He'd not seen another living man for two weeks, except the two men he'd killed. He was worried, but not overly so, that he had not yet encountered the Cummings wagon train. If another wagon train arrived within a day or two of when he set out after Martha Cummings, they could be all the way to Wagon Mound by now. What he did not know was that when he left the Trail and followed the Canadian River, he had actually passed them by.

On the ninth morning out from Point of Rocks, just east of Wagon Mound and not far from where he had camped that night, Rab encountered a cavalry patrol on its way to the eastern border of New Mexico territory to confront Comanche raiders who were on the war path there.

The men were rugged veterans, but they were still astonished to find a lone traveler so far off the Trail. The cavalry did not stop, but a captain approached and spoke with Rab.

"You know you're riding through Comanche territory?" the captain asked.

"I was following the Trail and provisions ran out. So I dropped down the Canadian River to do some fishing."

"You see any sign of Injuns?"

Rab shook his head and too advantage of the pause to fill the bowl of his pipe. As he puffed on the pipe he said, "Haven't seen a soul in a few days."

"You packing the trail alone?" the captain asked.

"I was guiding in a wagon train, but we were separated," Rab told him. "About two weeks ago. I'm hoping they joined up with another wagon train and might be waiting for me at Fort Union."

"Coming down the Cimarron Cutoff?" the captain asked.

"That's right."

"Most trains coming down the Cut don't stop at Fort Union, but we haven't seen anyone come from the Cimarron in a month or more."

"How many days out from the fort are you?" Rab asked.

"Just one day. We left yesterday and camped at Wagon Mound overnight. On your own, if you push you can be to the fort today and in Santa Fe in five days."

Rab gave the captain a wave and urged on the horses he was pushing so that he could make the fort before sundown.

***

Rab sold three of the four horses he took off of Pawnee Bill and Mickey Hogg to the army at Fort Union. The wagon train was not there and had not come in and left, so Rab rode on to Santa Fe.

He spent two days searching the town, visiting the hotels and riding out to the camps near the city. Though some wagon trains had come in over the last couple of weeks, no one had seen the Cummings party wagon train or any other group that came through the Cimarron Cutoff.

Rab camped outside of town where he could see the Trail as it curved south around Elk and Bear mountains, the southernmost mountains of the Sangre de Cristo range, that lay to the east of Santa Fe. The Trail dropped southwest from Wagon Mound to circle south of the mountains, and then it curved west and north up to Santa Fe.

When he could find no evidence that the

Cummings party had arrived either at Fort Union or Santa Fe ahead of him, Rab hoped that he had passed the wagon train when he left the Trail and followed the Canada River.

There were few other explanations, and none of them were good. It was unlikely they had been attacked by Indians. Indians would not have taken the wagons. He would have found evidence at the Point of Rocks of Indian attack. The other possibility was that they went on their own without a guide and were lost somewhere in the desert grassland.

His third day at Santa Fe, a stagecoach came in from Las Vegas, just on the east side of Bear Mountain. When he saw the coach coming along the trail, Rab saddled Cromwell and followed the coach into Santa Fe. There he questioned the jehu.

"We passed a wagon train on the way here, not far out of Las Vegas. They'll be in Santa Fe in three days," he said.

Rab returned to his campsite among the pines on a hillside, and he spent the next couple of days resting and wondering how he would tell Rachel about her mother and Amos Cummings about his wife.

Early in the afternoon of the third day, Rab saw them. They had joined a large wagon train with more than a dozen wagons, a real wagon master and a guide. Rab recognized the guide, though he did not know the man by name. The Cummings party had attached itself at the back of the larger train. Stuart drove the front wagon, and Rachel drove the wagon behind him. Amos Cummings was driving the next wagon. Rebekah Bancroft was driving a wagon. Jeremiah looked healthy in the driver's seat of the next to last wagon, and the oldest of the Bancroft boys was driving the last wagon. Paul was driving the livestock by himself, and Rab was glad to see the sorrel and the buckskin both looked healthy.

He had imagined a fond reunion with Rachel. In these days camped on the hillside waiting for the wagon train to come in, Rab thought maybe she would look up from the road and come dashing up the hillside and run into his arms. But she did not look up and see him and she did not dash into his arms. The news he bore was enough to keep him from running down the hillside.

Instead, he watched the wagon train pass. They were nearly done with their journey, but there was work yet to complete. Rab decided not to interfere with that work. Rachel was needed to drive the wagon. They would camp in the flats south of town, only a couple of miles away, and it was enough that he would join her there.

"All right, you old blue hawss," Rab said. "Are you ready to go and see Miss Rachel?"

He did not hurry. He took his time to saddle the blue roan. He could not explain it, but he had a raw feeling about going to her.

He smoked his pipe for a bit and packed his pannier and loaded it on the bay horse, the one he had kept of the four horses he'd taken off the two men. The bay was the best of the horses. It ran along with Cromwell pretty well and never had to be dragged or led. He thought he would probably sell the horse in Santa Fe once he was reunited with the sorrel and buckskin. Those had both turned out to be fine horses, and he would not sell them off.

The pannier packed and Cromwell mounted, Rab descended the hill and followed the road toward Santa Fe. When he crested a hill overlooking the flats, he rode down to where Paul was picketing the animals.

"Rabbie!" Rachel called to him when she saw him, and she tossed down a camp chair she was holding and ran toward him. Rab urged Cromwell forward and galloped the distance, and when he came up to her he leapt from the saddle and scooped her up in his arms at a run.

Rachel's face was bright with a smile, but the smile quickly fell and her expression turned dark as she realized what it meant that Rab was alone.

"My mother?" she asked, and Rab set her down from the embrace and took a step away.

"I was too late getting to her," Rab said.

Amos Cummings saw his daughter's shoulders drop. He saw her fall into Rab Sinclair's arms in a sob, and he knew the answer to the question that had burned in his heart for these past few weeks. Stuart Bancroft saw, too, and knew that his sister was dead. Jeremiah and Paul both went to their father to offer some comfort to him.

"I took her body back to the Point of Rocks, and I buried her there beside your brother," Rab said.

Rachel, crying into his chest, nodded her head. "That was the right thing to do."

She wept a bit longer. Rachel, more than any of the rest, had held onto hope that Martha Cummings would survive. Her hope was in Rabbie Sinclair and her belief that he was invincible in his element.

"Was she dead when you found her?"

"She was."

"I do not want to know any more than that,"

Rachel said. "I do not want to know where you found her or in what condition her body was. You have told me the things I wanted to know. But I have one more question for you. Did you kill those men who did that to her?"

"I did," Rab said, and unbidden the vivid recollection of their screams as he scalped them alive came into his mind.

"Do not tell my father that you killed them," Rachel said. "He is so torn with grief, and I am afraid the guilt would be too much for him."

Rab pressed his lips against Rachel's hair. As he did, she spoke a prayer into his chest, holding him tight in her arms.

"Lord in Heaven, I pray that you take into your bosom the soul of my mother to be with her son, and to be there waiting for her husband and children for the time when we come to join you. She was a kind and beautiful servant to You while she was on this earth, and I pray that she now enjoys her Heavenly reward. And Father, I pray for your servant Amos Cummings, whose soul suffers the loss of this good woman more than we can know. And I pray, too, for Mr. Sinclair. I pray that in Your blood you will wash the sin of blood from his hands, that you will ease his conscience and give him peace that he was Your instrument of judgment on this earth."

It had been many years since anyone had ever prayed over Rab Sinclair, and no prayer he'd ever heard from his Scotch father sounded so tender and heartfelt. And Rab found that through Rachel's prayer there was some easing of the vicious memory.

"I'm obliged to you, Rachel."

-33-

The Cummings party remained in Santa Fe for two weeks. They grieved and they prepared. They bought new provisions and sold two of the wagons. They found a wagon master who was leading a train to California and bought in with him.

Through those two weeks, Rab and Rachel stayed together every day. They walked in the streets of Santa Fe and hiked a short distance up the mountain to the east of the city. They rode Rab's horses out around the town.

But not once did Rachel talk about what it would be like when they were married nor how many children they would have.

The raw feeling Rab had never went away.

The afternoon before the wagon train was set to leave for California, Rachel and Rab rode a trail up along the banks of a narrow mountain stream.

They took with them a picnic for their supper,

and they ate beside the stream in a spot where they were also overlooking the town and the flats where the wagon waited for the next journey to begin.

Rachel was uncommonly quiet, and Rab did not have the voice for words.

They ate with almost no conversation between them. And when they had finished, Rachel took Rab by the hands and looked him in the face.

"I have to talk to you," she said.

"I don't want to hear what you're going to say," Rab said.

"Rabbie, I have to say it."

Her eyes were swollen and red. This journey had brought too much sadness.

Rab twitched his lips. He squeezed her hands and slid his hands out from hers so that he could fish his pipe and tobacco pouch from his pocket.

"Well, if I have to hear it, I'll listen while I have a smoke," he said, and he made some effort to smile at her.

He lit the pipe, and though he held the bowl in one hand, he resumed holding both of her hands in the other.

"I have never known a person like you, not even a little bit like you. And there is nothing about you that I do not love. Your courage and your wisdom. The things you have done and seen and the things you can do. You're like a real life Natty Bumppo. You're wild and scary, but tender and kind. And you are the handsomest man I ever have seen."

Rab blew smoke out the side of his mouth so that it would drift down wind and away from her.

"Those are all nice words, and I'm glad to have them. But I have this raw feeling that ain't what you intend to tell me," Rab said.

"It's so hard to say," Rachel said. "And I want you to know it pains me to say it as much as it pains you to hear it. You must know that. But Rabbie, I cannot stay here in Santa Fe with you."

Rab closed his eyes and nodded his head. "I know that."

"My poor father is heartsick. He has lost a son and a wife. And I have a duty to him. He needs someone to look after him. His faith is shaken, and he is suffering from terrible guilt. He believes all of what has happened was his fault because he brought our family west."

"It ain't enough that he has Jeremiah and Paul to look after him?" Rab asked.

"It's not the same," Rachel said. "My father is hurting, and men are not capable of tending to the injuries of the heart and the pain of the soul in the way that women are. Those are the wounds that need a tender touch, a softness and kindness that will only come from a woman. Surely you understand that. If it had only been Matthew and if my mother was there to care for him, then yes – a thousand times, yes! – I would stay here with you and go with you wherever you go. But he lost the woman who could nurture him back. And poor substitute that I am, I am all he has. My place has to be with my father."

Rab knocked the fire from his pipe and crushed it below his foot. He let go of Rachel's hands and put his hand on the back her head. He pulled her forward slightly and kissed her forehead.

"I should get you back," he said. "You'll need to rest tonight. The train you're with is large enough that you ought not to have to worry about Indians, but you're traveling through Apache country and they can sometimes be unpredictable."

Rab walked over to Cromwell and reached into one of his saddlebags. He drew out an elaborately carved pipe, the one Stuart Bancroft had returned to him.

"Like as not, it won't do no good with Apache. But if you are attacked, and you have the opportunity, show them this pipe. Some among those people know that it belongs to me, and they might let you be because of it."

Rachel took the pipe from his hand and looked at it. It was a beautiful piece of woodworking.

"I don't want to take something that's special to you," Rachel said.

"You already are, Rachel Cummings," Rab said, and though he did not intend it, the words landed sharp and stung Rachel's heart. "You're taking the thing that is most special to me. You might as well have the pipe, too. Maybe one day, if I ever get over to California, I'll see if I can find you to claim it back."

the end

OTHER NOVELS BY ROBERT PEECHER

THE TWO RIVERS STATION WESTERNS: Jack Bell refused to take the oath from the Yankees at Bennett Place. Instead, he stole a Union cavalry horse and started west toward a new life in Texas. There he built a town and raised a family, but he'll have to protect his way of life behind a Henry rifle and a Yankee Badge.

ANIMAS FORKS: Animas Forks, Colorado, is the largest city in America (at 14,000 feet). The town has everything you could want in a Frontier Boomtown: cutthroats, ne'er-do-wells, whores, backshooters, drunks, thieves, and murderers. And there's also some unsavory folks who show up.

JACKSON SPEED: Scoundrels are not born, they are made. The Jackson Speed series follows the life of a true coward making his way through 1800s America – from the Mexican American War through the Civil War and into the Old West. "The history is true and the fiction is fun!"

TRULOCK'S POSSE: When the Garver gang guns down the town marshal, Deputy Jase Trulock must form a posse to chase down the Garvers before they reach the outlaw town of Profanity.

FIND THESE AND OTHER NOVELS BY
ROBERT PEECHER AT AMAZON.COM

ABOUT THE AUTHOR

Robert Peecher is the author of more than a score of Western novels. He is former journalist who spent 20 years working as a reporter and editor for daily and weekly newspapers in Georgia.

Together with his wife Jean, he's raised three fine boys and a mess of dogs. An avid outdoorsman who enjoys hiking trails and paddling rivers, Peecher's novels are inspired by a combination of his outdoor adventures, his fascination with American history, and his love of the one truly American genre of novel: The Western.

For more information and to keep up with his latest releases, we would encourage you to visit his website (mooncalfpress.com) and sign up for his twice-monthly e-newsletter.

RETURN TO PARKSHORE LIBRARY

Made in the USA
Monee, IL
24 September 2019